PERSONALITY, DIVINATION AND THE TAROT

By the same author

Astrology of Rising Signs

PERSONALITY, DIVINATION AND THE TAROT

Carl Sargent

DESTINY BOOKS

Rochester, Vermont

Destiny Books
One Park Street,
Rochester, Vermont 05767

Library of Congress Cataloging in Publication data

Sargent, Carl
Personality, divination and the tarot/by Carl Sargent.
p. cm.
Bibliography: p.
Includes index.
ISBN 0–89281–219–2 (pbk.)
1. Tarot.   2. Occultism—Psychological aspects.   I. Title.
BF1879.T2S33 1988
133.3'2424—dc 19   88–20301 CIP

Printed and bound in Great Britain

10 9 8 7 6 5 4 3 2 1

Destiny Books is a division of Inner Traditions International, Ltd.

Distributed to the book trade in the United States by Harper and
Row Publishers, Inc.

Contents

Preface

The Tarot is an extraordinary thing, much more than a pack of cards. The strange symbols on them capture our imaginations, even in our allegedly 'rational' age. This book seeks to make the wisdom of this very old picture-book come alive, as a story about ourselves, about our lives and our personalities.

For some ten years, I taught abnormal psychology and the psychology of personality in the Psychology honours course at the University of Cambridge. This gave me a great familiarity with the psychologists who have written about human personality, including that giant Freud and his many descendants. When I first became interested in the Tarot, the parallels between the images within it and the writings of these psychologists were blindingly obvious. As I delved deeper into this, I found that this had in large measure escaped other writers. To be sure, some of them had linked the Tarot with the psychology of the Swiss Carl Jung, but going beyond that single theory (and there are many theories of personality!) was very rare indeed. This book takes up the task, linking the Tarot with many personality theories, and claiming that the Tarot is almost a 'super-theory' of personality. One can hardly find an original insight in personality psychology which is not foretold in the imagery of the Tarot. The Tarot is the *ultimate* tool for understanding ourselves, if we know how to use it. This book is a signpost to that fuller usage of this very old tool.

It may seem strange that someone like myself, trained as an experimental scientist (admittedly one with interests in some rather *strange* things, like ESP and astrology), should take the Tarot seriously. All I can say is that I have found, by experience, that it is a valuable thing. One standard scientific dismissal, that people who 'believe' in the Tarot find justification in their beliefs by interpreting the vague pronouncements of Tarot readers in accordance with what's going on in their lives, seems nonsense to me. I've had the good fortune to know two Tarot readers who gave me information which did anything but pander to what I might have *wished* to hear, and accurately predicted several events (some of which were highly improbable) which later happened – things I had little control over – so the prophecies couldn't have been self-fulfilling. Furthermore, when I came to use the Tarot myself, something distinctly odd happened. At first, I used two of the many Tarot decks available – the Marseilles deck and the Thoth deck of Aleister Crowley. In both cases, I found that they produced intelligible and seemingly correct answers to my queries when I used them. Then, I acquired a third pack for use (I have many others which I don't actually use) – the Waite-Rider deck. This is a very pretty, very attractive deck, and I eagerly looked forward to using it. So, given my enthusiasm and liking for it, by the standard explaining-away theory of self-deception, I should have had a wonderful time with it. I didn't. Every reading I produced was inconsistent, even incoherent. I simply couldn't use this Tarot pack at all. It was as if the 'magic' of this deck just didn't mesh with me, and my personality, at all. I simply could not explain this away. And, just after this, one of my Tarot readers produced a series of highly accurate readings, mostly concerning matters she knew absolutely nothing about and wasn't involved with in any way. The Tarot was firmly entrenched in my life.

So, here is the book which has been struggling its way out of me for some time now, against some of my conscious inclinations. Just as every worthwhile theory of human personality deals with our development as human beings, and as the Tarot itself is a picture-book of our voyages through life, this book strikes me as having something of a voyage of discovery about it. I hope the reader picks up something of that, to help with his or her journey.

In addition to my Tarot readers (who don't want to be named, so I shall respect their wishes), some other acknowledgements are due. Thanks to Nick Thompson for everstimulating discussions about this (and almost anything else; how can one person know so many things?), to Oliver Caldecott at Century Hutchinson for his encouragement and time and *more* stimulating discussions; and thanks to my very good friend Trevor Harley for getting me into the Tarot in the first place, although he probably never realized where it would end up – this book is for him.

Carl Sargent
Cambridge, 1987

1

What is the Tarot?

1

What is the Tarot?

The Tarot cards are at least six hundred years old. Although their history is uncertain, they are probably even older, dating back to the twelfth century. There are many exotic theories about their originating with Egyptian mystics and suchlike, but most likely they are of Western European origin, quite possibly Italian. Over the centuries the appearance of the seventy-eight cards of the Tarot pack have changed in many ways. One only has to look at all the packs in a shop which sells Tarot cards to see how many different versions exist today. Yet two things remain unaltered. For one, the core symbols of the cards have a lot in common, even in packs which look very different at first sight. The *essential* structure of the Tarot has not changed so very much over the centuries. The second thing which is unchanged is our reaction to the cards. They are still as mysterious as they ever were, their curious symbols fascinating some people and even making a few afraid of them. Before looking at the structure of the pack, or deck, of seventy-eight, just turn to page 90 and look at the card there – the Major Arcana card (we'll see what 'Major Arcana' means shortly), 'The Hanged Man'. What an extraordinary card this is! This is no criminal swinging on the gallows; for a start, the man hangs by one foot, not by his neck. If we bow to the almost irresistible urge to turn the card upside-down, we see the expression on his face. He clearly isn't suffering. If anything, a smile plays around the edges of his mouth and in his eyes. Again, he hangs not from a gibbet but from wood which is *alive*, sprouting with buds. What can possibly be the meaning of this compelling card? Just from a quick look at this single

1

card, we can see why the Tarot retains its centuries-old hold on our imagination.

Picking up our story about the origins of the Tarot, we see that in some ways it resembles our modern decks of playing-cards, although the Tarot contains seventy-eight cards as against a conventional deck of fifty-two. It is probable that the Minor Arcana of the Tarot gave rise to the playing-cards now used to play bridge, poker, and so on, just as the Tarot itself can be used to play the game of Tarocchi. The Tarot deck can be divided into one group of twenty-two cards, the Major Arcana, and another group of fifty-six, the Minor Arcana. It is the latter group which looks like playing-cards. These cards are arranged in four suits (wands, cups, swords, and coins) which have become the clubs, hearts, spades, and diamonds of playing-cards. The suits of the Minor Arcana each have fourteen cards, the Ace, nine cards numbered from 2 to 10, and then a Knave, Knight, Queen and King. Clearly, in playing-cards, either the Knave or the Knight has become the Jack, and the other card from the Minor Arcana has become lost (or the two fused into the single image of the Jack). But the others remain much the same. Of the Major Arcana, though, there is nothing left, with one exception: the single card 'The Fool'; the Major Arcana card numbered zero (the others are numbered 1–21) has become the Joker in the pack of playing-cards. Perhaps he was too tricky to keep out. It's peculiarly appropriate that, of all the Major Arcana cards, this card still lives on in playing-card decks, since the Fool stands for the uncontrollable, the unpredictable and the entire gamut of possibilities in our lives.

So, we can see that even if we've never looked carefully at a Tarot deck in our lives, we will certainly have idled away some time playing with a derivative of this old and curious pack of cards. Before we take a closer look at the Tarot, we are faced with the puzzle of the many different versions of it. Which deck should we use? As I've noted, all Tarot decks have much in common, but many decks, particularly twentieth-century ones, diverge greatly from older, 'classical' designs. Many modern authors and designers of cards have strong ideas about the Tarot which have influenced their designs. To take one example, some writers have claimed that the Major Arcana cards are strongly linked with the variety of Jewish mystical knowledge known as the Qhabbala. We need not go into the details of this, but what has happened is that several Tarot decks have appeared since the late nineteenth century which have been deliberately redrawn to emphasize parallels between the images of the Tarot and elements within the Qhabbalistic Tree of Life. Again, one can find various 'Aquarian' and 'New Age' Tarot decks, which claim to show the Tarot images in a form suitable for our changed lives and circumstances in the modern age. Some people suggest that many Tarot symbols are sexist, and that illustrating a *psychological* principle of femininity or passivity using a *female* figure doesn't do justice to the changing roles of women in modern society nor does it reflect the fact that all of us, male or female, have both masculine and feminine traits in our psychological make-up. So, back to the question: which deck shall we use?

Those who are knowledgeable about the Tarot probably have their own favourite deck(s). In this book, I'll be using one deck as a standard reference, the relatively old Marseilles deck (it's not entirely certain just how old this is). In explaining my preference the reader will, I hope, pick up some of the reasons why the Tarot is a powerful tool for understanding ourselves.

Above all, what I prefer about the Marseilles deck is that it *isn't* particularly pretty or eye-catching. Many of the elements in the cards are seemingly awkwardly placed, not at all neat, and the pictures certainly aren't prettified (unlike the popular Waite-Rider pack, one of the best-selling versions, in which all the human figures are handsome and attractive and the lines are always smooth and clean). Our *lives* are not clear-cut and often not pretty, and the Marseilles deck reflects this. There is a more realistic, almost gritty, quality to many of the cards and in some cases this is crucial to an understanding of them. What I mean by this will be illustrated when we look at a card such as the Magician, from the Major Arcana. Also, the cards bear only their numbers and the formal titles for the Major Arcana and the court cards of the Minor Arcana. In this the Marseilles deck differs from the celebrated Thoth deck of Tarot cards, designed by Aleister Crowley, in which all seventy-eight cards are given names (many being contentious) and also symbols to show their correspondences with Qhabbalism and astrology. Too much clutter! The Marseilles cards show us starkly the essential features of Tarot designs, with little superfluous dressing-up and, almost alone, this deck does *not* come accompanied by a little book of interpretation. Although these books appear helpful to the beginner, often they divert attention away from the stories that the images on the cards are telling, and demote them to the role of illustrations to the book. The Marseilles deck, on the other hand, forces us back upon our own imaginations and understanding. Lastly, the Marseilles is as close to the now-vanished original Tarot decks as we'll get, and hand-in-hand with that is the fact that here we are not being subjected to one individual's particular views on the Tarot reflected in the design he has made up for us. We get closer to the essence of matters by not being distracted by an unusual and unorthodox appearance. There is also the point that the Marseilles Tarot is to be found in many shops which stock Tarot cards. This is important. It wouldn't be very helpful for the reader to be told that the 'best' deck was one which was almost impossible to get hold of!

So, we'll be working through the Marseilles deck here. But what is this? How are we to regard these cards? We should see the Tarot as a picture-book which tells a story in images. It is a story about ourselves, our lives and our personalities, both the best and the worst things about us. It is surely that common human weakness, the dislike of having, and even inability to face up to, the things we don't like about ourselves which makes some people fearful of the Tarot, recoiling from its darker images, and even giving it foolish labels such as 'The Devil's Picture Book'. In this way, such people can gain comfort by pretending that the Tarot is some evil thing from outside ourselves, inspired by the devil – or used by witches! ! – and not have to face the awkward truths that the Tarot reflects back to us. Mention of this old psychological trick, known as *projection* to some psychologists (pretending that something worrying *inside* ourselves is actually an *external* threat), brings us close to the basic idea of this book: the Tarot is a model of human personality. Indeed, we can go further. In the structure and images of the Tarot we can see clearly virtually *all* of the major theories of personality which psychologists have described. The Tarot is, if you like, a *super-theory* of personality. There is little that psychologists have discovered about human personality which isn't contained within the Tarot, and can be seen and understood in its images. The Tarot can tell us as much about ourselves as any theory of personality. More, in fact, because many theories of personality simply don't attempt to cover all the ground that the Tarot does.

This is a pretty strong claim: that Freud and all the other eminent psychologists who have studied the secrets of the human mind had their discoveries pre-dated in a mere pack of cards. It seems almost incredible. But later in this book, as we look through the seventy-eight cards and their meanings, we will see that the conclusion is inescapable. It really *is* this way. At this stage, though, we can look at some general arguments which make the case plausible – and some complications, too.

First, I'm *not* claiming that every detail of every personality theory which psychologists have postulated is predicted and shown in the Tarot. That *would* be ridiculous. It is the *key* insights of different writers about personality which are shown in the cards – the significant thrust of the writer's ideas. The minor details could not all be covered in a single deck, and, don't forget, many of the details of theories of personality are *wrong*, so we wouldn't expect them to be prefigured in the Tarot if it really is a source of wisdom and understanding!

Second, we have to keep in mind that the Tarot is a collection of *symbols*. We have to be able to interpret these symbols to be able to see how they match up with psychologists' theories of personality. In some cases the correspondences are obvious; in others, they have to be ferreted out. This shouldn't worry us; after all, most psychologists accept that they have to interpret behaviour and emotions and what goes on inside us in order to understand personality. That may be interpreting the causes of anxiety, or the structure of our dreams (and interpreting Tarot is probably much less tricky than interpreting dreams!). But, to understand Tarot, we will sometimes have to range a little far afield from what looks like the province of a psychologist studying personality, into folklore, fairy tales, legend and myth. But is it so very far? After all, these stories and tales were composed by people like ourselves, with similar emotions and feelings, and something of their personalities is reflected in the tales they wove. It is hardly ridiculous to claim that something about personality can be understood from these sources, even if few psychologists have ventured to study them.

Third, the Tarot is a *dynamic* structure. The story it tells is of the way in which people develop, of how they grow up, of the struggles they face as children, as young adults and in old age. It is a story of personality as something which is ever-developing. We will see just how strong this current of growth and development is as we look through the Major Arcana later. This is an important point to bear in mind as the argument develops. The Tarot shows not just how, and who, we are, but also tells us something of what we have been and what we will become. This is actually beyond the scope, remarkably, of many theories of personality, as we shall see. This is part of the greater power of Tarot in helping us understand ourselves.

Fourth – and this is important also – just as there are many Tarot decks, there are many theories of personality. This fact shows us just how uncertain an enterprise any meaningful psychology is. It also shows us that the notion that any one particular theory is 'the truth' about the way we are, is nonsense. There are different theories of personality which have almost nothing in common at all, differing in almost every respect about what sort of creature the human mind is and how, and what we can learn about it. There's no point in trying to get at the real *truth* about it all; quite possibly there isn't one. Rather, what we *can* ask is: what ideas, in which theories, are valuable to people? Which ideas help to alleviate mental suffering, anxiety or even mental illness, and therefore are useful in practice? Which ideas seem to explain much (rather than little) about our feelings and what we do, and are therefore important rather than trivial? Perhaps most importantly, when do we find ideas in different psychologies which match up? If there *is* any 'way that we really are', such agreements must come closest to pointing to the direction of that. Although we will take a closer look at theories of personality in the next two chapters, I can give an example of this now. In both the psychologies of Carl Jung, a disciple of Freud later to develop his own model of personality, and in the humanistic psychology of writers like Abraham Maslow, a dominating (possibly *the* dominating) drive within people is the instinct to grow, develop, differentiate, and to nurture our 'spiritual' feelings. Don't misunderstand that term. Both these psychologists (as we'll see) are quite precise about what they mean by this. This isn't some wishy-washy, vague and nebulous waffle. This central drive is the central story of the Major Arcana, and the details of its symbols show very close parallels with the details of the stories Jung and Maslow tell us about just how we can develop as people. (Note I say *can* develop. This is a *potential*, not something which inevitably happens.)

We can even play around with one idea which provokes some thought: Tarot decks have changed a lot in this century as new decks have proliferated. Theories of personality have proliferated too, with new ideas being developed into formal theories. Perhaps both sets of changes reflect similar changes in our culture, and consequent changes in our personalities. That is, they have the same basic cause. If that is true, then the claim that the Tarot is a picture-book about ourselves and that it is a theory of personality itself becomes almost obvious!

So, our first point of inquiry is a look at some major, influential, theories of personality from Freud onwards. Then we shall move on to look at the structure of the Tarot more closely, and to deal with the meanings of the cards, seeing how many elements of the personality theories we've looked at will match up with what the cards show for us. Finally, we look at the extra information in Tarot; what there is in addition to its story about personality, and what it shows us that personality theories do not. And how do we use this picture-book? How do we put to use the wisdom and insights within it? For they are there, if we only know how to see and understand what the Tarot tells us when we ask.

2

Psychology and Personality

2

Psychology and Personality

In this chapter we will be looking at some major theories of personality, and isolating the central ideas in them. These are Freudian psychoanalysis, Jung's analytical psychology, the humanistic psychology of Carl Rogers and Abraham Maslow and the personal construct psychology of George Kelly. Perhaps some explanation of why I've chosen these is called for.

No one writing about personality could fail to include Freud but the other choices need a little more justification. Jung's psychology is important because some of his ideas are commonly accepted in academic psychology, most obviously his writings about extraverts and introverts, and everyone knows these terms; also Jung was the originator of the term *complex*, as in having a mother complex – also a familiar term. Further, he is an important writer on the development of the personality after the early years, and he is virtually the *only* author to have looked into seemingly obscure areas such as mythology, folklore and alchemy, in search of knowledge about human personality. Jung's psychology is too extensive to be ignored. The humanists are important because they too consider human growth and development. Maslow in particular strove to ally clinical evidence with personal experience and experimental studies. Humanistic psychologists have a reputation for being vague and rather wishy-washy in some quarters, a myth we'll soon explode. Kelly's inclusion might surprise the knowledgeable. He's a difficult writer and the psychology doesn't seem to have anything at all to do with the Tarot, which is one very good reason for looking at it. In essence, Kelly took a model of 'man as scientist' as his inspiration and sought to examine how much

9

of human behaviour could be explained in terms of this model. That's putting matters a little simplistically, but the details come later. Kelly's work predates research on artificial intelligence and 'smart machines' by decades and few of the people working on such matters have ever heard of him, but his theory is surely inspired by the same ideas which guide this more recent research (and is a lot more sensible). This is a very twentieth-century idea in many ways (although it harkens back to the seventeenth so far as Kelly's intellectual ancestors go – at least that far!) and it's interesting to see how this can be compared to the Tarot.

There are some theories of personality which I'm not going to be considering here. This may seem like a cop-out from the claim that the Tarot shows the significant insights of all major personality theories, but this is not so. For one thing, there are obvious space limitations – I *could* have discussed lots more theories but then this book would have been as long as *War and Peace* and twice as tedious. But it could have been done; for example, Alfred Adler's theory of personality stresses a primary drive to power, competence, and effectiveness (a very masculine idea). It will be clear to the reader as we go through the Tarot later that there are many symbols of this drive, shown in cards such as the Chariot (material power), the Devil (temporal power and control), and many Minor Arcana cards. The parallels are there. Further, there are quite a few theories of personality which don't have anything *important* to say which isn't covered by the theories we're going to be looking at anyway. Many post-Freudian psychoanalytic theories would be examples of this.

Although Kelly's cognitive theory *is* considered there are also certain 'scientific' theories of personality which I have not covered here. Such theories are those based on experiments and questionnaire study. I should explain why these are not included in my survey.

For one thing, many readers will be familiar with many of the terms of Freudian psychoanalysis, such as *repression* or *denial*, and likewise terms such as Jung's *introvert-extravert* are part of everyday language. But the methods and substance of statistical *trait theories*, as the scientific models of personality offered by writers such as Hans Eysenck in Britain and Raymond Cattell in America are known, are unfamiliar to non-experts. Trying to cover these would mean deluging the reader with many unfamiliar and technical terms, which I have no desire to do.

Second, there is in fact a set of correspondences between these trait theories and the theories of personality I will be considering. For example, the trait of introversion-extraversion is common to all such theories, and to Jung's theory of personality. The most detailed trait theory, that of Cattell, also includes factors such as ego strength, superego strength, and tension level (which Cattell makes clear is a form of instinctual energy). There is a very strong similarity between these scientifically derived traits and the ego, superego, and Id of Freudian theory. We shall be considering those Freudian terms shortly. For now, though, we may note that if we tie in such elements of Freudian theory with the Tarot, we are also tying in part of Cattell's theory, so that we are not actually failing to establish any connection with scientific personality theories. A full exposition is not within the scope of this book.

In this chapter, what I shall do is to give a précis of each of four personality theories; those of Freud, Jung, Maslow and Kelly. I shall only make a few brief references to the Tarot at this stage, for what is important for the reader here is to understand the basics of each personality theory. We shall then consider the Major Arcana of the Tarot, and when doing so I shall point out parallels with the personality theory in detail. Likewise, the parallels with the Minor Arcana will be established in Chapter 4. Our first business, however, is to establish the basic principles of the personality theories, and the obvious starting point is with Freud.

Sigmund Freud: Mapper of the Unconscious Mind

The key message of Freud's theory of personality is simple. *Unconscious* processes are of major significance in our lives. Freud claimed that evidence of the unconscious could be found in the symptoms of neurotic people, in our daydreams, fantasies and dreams, in slips of the tongue, errors and mistakes, jokes, and in art and literature. He developed a technique for exploring the unconscious, known as *free association*. Often used to interpret dreams, this is simply allowing the conscious mind to wander freely and come up with associations to what is remembered of dreams without censoring anything as absurd, ridiculous, foolish or embarrassing (this is the 'free' in free association). This is an ideal since, in practice, the conscious mind will certainly reject at least some associations as being absurd or embarrassing. The aim is to generate ideas and recall memories, as free as possible of this censoring process. But what *is* the unconscious, why is it so powerful, and what is the relation between our conscious and unconscious minds?

In his earlier writings (Freud changed his ideas over the forty-five or so years during which he wrote about psychoanalysis), Freud defined three types of mental processes. One set are those of the *conscious* mind – that part of us which perceives the world around us, reflects and thinks, and tends to be verbal, logical, and adept at 'reality testing'. The *preconscious* mind is a system of no major importance for Freud. This part of the mind is unconscious, but from it we can summon up contents into our conscious awareness more or less as we wish. Let us say we are trying to remember some place we once visited. We conjure up memories of it, recall names and faces, see buildings in our mind's eye, and so on. These thoughts, images and impressions were obviously not in our conscious minds before we made an effort to start thinking about them, and they won't be conscious after we've pondered them and gone on to something else. They were preconscious. It is the (fully) *unconscious* mind which is the nine-tenths of the iceberg, unconscious memories, emotions and instincts which we *cannot* summon into consciousness. For Freud, it is here that the central human drives and motivations are to be found, using such tools as free association and dream analysis. We have to use such roundabout methods because the conscious mind is generally in sharp conflict with the unconscious. We don't recall what is unconscious because the conscious mind won't let us; this is not so much a *can't* as a *won't*. Much that is in the unconscious mind is unacceptable to our conscious way of thinking, and the conscious mind uses *repression* (a familiar term) to prevent the feared material in the unconscious coming into our awareness.

Why? What are the roots of this war between our conscious and unconscious minds? To understand this, we need to know more about how the unconscious works, and to look at Freud's views on how the mind develops. This is the key to understanding the origins of the conflict. One crucial element of the unconscious is that it is the seat of the instincts or drives. Freud considered that there is even a perpetual conflict *within* the unconscious, instincts with incompatible aims which are at war. Sex, the drive of libido, was always considered by Freud to be one of these central instincts. At first he thought this was opposed by the drive to self-preservation. Later he dropped that view and seemed to consider that libido was the only major instinct. Lastly he considered that a form of destructive aggression was the other major instinct with which libido was at war, driven to that view by a number of observations (on sexual sadism and masochism and some other less exotic phenomena). Conflict is rife even within this single realm of the mind.

Next, we need to understand the major difference between the conscious and unconscious minds so far as their style of operation and aims are concerned. The unconscious is very different from the conscious mind; it has its own language, a totally different one from the logical, precise language of the conscious mind. The unconscious expresses itself in symbols; it shows desires in the forms of symbols, analogies, puns and fantasies, and it has no connection with external reality. It wants what it desires and wants it *now*. We can see at once one major reason for the conflict with consciousness; the unconscious has absolutely no tolerance for frustration. The conscious mind has to develop such a tolerance, and it also has the rational awareness to see that sometimes postponing an immediate gratification can lead to much more satisfying rewards in the future. Indeed a major part of our growing up and becoming social creatures, is learning to tolerate frustrations, to postpone gratifying our desires until the time and place are right and acknowledging other people's needs and desires. The conscious mind learns these things. The unconscious won't stand for it. Conflict results.

As infants, Freud asserts, we are largely unconscious beings. We have to learn about the world outside, and slowly consciousness and an awareness of who, and what, we are develops. The ability of the child to think in logical terms is a hard-won and difficult development. As consciousness develops and perceptual memory and thinking skills improve (Freud saw this as a built-in maturing although the environment could certainly exert effects on it), the conscious mind comes to reject many of the wishes of the unconscious. Let us consider an example.

A young child finds that his pregnant mother produces a new sibling, a younger brother or sister. The attitude of the unconscious to this new arrival is pretty unequivocal: the sibling is a rival for mother's affections. The unconscious desire is to see the sibling removed, to kill it. But the conscious mind rejects this wish. It knows that mother would never stand for this and indeed mother has probably told the child to love his new brother/sister. The conscious mind is afraid of the wish because it threatens the child with the loss of love and with the punishment which it realizes would occur if it did kill the hated rival. So, the conscious mind uses certain tools at its disposal (repression and the other *defences*) to drive the wish out of awareness, back into the unconscious where it came from. There will be more about the defences, which are a crucial part of our personality development and structure, later.

But what if there is no such sibling? No matter. Conflict between the conscious and unconscious will be intrinsic right from the very start in any case. Very early in development, the conscious mind is aware of just how strong the unconscious is. The conscious mind is still weak, still developing, still growing and trying to develop a better awareness and mastery of the world outside. The infant is very weak and helpless and dependent on others and the conscious mind mirrors these qualities. The power of the demands of the unconscious is frightening; even something as simple as a hunger pang has a fiendish intensity. The sheer tension generated by an unsatisfied unconscious desire like this is experienced by the conscious mind as an intense anxiety, a fear that it could be destroyed by this elemental, instinctual power which could overwhelm and shatter it. The conscious mind simply *has* to be able to defend itself against the threat of instinctual energies. Conflict must ensue. The incessant clamour of the instinctual drives must be countered. The child's conscious mind realizes that the mother cannot always be around for food and comfort as and when the unconscious wishes it to be so, that tensions due to unsatisfied drives will accumulate, and therefore defences develop.

This basic pattern of conflict will intensify during childhood development. Sexual desire, libido, is active in the unconscious of the child; this is Freud's theory of infantile sexuality, which earned him so much notoriety in his contemporary circles. That now we are not so uncomfortable with the notion that children have sexual instincts reflects the enduring influence of Freud's writings. For Freud, the child will inevitably be drawn towards the cross-sex parent as an object of desire, son to mother, daughter to father. There are too many people running around who fit the bill as 'daddy's girl' and 'mother's boy' to reject this notion out of hand, I think. This particular unconscious desire is absolutely unacceptable to the conscious mind. A male child fears his father's retribution and punishment for his desire to take the father's place and possess his mother. A massive repression of the unconscious, incestuous wish is set in motion. Other defences are employed also. For example, the boy takes on and develops the masculine traits of his father, he *identifies* with him, as if by doing this two aims can be achieved at once. On the one hand, by being like his father he can placate him and avoid punishment; on the other, by being like his father he is in some sense taking the father's role and possessing his mother. Of course this is illogical but then the unconscious doesn't work by logic. This defensive manoeuvre manages to gain something for the unconscious out of the repression of the wish; our defences may be deployed in the service of the conscious mind but they utilize unconscious energies. The story for the female child is more complex and rather less satisfying, but it would be hard to deny that Freud here homed in on something very important in our psyche.

We cannot escape the conflict between the conscious and unconscious. It is inevitable, as certain within us as the succession of night and day is in the external world. All that is left to us is to examine the details – the defences the conscious mind uses, how the unconscious can be tracked down and how it reveals itself to us.

Defences develop as the conscious mind grows and they act in its service, although their operation is not voluntarily controlled. They operate as defensive reflexes. The most important of them is *repression*, the elimination of unacceptable wishes from conscious awareness. If these wishes, and the memories and fantasies associated with them, are powerful enough to threaten an eruption into consciousness, they must be repressed. To do this, the conscious mind uses some of the 'psychic energy' available to it to block the entry of the unacceptable memories and thoughts into consciousness. Think of this as damming up a stream. There is a build-up of tension (unsatisfied desire) in the unconscious which forces the conscious mind to create a repressive barrier against the wish becoming conscious through the force of the energy it carries. There is a price to pay for repression. For one thing, the wish will not go away, and since there is a build-up of tension a vicious circle of more repression and more tension may result. This may be partly defused by the indirect expression of the wish in dreams, jokes, errors and (if repression is very severe) neurotic symptoms. Another problem is that repression must weaken the conscious mind. For one thing, it drains psychic energy, leaving less available for other activities. Also, the repressed memories, thoughts and images associated with the drive were at one time part of the conscious mind or at least available to it; the conscious mind grows from the unconscious. To repress these mental contents leaves fewer mental resources available to the conscious mind. Repression drains energy and impoverishes content also. It may be necessary, but it's harmful in excess.

Other defences may also be used. *Projection* is a defence which says (in effect), 'It's not me that has this nasty desire. It's *him*' and the conscious mind perceives the feared desire as being *out there*, and not part of the inner self. In extreme cases, this can produce paranoia, the experience that everything out there is threatening. Projection can clearly be seen in white racialists who accuse blacks of being sexually immoral and promiscuous. To be sure, other vices are usually listed (notably laziness and disrespect for authority – people like this see the latter as a vice!), but sexual immorality is always in the list somewhere.

Denial, which at first sight looks like repression, is another defence of importance. The conscious mind effectively says, 'Absolutely not. Of course I don't think/feel this.' The extra content of denial above and beyond that of repression is shown by the efforts the defence makes to change perceptions into opposites which support the denial. Thus, the boy's feared father becomes the champion of the world, supremely powerful, a great hero and protector. This is also acceptable to the unconscious, since the boy identifies with his father and is, in effect, indulging a fantasy about his own omnipotence at the same time. Defences strive to try to gain *something* which will satisfy the unconscious at the same time as serving the needs of the conscious mind!

Reaction-formation is a linked defence. Not only is the unconscious desire repudiated but the exact opposite is true! This defence builds a polar opposition to the feared wish. A hallmark of reaction-formation is its compulsive, rigid, obsessional quality. The wish is not just denied but even negated into the bargain, so such rigidity seems mandated. As an example of how this defence affects personality, we need to develop some further detail of Freud's theory of childhood development.

Not only is there an opposition of unconscious libido and the conscious mind, but libido has its own development timetable, according to Freud. Libido tends to focus, at different stages of development, on different body zones which are of particular importance. The first of these is the oral zone, important during early feeding and teething. Later, as the child is toilet trained and develops the capacity to control its bowel movements, the anal zone is a major focus of libido. Later development is to the phallic and then genital zones (identical only for the boy, according to Freud; I think I'll duck this issue here) but the 'anal stage' of development is the one we want to look at here.

Freud considered that the development of libido was paralleled by a development of defence mechanisms, and that reaction-formation was a defence strongly associated with the anal phase of libidinal development. In the child's development, reaction-formation is the defence brought into play to deal with messy, 'anal' habits which the child's parents discourage (the propensity of children to play with faeces is surely well-known). The rigidity of reaction-formation can create a typical personality obsessed with cleanliness, orderliness and control, and with meanness and a stingy nature. Freud claims that money and faeces are symbolically equated, an intriguing idea we don't have the space to explore here, but just consider it – British readers will know the expressions 'filthy lucre', and 'where there's muck there's brass', and many other cultures have similar expressions. This personality structure is closely associated with this particular defence, and this stage of libido development. If the idea seems bizarre, there is excellent evidence of an 'anal personality', much as Freud described it, from scientific study using questionnaires and observational studies.

Regression is a defence which can also be understood in terms of Freud's theory of libido development. Different types of conflict and different defences are associated with different stages of development, and when a conflict at a later developmental stage is very difficult, the person may regress to more childish, primitive modes of self-expression and gratification to evade the conflict. Childish and immature patterns of behaviour take over. We can surely remember times when we behaved like this. Lastly, the most mature of defences for Freud because of its socially valuable nature is *sublimation*, the indirect expression of a wish in a socially acceptable form. As an example, works of art and literature reflect unconscious wishes in highly symbolic and sublimated forms, but the symbols used manage to express unconscious wishes, nonetheless. And this brings us back to the issue of how we can track down the wishes and instincts of the unconscious mind.

Given that the instincts in the unconscious, and memories and fantasies associated with them, are repressed from consciousness, it is obvious that only in areas of our mental life where the conscious mind does not hold complete sway can we see unconscious factors clearly revealed. Hence Freud's famous formula that 'dreams are the royal road to the unconscious'. The chaotic, seemingly unintelligible, language of dreams is *almost* the pure language of the unconscious. Not quite, though. When we wake, the conscious mind tries to repress much of the dream so that we cannot recall it. It also tidies up the dream by a process Freud termed *secondary elaboration*, making the dream (as we remember it) a little less chaotic and strange, and managing to make its true meaning still more obscure. One reason our dreams are incomprehensible is that our conscious mind does its best to make them that way! But if we can free-associate to what we do recall of a dream – the *manifest* content of the dream – there is a chance that we can find out about the wishes the dream portrays, the *latent* content of the dream. Linking the two is the *dream-work*, the arcane process of symbolization and other elements of the language of the unconscious. Dreams are *not* just a random chaos; they are *hallucinated wish-fulfilments*, for the unconscious does not readily discriminate between fantasy and reality and the dream shows fantasied gratifications for repressed wishes.

In understanding dreams, there is a key role for understanding symbols – and this is going to be of obvious importance to us when we try to relate Freudian theory to the Tarot. Freudian dream symbols are very concrete, representing body parts or others who are significant as the objects of desires and wishes. Thus long, sharp and pointed objects are phallic symbols, whereas hollowed-out, smooth, rounded objects are female/vaginal symbols. A figure such as a King or Emperor may stand for one's father, and so on. Actions may be symbolic, for example, climbing a staircase may be a symbol for sexual intercourse. The symbols are clearly very much physical in terms of what they indicate. In the dream, such symbols may often be worked into memories of recent events ('day residues') to build up the structure of the dream in images.

Rather than give a dream-analysis (which is lengthy) to show how symbols can be interpreted and understood, we can look at an amusing case from another realm in which unconscious wishes may be expressed – errors and mistakes ('Freudian slips'). Mistakes are *never* random for Freud. Of course, they may be likely to occur when we are bored or tired or slightly intoxicated, but those factors just make it easier for mistakes to occur – they 'lower the threshold of consciousness' so that unconscious determinants can influence our actions more readily. The *form* which errors take are crucially determined by repressed wishes.

I can recall giving a series of seminars on Freud to a group of students which included several distractingly pretty girls. At the time I was engaged, which explains why my defences may have been giving me a hard time of it. In the course of one seminar, I mentioned an example of forgetfulness as a Freudian slip – a young man leaving his umbrella (a classic phallic symbol) behind in the hallway (a classic vaginal symbol) of the home of a young woman he had met. This expresses an obvious wish. I spent some time after this attacking the Freudian notion of symbolism, suggesting that it was too limited and too concrete. As I prepared to leave at the end of the seminar, and walked towards the door, a girl sitting at the back of the class pointed out to me with a sweet smile that *I had left my umbrella behind*.

The error doesn't end here. When typing this first time round, I made another error which I didn't see at first. Instead of umbrella, I typed in unbrella, a negating prefix (un-) which denied the symbolism. Not satisfied with *that*, my unconscious subsequently managed to delete the word-processor file the text was stored in. Sometimes one simply cannot accept mistakes like these as random!

Rarely do we realize, though, that our mistakes give us away so completely as this. This is hardly surprising – our conscious minds censor out any awareness of the mistake as reflective of any unconscious wish. But nothing is random for Freud; many cases may be obscure in their interpretation but by using free-association and linked techniques it is always possible to track down the repressed wish. If the dream or error does not clearly show the wish, ideas and images which one associates with the dreams and errors will. Tracking down the repressed wish is the basis of Freudian therapy. Neurotics need freedom from repression and it is necessary to release some of the dammed-up instinctual energy by lifting the repression. *Catharsis* is the name given to the diminution of tension and anxiety when some repressed wish is accepted by consciousness. Know thyself is indeed the ultimate commandment for Freud, but simply knowing something (in the intellectual sense) is a quite different matter from apprehending it with the emotional release of catharsis. Conflict is intrinsic to the human personality but lifting repressions caused by major traumatic events (either real or fantasized, as with incestuous wishes) makes us less neurotic and more healthy people.

Still, this is a pessimistic view. Our much-prized intellect is almost helpless in dealing with the dynamics of our own inner conflicts, and we have a mind irrevocably at war with itself. We hardly seem to know what we do and why we are doing it. Perhaps the greatest shortcoming in Freud's model is the lack of anything satisfying about our creative, healthy drives. Freud was once asked what someone should do if reasonably free from repressions and neurosis. His reply was that we should dedicate ourselves to work, and to love. Very edifying, but one might have hoped for something more illuminating and detailed than this. For Freud, art, poetry and literature are just sublimated libido; spirituality and religious faith just delusions. Freud never could get to grips with the psychopathology which has increasingly dominated the twentieth century – the schizoid alienation of so many people, the feeling of futility and meaningless and inner emptiness. Freud's very last paper concerns this topic and he has nothing to say save for expressing a deep, defeated, pessimism. The common claim that Freud did a good job in the basement (base drives) and never went near the light, airy spaces of the skylighted loft (creativity, spirituality) seems to many critics to be a valid criticism. Not so. It is actually quite inadequate. To understand humanity's finest aspirations and the better qualities which make us complete personalities, it is very necessary to study the unconscious, as Jung shows.

But it would be monstrous to belittle Freud's achievements – the discovery of the grammar of dreams, the descriptions of defences in the personality, infantile sexuality, the dynamics of much neurotic illness. These and many others are achievements which may be reformulated or rewritten, but later writers will always owe a great deal to Freud's pioneer efforts. Freud may not have been the first to discover the unconscious, but he gave future writers a map of the territory which was infinitely more useful than anyone who had been there before him.

Still, we will need to look further afield. How do our personalities develop as adults? This was something Freud said relatively little about. Is it *really* true that our unconscious minds are almost entirely fuelled by the energies of sexuality and destructiveness? Are religion, art, altruism, philanthropy and creativity all just expressions of neurosis, with a dash of sublimation if we are lucky? Or is there more to it than this?

Carl Jung: Beyond the Individual

Jung, when he broke with Freud (and afterwards), did not dispute the validity of many of Freud's claims. He accepted that many neuroses could be explained in Freudian terms, as a function of repressed sexuality. But he argued that Freud had missed much about the human personality. Also, while there might indeed be conflict between the conscious and unconscious minds, perhaps that conflict was not inevitable. Perhaps conflict within the mind could be *creative*; perhaps it was a spur to development, even a sign that such development was foreordained. If there is struggle, then at least the personality is *alive*; the struggle is a struggle to *grow*, to develop.

One key theme in Jungian psychology is the notion that the conscious and unconscious minds stand in *complementary* relation. What is strongly accentuated in the conscious mind is compensated for in the unconscious, which has the exact opposite qualities. So, naturally, there is struggle; the unconscious struggles to express the underdeveloped sides of ourselves, to balance the imbalance of the conscious mind. This is a theme which underpins all the interactions within our minds. Let us see exactly how this works.

A first point made by Jung is that our conscious minds are typified by certain dispositions of temperament – we tend either to be extraverts or introverts (these terms are surely familiar to us). For Jung, these terms have a precise meaning. Extraverts tend to direct their libido outwards – into the world of 'objects' around them (other people, significant activities, and so on). Extraverts look outwards; their attention is ever drawn beyond themselves. Libido is drawn outside the person. The term 'libido', for Jung, means *not* the sexualized energy of the Freudian view, but rather a general 'psychic energy'. It is a quantity of arousal and attention which dictates our actions, feelings and emotions, and even comprises them. Jung gives a telling example for rejecting the Freudian sexualization of libido – a baby derives obvious pleasure from suckling at its mother's breast. But why regard this as a sexual pleasure? Isn't it obviously nutritive, and shouldn't we accept a more general nature of libido? On the other hand, introverts direct libido inwards, inside themselves, onto thoughts and fantasies within their own minds. We all tend to one or other *type*; some of us are so extreme that we develop pathology as a result. The extreme extravert is a shell of a person, with no rich inner life, no fantasy daydreaming and no creativity within himself. The extreme introvert lives in a fantasy world, with no sense of reality or the joys and pleasures of the world around him, narcissistic and self-involved. Imbalance is pathology; this is a standard formula for Jung. As our conscious minds are inclined one way, the unconscious is inclined in the opposite direction. If we are consciously extraverted, then our unconscious will be introvert, trying to drag us back within ourselves, to find those things deep within ourselves which cannot be denied. This will show itself in our dreams and in our untypical actions and feelings, as we'll see shortly.

In addition to this temperamental factor, Jung also suggests that there are four typical mental *functions* by which we relate to the world. Again, one or two of these will be highly developed in our conscious minds, while the unconscious has the exact opposite qualities. *Sensation* says to us, 'this is'; it registers what an impression is, without analysing it or evaluating it in any way. *Feeling* is that function which tells us what something is in terms of whether it is pleasurable or unpleasurable. *Thinking* is the function which deals with things in terms of analysing and dissecting them, using logic and analysis to deal with the objects or impressions which impinge on us. Lastly, *intuition* is that hard-to-define mental function which whispers to us of what things *might* be, what they could become, what their possibilities are. On a moonlit night, trees and bushes can cast strange shadows and generate odd appearances; clouds take on peculiar and suggestive forms . . . if I seem almost to be using semi-poetic language here, this is the language that intuiton employs. It is never precise or logical. Intuition never speaks to us as a mental function; it whispers and insinuates.

Is this just arbitrary? Jung thought not. For him these four functions were a discovery, because they were all clearly exclusive of each other (how could one define intuition in terms of thinking?), and all four together seemed exhaustive. There was no need to postulate any fifth function – the four encompassed all possibilities. And, just as extraversion and introversion were polar opposites, so the four functions paired off into opposites. Thinking and feeling were opposed; they were *rational* functions because they attempted to evaluate what we perceived. Likewise, sensation and intuition were opposed; although both *irrational* (for they do not seek to analyse or evaluate impressions in any way), one function (sensation) accepted things just as they were while the other (intuition) was entirely absorbed in projecting beyond the given. Again, the standard rule of conscious-unconscious opposition applies; a person whose conscious mind is dominated by one function would have an unconscious dominated by the polar opposite. If a person has consciously developed thinking (the *superior function*) then feeling (the *inferior function*) would dominate within the unconscious.

For most of us, the imbalance is not so extreme as to cause pathology within our minds. But if it is, then an example will illustrate what may occur. A person dominated by the thinking function within his conscious mind to an extreme extent will be subject to the feeling function erupting at times of stress (or in dreams, or errors, or uncharacteristic behaviour). Just how this may happen we will see later, when the nature of the unconscious (which will erupt into explosive action) in Jungian psychology becomes clearer.

Thus, a balancing act between the conscious and unconscious minds exists. There is always struggle as the unconscious seeks to compensate for the excesses of the conscious mind, but whether this develops into open conflict and disturbance within our minds and personalities depends on how extreme the imbalance is. We need first to consider Jung's ideas on the early development of personality and then his ideas on the nature of the unconscious mind.

For Jung, the mind of the very young child has a balance within it, a balance of attitudes (extraversion-introversion) and functions; as with Freud, consciousness has not developed, and a balance still exists. Importantly, we'll consider this balance as *childishness* as opposed to being *childlike*; this distinction will become clearer when we look at the zero card of the Tarot Major Arcana, the Fool. As consciousness develops (and this is strongly affected by the environment around the child), a process of *differentiation* begins. Typically, extraversion will tend to develop in the child – after all, the child is a helpless creature, and the objects in the world around him (or her) are of major importance. He depends on those around him for sustenance and survival. Which function predominates is less clear-cut, but imbalance necessarily develops; this is essential for dealing with the world. It must be said that Jung's theory of the developing personality of the child is less complete and persuasive than that of Freud, although he is able to show from his studies that the psychology of the Self and the archetypes (see below on this) can be seen in the child. Jung does not deny that

sexualized and even incestuous desires within the unconscious are important in the child, but he does not ascribe to
them the dominant role which Freud claimed.

Nonetheless, the growing child and the developing child
will develop imbalances between the conscious and unconscious mind. There are cultural factors which create this, and
(perhaps) pre-programmed, genetic imperatives. The role of
the developing young adult (Jung stressed this for men, but
a similar analysis could easily be given for women too) is to
be the extravert, conquering dominator; to carve out for
oneself a career, a home, a spouse, those attributes and
possessions which almost all societies deem appropriate for
the young adult. This is the process of differentiation, and it
generates imbalance. But what is to come, after the young
person has 'qualified' as an adult within his society, is a
strong urge from within the unconscious to transcend this,
to create once more the balance of childhood, but in a
superior way; *individuation*. In the child, an early and primitive balance existed between the undeveloped attitudes and
functions; in the adult, an imbalance necessarily must exist.
In the middle of life, this imbalance nags away at the
conscious mind as the unconscious insists on being heard. If
the imbalance is severe enough, a 'mid-life crisis' may be the
result. The individuation process is the one by which balance
is restored, with the neglected and undeveloped attitude and
functions of the unconscious and mind becoming developed,
being 'raised into consciousness' if you like. Understanding
how this happens brings us to one of Jung's most important
claims: that our unconscious is in large part a *collective* unconscious. Certain structures, images and forms are common to
all of us, and Jung calls these *archetypes*. This claim has met
with some disfavour because (so it is said) Jung regarded
these archetypes as acquired through the racial history of
mankind. A careful reading of Jung shows that this is not
so. His later writings view the archetypes as part of the basic
structure of man's psychology, genetically wired-in predis-
positions within the human brain. The archetypes are predis-

positions to experience our lives in certain ways rather than others.

The archetypes cannot be understood directly; they lie very deep in the unconscious and they can only be comprehended indirectly through the images and themes associated with them. One can think of mountain peaks, covered with snow; one cannot see the mountains themselves, but it is obvious that they are there underneath the surface appearance.

The *persona* itself has an archetypal quality – by persona, Jung means our social appearance, our interactions with others, the compromise between ourselves and society as to what we should be like, and how we should behave. Development of the persona has a timetable in development, in our early lives: the specialization of our superior function and a dominance of one or other attitude, in the face we present to the world. If things go well, then the persona is a mask we can let drop when we need to and want to; but we can also become imprisoned in the mask, even identifying ourselves with it and feeling that this is what we really are. In the well-known book, *The Divided Self*, the pathology of the 'false self' which R. D. Laing describes could be seen as the pathology of this part of our personality. We become what the world expects of us, and our inner self wastes away. To compensate, the appearance of another archetype during individuation – the Shadow – may be very threatening and frightening indeed.

The *Shadow* is all the things which we fear and want to deny within ourselves. As the conscious personality (the *ego*) develops, everything it sets aside as useless or undesirable – the inferior function, the undeveloped attitude and unacceptable emotions and feelings – grow within the unconscious and constellate together. The Shadow, the 'dark brother' in one elegant formulation, grows within. For Jung, material from the Shadow side is what Freud spent almost all his time dealing with, and Jung used similar techniques to deal with it – the Shadow must be made conscious, the ego must accept as much of Shadow content as it can. Not everything about the Shadow need be negative. For someone who is living well below his potential, the Shadow may even contain the positive, creative qualities so lacking in that person's conscious life. Indeed, the Shadow is a fundamental part of our creativity – without this dark side, we are just two-dimensional, not even fully human, for within it lies the rejected and the undeveloped, those things within us without which we will never be complete and without which the Self cannot develop. The Shadow is also of interest because we have both a personal shadow and a collective one. Much of what forms the images of the Shadow is drawn from our personal unconscious, events and people and experiences from our individual lives; but as an archetypal form, the Shadow also lives on the borderlands of the collective unconscious. We can now bring in one of Jung's reasons for claiming that certain elements of personality are archetypal – that they are ubiquitous, little modified by culture and that their images can be seen throughout history, in art, literature, myth, and legend. Such all-pervasive influence marks certain themes as truly collective. Images of the collective Shadow are easily found in such sources: the German *döppelganger* would be an obvious example, and in mythology there are many Shadow figures – the Norse god Loki is a prime case. Most often, the light and dark brothers, ego and shadow, are seen together: Castor and Pollux, Cain and Abel, and many others.

The task which the Shadow demands of us is that we have to accept our weaknesses and failures, and face what we dislike about ourselves. If we continue in life collecting all the advantages of material success, being driven on to more and more effortful striving, then we will pay a savage price for it. The Shadow becomes darker and darker as more of ourselves is repressed into it. As Jung says, if the Shadow were merely evil, this might not be a bad thing. But it isn't; it also contains the childish, the undeveloped, the primitive and inferior, and these things are vital to our creativity. Denying the Shadow access to consciousness inevitably leads to neurosis; inability to accept it blocks any further development. It will erupt forth in behaviour eventually – this is, perhaps, why some people behave anti-socially or even violently when drunk, when the threshold of consciousness is reduced. 'He's the very devil when he's in his cups' – the personal devil of the Shadow can be readily seen in some of us at such times. One common defence against it is projection (a term familiar to us from Freud); the Shadow is *out there*, and not inside us at all. Many of the Major Arcana cards show hints and symbols of the Shadow, such as Strength and the Devil, as we shall see later. This ubiquity parallels Jung's description of the Shadow as an ever-present companion.

Frequently, the images and messages of the Shadow, as they develop in dreams and behaviour (and more on this later), are additionally confusing because another archetype from the unconscious presses for recognition in the conscious mind. This is the *animus/anima*, the cross-sex archetype. The anima of a man is the internal representation of femininity within him, and likewise the animus of a woman is her internal representation of masculinity. The anima/animus is strongly influenced by undeveloped attitudes and functions, and is very difficult to raise into consciousness. Perhaps the way we will first meet this internal figure is by projecting it onto someone of the opposite sex; when this happens, a very dangerous game is set into motion, as the person reacts not to another person, but to a fusion of that other with his/her own internal images.

Jung's writings about the anima suggest that he considers that thinking is typically the mental function which society demands men develop in their personas. Hence the anima is the direct opposite: dominated by the feeling function. The anima can appear as a feared siren figure, typically possessed of a mysterious power before which the man feels himself helpless. He does not comprehend the nature of this power. He knows, in some way which cannot be put down to the operation of thinking alone, that this figure shows the way to a possibility of his being a more complete person, but has to learn painfully how to accept this unconscious part of himself. Repressed feminine traits – nurturing, compassion, feeling – must become part of the man's Self.

Likewise, the animus figure in women is often dominated by the thinking function, and sometimes by possessing clear attributes of physical and material power rather than the emotional power of femininity. The animus can appear as warrior, hero, or – on a lower level – a well-known powerful male figure in public life (a sportsman, a political or military leader). Unlike the anima of the man, which is often a singular figure (or type), the animus figure may often appear in several guises – perhaps, as men have polygamous tendencies in their consciousness, and women more monogamous ones, in the unconscious matters are reversed. June Singer, a female Jungian writer, suggests that the animus in women is the masculine drive which enables them to break through the limitations they impose on themselves, and which society imposes on them also, and use the part of themselves which can think coolly, has a natural authority and can use logic, strength, and determination, *without* giving up the nurturing and compassionate traits their conscious minds accept and emphasize for the female role. That's the ideal: bringing the two together. But things will often go wrong, so that a person is almost possessed by the anima/animus, the woman becoming a carping harridan, the man a childish, moody, petulant creature.

What makes this process difficult is the great power of the archetype. It is very hard to accept what the unconscious says and assimilate it gently, hard to keep equilibrium in the face of powerful imagery coming from the unconscious without being overwhelmed by it.

Deeper still within the recesses of the unconscious mind are the same-sex archetypes; what is most specifically masculine in the man, what is most specifically feminine in the woman. These archetypes are truly collective; whereas the Shadow was partly personal, partly collective, and the animus/anima mostly collective but somewhat affected by personal experience, the archetypes of the Wise Old Man and the Great Mother are purely collective, untouched by any personal experiences we have had. The basic masculine principle in the Wise Old Man archetype is a spiritual one; by this Jung means an artistic, religious, philosophical, ethical principle, spirit being the power behind these 'highest' attainments of civilization. The feminine principle is a material one; fecundity, nurturing, mothering, fertility. This is *not* to imply either that femininity is an inferior quality, nor that it is lacking in what might be termed 'spiritual' qualities in a more vernacular sense than that used by Jung. Great Isis, fertility goddess of the Egyptians (this is a classic Great Mother or *Magna Mater* image in mythology), was possessed of great wisdom and was supreme goddess of Magic. The term 'material' shouldn't be read in too limited a way.

These archetypes are *mana* figures for Jung – that is, they are possessed of extraordinary power. When we encounter them, they seem awesomely powerful and ever-mysterious. They have a *numinous* quality – we are profoundly emotionally affected, but we are not certain why this is, and we could not explain our fascination. This powerful subjective factor is also part of the definition of 'archetypal', together with the objective factor of the ubiquity of archetypal forms – the definition involves both areas. The images of the High Priestess, the Fertility Goddess, the Magician, and Charon the boatman ferrying the dead across the Styx, still have a power of fascination for many of us, and these are all images of the Old Man/Great Mother archetypes.

Dealing with these archetypes is dangerous, precisely because of their power. Their *mana* may not be assimilated into the conscious mind, but rather inundate it and possess it, producing megalomania and self-glorification as the person identifies totally with the archetypal images. The form of Nietzsche's madness, his identification with the god-like Zarathustra, would be one tragic example. The final megalomaniacal writings of the sexual radical Wilhelm Reich would be another – in his last books, in addition to comparing himself with Christ and other great figures, Reich even took to writing about himself in the third person.

But if the dark Shadow has been accepted, the cross-sex part of ourselves differentiated, and our relation to our deepest nature worked through, then we will have brought a great deal of what was unconscious within us into the light. The loss of balance which the unconscious threatened us with has become a new balance, a partnership of the conscious and unconscious (for deep collective unconscious material can never be made entirely conscious). The archetypal image of this balanced system is that of the Self. This is the final goal of individuation; full Selfhood is attained when a man or woman has solved the problems of relations with the inner and outer, conscious and unconscious, realms. Because conflict is minimized, neurosis fades away – which is not to say there will not still be struggle within the mind. Without struggle, one is dead; any creativity involves struggling. The Self embraces *all things* within the personality; the persona, ego, the personal unconscious, the collective unconscious, and also stands as the centre of the system. Of the many symbols and images of the unconscious, the one most commonly associated with the Self is the *mandala* – a structure in which everything is balanced within a circle or a square, showing all things in detail (differentiated) but in a stable balance.

This is an idealized state of affairs. Attaining Selfhood is an ultimate goal. Perhaps we can never get all the way there. Many of us – even most of us – will be doomed simply to struggle with our Shadow, never progressing any further. Jung does not claim that human personality will always develop along the lines he indicates; but he does claim that to try to develop in this way is a goal which personality attempts to achieve. If no growth can occur, the result must always be neurosis and sickness.

But how do we apprehend and understand these seemingly increasingly obscure unconscious forces within our-

selves? What does Jung mean by 'making the unconscious conscious'?

Jungian psychologists use certain of Freud's techniques, most notably dream analysis, but how dreams are approached is fundamentally different. For one thing, attention is paid not just to single dreams but to dream series. The reason is simple: the individuation function is progressive, it has a goal, and is orientated to the future. Looking at how the journey is progressing needs more than a single freeze-frame of the unconscious. If one thinks that dreams are only affected by past events, there is less need to look at an unfolding, progressive series. Jungians would also accept that by no means all dreams are archetypal; many may simply reflect current circumstances of the dreamer, and have no link with deeper emotional factors. Also, rather than using free-association and interpreting the dream exhaustively, Jungians use the technique of amplification: to understand some motifs in the dream, the analyst may find similar motifs in literature or art, and give these to the dreamer to think about and try to relate to his own dreams and fantasies. These common images are used as a jump-off point for creative imagining.

Jung considered that people can well subjectively recognize archetypal material in their dreams and fantasies. Also, repression is often not so much suppressing the taboo as a matter of not developing the seemingly useless, which loses the ability to influence consciousness. A man rejects his feeling function by not developing it, but he is capable of understanding that this function is having its revenge on him when he becomes inexplicably prone to bouts of moodiness and childish behaviour. The conscious and unconscious are not so much at war because they hate each other, but are opposed because they simply don't understand each other – the task is for the ego to accept the opposite side and promote an armistice.

A dream involving penetrating a dark basement may mean for a Freudian a representation of sexual drives. For Jung, it may equally well mean that the dreamer is accepting a need to deal with his unconscious – that dark, subterranean realm. In Jung's own case, he gives an example of such a dream in which he found relics of great antiquity in the gloom. Now one *could* give a Freudian analysis of this, but Jung's suggestion that the dream is pointing to a need to grapple with the wisdom of the unconscious, and to understand the repressed material lost there, is surely more plausible.

The understanding of dream symbols is also more complex with Jung. There is no question of symbols being exclusively physical, standing for body parts and other people. Indeed, Jung was rather doubtful about the job of interpreting symbols at all. He felt that the dreamer could often intuitively grasp the meaning of the symbols himself. Crucially, part of the definition of 'symbol' for Jung is that it *cannot* be entirely explained and understood, especially if it partakes of an archetypal quality. Why are the mana figures of the Wise Old Man and the Great Mother so potent? One could write a great list of associations and reasons, and still one would not feel that the power of the image was exhausted and completely explained. Archetypal symbols retain an irreducibly mysterious quality. A symbol cannot be reduced and its meanings exhausted. Freudian 'symbols' are, by contrast, usually only *signs*; an umbrella is a sign for the phallus. That's it, the whole of the content, and there is no numinosity here.

Insights into the unconscious can also be had by dealing with the *complexes* of a person. These are groups of associations, memories and images, which are in some sense split off from the integrated conscious personality. The libido attached to them has an unconscious source, and is associated with a repressed or unexpressed unconscious force. Jung pioneered the use of word-association experiments to tap complexes, showing that blocking of responses to words which triggered the complexes, and odd and stilted responses, betrayed the existence of these structures. Much of the material in a complex is derived from the personal, rather than the collective, unconscious, and some emotional trauma is often the source of the problem – but there will almost certainly be some archetypal energy at the root of matters as well. A complex may point to some area in which the development of the personality, individuation, is being frustrated; some particularly painful aspect of our Shadow, for example, so that a meek man with a self-effacing persona may have complexes relating to the anger and aggression he cannot accept within himself.

Accepting the unconscious into the conscious is not difficult in theory; it's just trickier in practice. By fantasizing and using the amplification method, just keeping the unconscious images in the conscious mind, in some way the 'threshold of consciousness' is lowered, and the repressed material accepted and tolerated by the conscious mind. This is perhaps most difficult with Shadow material. Also, frightening images and associations can be mastered by repetition, especially by drawing the images again and again, using one's imagination to re-create them, and slowly gaining mastery over them. Familiarity is always a powerful tool for eliminating apprehension and fear. To my way of thinking, Jung never truly explained this process very well but, on the other hand, he does say that much that is archetypal cannot be made conscious. There is also the matter of trusting the unconscious when we cannot understand it, of refusing to deny the inner voice when some small intuitive whisper tries to gain a place in our conscious thoughts and behaviour. We will not understand why this voice speaks as it does, and if we try to use thinking to evaluate what the inferior function says we cannot succeed. We may never make this function fully or even mostly conscious but the individuated person can accept the validity of the message just the same, and still strive for a deepening and broadening of consciousness.

This certainly doesn't mean an acceptance of everything, a failure to make any kind of evaluative choices. Quite the reverse. For Jung, man is a naturally moral, even religious, creature. The world's great religions have mythologies, histories and practices soaked in archetypal content; a familiar example to some readers may be the traditional Catholic Mass, which contains powerful symbols of undeniable numinous quality. Man's spiritual nature is revealed by the collectivity of the collective unconscious, and the rooting of the deepest archetypes in the very processes of nature itself (such as fertility). We'll see more of this when we come to look at such images as the Sun within the Tarot. Man yearns for a sense of meaningfulness, of the completeness of things, as he yearns for the latent completeness within himself. Many religious paths to spiritual enlightenment are collective individuations, just as Jung found evidence of this in other collective enterprises such as alchemy, the search for the transmutation of base matter (the personality) into the radiant gold (the Selfhood) the alchemists so vigorously sought.

One final, very controversial, part of Jung's writings cannot be evaded because it is important to our understanding of the Tarot. As archetypes were part of man, so Jung considered they were virtually an objective part of nature, and archetypal forces could operate in the world around man. Sometimes a focus of archetypal energy would be made clear both in the subjective life of a person and in the objective world too. Jung's famous example is that of listening to a person telling him of a dream about a scarab beetle, and at that moment precisely such a beetle (extremely rare in Switzerland) flew in through the window. Jung invoked the principle of *synchronicity* to explain such events – a connecting principle reflected in 'meaningful coincidences', where archetypal forms linked the subjective and the objective. If this sounds like mysticism, the physicist Wolfgang Pauli was sufficiently intrigued and captivated by the idea to write a lengthy essay on archetypal forms in nature, and in the processes of scientific discovery.

It is not easy for many people, worried about unemployment, the cost of living, unruly children, and the other problems of everyday life, to accept Jung's lofty writings. 'What does this have to do with my problems?' seems an obvious rejoinder. I don't think that Jung can be dismissed so easily. What Jung has to say about the Shadow, and how we treat others badly because we project our own undeveloped and repressed tendencies onto them, is important for understanding so much social conflict. What he has to say about the dangers of projecting our anima/animus onto people we are attracted to is a powerful insight into why relationships often do not go as well as we hoped when we first became infatuated with that other person (infatuation is a sure sign of anima/animus involvement). If the later steps along the pathway of individuation seem more obscure, more mystical, then we should still not dismiss them out of hand. It would be a great mistake to dismiss as an obscurantist mystic a man who said that material well-being was important for psychological health, and that one should not underestimate the value for emotional health of owning one's own home, and a garden too. This seems a pretty commonsense attitude to the practicalities of life, but perhaps it will be easier for us to grasp something of the same ideas, expressed in a manner more in accordance with our day-to-day experience and language than Jung's arcane and often obscure writings. The work of the humanistic psychologists offers us the chance to assimilate the same message about our development as people, in a language we may find easier to understand.

Abraham Maslow: The Needs of Man

As a young man, the American-settled Abraham Maslow was a 'rat runner' – that species of psychologist which spends its time deluding itself that the intricacies of rodent behaviour have great importance for understanding anything else. One powerful factor influencing the complete change in his direction in life was observing the neurologist Kurt Goldstein working with brain-damaged soldiers from World War II. Goldstein found that, despite major injury to the brain, people struggled to regain lost abilities by finding new strategies for achieving what they had once been able to do. If an old way of doing this was now impossible, behaviour slowly began to reorganize to achieve the same ends using different means. There seemed to be a great plasticity in the brain, and in human behaviour, and Maslow began to give thought to human motivations – specifically, the drive (and the ability) to grow and develop, even in the face of such massive disadvantage.

At much the same time, Carl Rogers – a psychotherapist – was beginning to formulate his ideas about human personality and drives from a different perspective. Dissatisfied with the Freudian emphasis on sickness and neurosis, Rogers tried to grapple with the healthy drives of humanity, arguing that there is a fundamental drive to growth, development and increasing one's range of abilities and talents. Human beings, he argued, naturally tended to grow towards greater independence, greater self-responsibility, but this was not some selfish, anti-social urge. Far from it. Humans were naturally gregarious and socialization was important to them also. After all, their goals were to be achieved in a social world.

Unfortunately, this rather idyllic picture tended to get despoiled by society and culture. Most distortions of self-perception, and the origins of neurosis (which for Rogers was the inhibition of the desire to grow and develop), could be traced to social inhibitions on the person. Rogers always viewed the educational system as one of the major instruments of this inhibition. Because basic human drives were frustrated and denied, the person's self-concept, his idea of himself, grew distorted also, and if you can't feel integrated and comfortable within yourself, you will never be understanding and accepting of others. Other people will tend to be seen as threats, and will certainly be perceived in a distorted way (for Rogers, how we perceive the world is always intimately influenced by our personalities). For Rogers, a naturally healthy and sociable set of human drives is distorted and warped by the inhibitions and strictures of society.

This looks like a very naive view of human nature; it harks back to the dewy-eyed optimism of writers like Rousseau, and certainly Rogers has a great deal to answer for as the guru of that ghastly and peculiarly American horror, the *encounter group*. But it is Maslow rather than Rogers whose theory I want to look at, because it is less romantic in certain respects, and is better worked out in detail. Also, Maslow has a deft touch as a writer which makes him much more fun to work through.

Maslow followed Goldstein and Rogers (and others) in adopting a 'holistic' view of man long before that word became the trendy term it is today. Maslow insisted on treating the motivations and personality of man as a whole entity. Even a drive as simple as hunger would have to be looked at in the context of the whole person. *Nobody* says, 'My stomach is hungry,' even though that's where the hunger pangs are felt. We say, '*I* am hungry.' And, because *I* am hungry, this drive affects a great deal of me: my perceptions change (I notice the smells of food more readily and experience them more strongly than I did before), my memory changes (I start recalling foods that I enjoy eating and have eaten in the past), and my emotions change (I may feel more tense, anxious, dissatisfied). You cannot separate off even this seemingly simple drive from the whole of the person. Actually, one can even project this argument beyond Maslow's line of thinking as I've recounted it above: even simple drives have far more than a simple significance. Consider what hunger and eating means in a wider context. One eats with one's family or friends much of the time; this is a social affair. Going to a restaurant is a social business. Entertaining people at a dinner party does a lot more than satisfy the appetite of hunger. Many meals have a significance far beyond hunger – Thanksgiving, Christmas, the ceremonial of taking unto oneself the Body of Christ in the Catholic communion. French readers would probably understand this a lot more readily than the British, with their peculiarly puritanical attitude towards food. Enough; it should be clear that a 'simple drive' is anything but.

What is more, we are dynamic creatures. No sooner is one drive satisfied than something else clamours for attention. After pandering to narcissism by bathing and dressing, one may go to a restaurant, eat and drink, go on to a cabaret club, come home with one's boyfriend/girlfriend, want a cigarette after satisfying an obvious drive, and then decide (if one is neither tired nor particularly romantic) that a late-night TV film would be fun to watch. This echoes one of Jung's criticisms of Freud: one cannot reduce the unconscious to inactivity by eliminating conflicts, because the unconscious is always trying to achieve something positive; likewise, for Maslow there is an endless dynamism to our motivations. It is these motivations which are the key to our personalities.

Maslow eschewed giving some kind of list of motivations. For a start, any sort of listing tends to carry an idea that the motivations are equals in some sense, that they are equally strong and have similar probabilities of appearance, which isn't true. It also suggests that they are discrete and isolated, which is hopelessly wrong (consider the many motivations involved in eating again). A list does not reflect the fact that motivations are *hierarchical*. With the introduction of this term, we are getting closer to the Maslovian model of what motivations are.

Before presenting Maslow's postulated human motivations and needs, one point Maslow makes is worth pausing over. Maslow notes that our motivations are more realistic than many explorers of the unconscious would give them credit for. He notes wryly that people earning low salaries do not, by and large, yearn for yachts and aeroplanes, even though these things might be yearned for by someone who (as an example) has his snout in the trough of the insider trading of our major Western financial institutions. Motivations have a better 'reality awareness' than they are sometimes thought to have. On the status of the unconscious mind, Maslow was rather uncertain. He accepted that the unconscious mind had creative potential, and that drives which did not affect our conscious thinking strongly almost certainly did have some unconscious force. Putting the two together surely suggests that the unconscious has some power creatively to force an awareness of better elements within us into consciousness, for our higher drives are the hardest to realize, but Maslow seemed somewhat reluctant to draw this conclusion. It is something we will have to return to later.

Basic needs formed the most potent drives for most people, in Maslow's view. There are the simple, physical needs governed by homeostasis – the physiological self-regulating principle. Hunger and thirst would be the most obvious examples; sex is a much trickier case to consider. These drives are *prepotent* for us; that is, if all our needs were unsatisfied, these needs would be the most important, the ones we would seek to satisfy first. Again, as we've seen, these needs affect everything in the personality; Maslow wrote, provocatively, that for a desperately hungry man, Utopia could be defined as a place where there was plenty of food. Put another way, man may not live by bread alone, but without it he doesn't live at all. However, such cases are very extreme. When the basic needs are satisfied, others will come to the fore. The relative potencies of drives and needs change; this is always a dynamic process, some needs fading and rising again as others recede. As we will soon see, this dynamism and the appearance and re-appearance of needs and drives is a central theme in the whole of the Major Arcana of the Tarot.

Safety needs are our desires for security, stability, protection, freedom from fear and chaos, our needs for structure, order and lawfulness. These can be every bit as dominating as being-needs. Such needs may be very powerful in the child, who is a helpless creature dependent on adults for safety and protection. Their power is reflected in the damage which experiences such as the death of a parent, divorce or separation, or just endless parental arguing can do to a child.

Belongingness and *love needs* are the next hierarchical elements. These are our needs for friends, spouses and sweethearts, children, affectionate relationships, a feeling of place in a group and a family. When such needs go unsatisfied, the person feels pangs of ostracism, rejection, rootlessness, friendlessness and a frightening alienation. Maslow argues that the current strong interest in such enterprises as encounter groups, counselling groups and self-help organizations surely reflects a major inadequacy in our society to address these needs. It is difficult to argue with this, I think.

Esteem needs are our desires for strength, effectiveness, achievements, a sense of adequacy and mastery, freedom and independence, reputation and recognition of ourselves as valued by others. There is a subtle difference from belongingness needs, for they are very much concerned with the reactions of personally significant others, but esteem needs are clearly in part much more concerned with one's *inner* sense of one's own worth. Esteem needs are concerned not just with getting affection from others, but getting *respect*, and above all getting *earned* respect. That which decides whether the respect is earned or not is an *internal* judgement about how deserving we are; it is a judgement made by an internal moral agency, if you like, which is intrinsic to our deepest nature.

So far, so good. Maslow's claim that these needs are a hierarchy, and those at the bottom are more potent and more pressing and in some sense more obvious than those higher up the ladder, seems a plausible one. However, we haven't got to the apex of the pyramid yet.

Even with these other needs satisfied for much of the time, Maslow suggests, a certain restlessness often develops. There is a need to create, to *be* the right thing, the right person, *to be true to one's own nature*. For Maslow, this is the highest need: the *self-actualization need*. Putting it in rather an abstract way, this is the drive to actualize and make real what one is *potentially*. The specific form this takes will vary with different individuals and as a function of their circumstances: it may be the urge to be a great artist, a pioneering scientist, or a wonderful parent to one's children. Maslow does not regard such allegedly loftier pursuits as art or science as in some sense superior to more mundane matters. One of his most telling dictums is, 'It's better to bake a first-rate cake than produce a second-rate painting.'

Shortly we will see exactly what Maslow means by self-actualization, but some further points and reiterations about the higher and lower needs are worthy of note first. Lower needs are imperative for physical survival, and there are generally fewer preconditions involved in satisfying them. But higher needs, when gratified, produce more powerful subjective results – greater happiness and serenity. Their pursuit is a step away from mental sickness, which is so often tied up with chronically unsatisfied safety needs or other needs low in the hierarchy. Higher needs are less selfish, and they involve others in more co-operative and less manipulative ways.

Maslow also speculates about specific pathology linked with certain areas of needs. People suffering from obsessional-compulsive neurosis, he feels, may have chronically unsatisfied safety needs: their bizarre rituals and obsessional thoughts ward off the feared instability of an unprotected, insecure, existence. Psychopaths have an obvious and major problem with belongingness and love needs. Perhaps most importantly, Maslow writes of the pathology of futility and meaninglessness; the absence of fulfilment in life. This is due to the frustration of self-actualization needs, not least because these bring into play our ever-present love of exploration, curiosity, play and experimentation, most freely and easily (higher needs always have this quality). With no sense of inner purpose and a wretched creative life, an insidious psychopathology – in some sense the ultimate mental sickness – is the inevitable result.

We can understand the self-actualization need by considering Maslow's descriptions of what self-actualized people are actually like. Just trying to reel off a list of adjectives would not be quite so useful here. Maslow did not find very many people who fitted the bill, which is interesting; despite interview and questionnaire and other research, few people came up to scratch. Again, there is an echo of Jung here: we do not attain our ultimate goal, although we can come close to it. There is no perfect human being!

There is an important balance between acceptance and evaluation in self-actualized people. They are tolerant of others, and accept the weaknesses and frailties of human nature, but are not self-satisfied. They certainly evaluate, but are not as ready to condemn as many. They are accurate perceivers and judges of others, and Maslow even asserts from experimental studies that they have superior perceptual faculties. They are often detached, liking solitude and privacy, avoiding pointless conflicts, but Maslow is swift to dispel any ivory-tower image. Far from it; such people have a very keen sense of justice and rightness and will work endlessly to promote these values, providing that they can do something about things – as practical people, futile confrontations are to be avoided. They will reject cultural norms in many cases, but not by substituting some infantile social rebelliousness for conformity. So far this all sounds deeply wonderful and one wonders why they do not all wear halos.

Maslow is quick to counter such idealizations. Just like anyone else, self-actualized people can be boring, stubborn, and irritating. They can even be ruthless – they are very strong personalities, after all. Maslow gives an example of such a person abruptly cutting off all ties with a lifelong friend who turned out to be dishonest – a ruthless action indeed. No angels, these. But two final pieces of the picture remain for us to see.

Quite simply, self-actualizers have more vivid and intense lives and experiences than others. Not least, it is this criterion which permits us to say that in some sense these people have more completely fulfilled the potential of what it is to be fully human. Maslow puts much emphasis on what he terms the 'peak experience' – the experience of something awesome, an experience of great wonderment and joy, an awareness of something beyond one's own Self which is invigorating and powerful. Such an experience may be mystical, sexual, a response to some timeless piece of music, or the 'oceanic feeling' some writers describe in response to a communion with nature. The sense of one's place in space and time is wholly lost, so that a feeling of timelessness or the eternal is strong, and there is a quality of freshness, even naivety, about the experiences and impressions. The definitive hallmark, Maslow says, is that the person has a powerful conviction that something very important and very valuable has happened. It is almost impossible to express the sense of experience to others, save perhaps through poetic images. These peak experiences are most common for self-actualized people, but not confined to them, and for others the compelling nature of them can draw them further towards the goal of self-actualizing. In his writings in this subject, Maslow surely does justice to one of the most profound of all human experiences.

A subtle, and telling, point we could finish with is Maslow's claim that many conflicts simply evaporate for self-actualized people because *the conflict was never 'real' in the first place*. The struggle between intellect and emotion, reason and feeling, disappears because the two fuse: empty intellect with no deeply felt ethical conviction atrophies away as it should, and irrational emotions (such as guilt and shame and fear) become fused with the light of reason and the feared dark spectres vanish. One dichotomy which is seen to be equally false is that between selfishness and selflessness; the acts of self-actualized people are mostly good both for themselves (selfish) and for others (unselfish). As Maslow writes – if duty *is* pleasure, and work *is* play, where's the problem? He also wrote that such a state of affairs shows that the higher and the lower are not in opposition but in agreement – an obvious affinity with Jung.

Human beings *can* choose this path of development if the choice is possible for them, Maslow asserts. Often it is not. Adverse material circumstances, a repressive educational system and the inhibitions of society do not make matters easy. Maslow recounts a telling anecdote from a seminar with some students, in which he asked them to write down their ambitions for their future career. He was appalled by the utter mediocrity of their expressed desires – he railed at them, for nobody wanted to be the President of the United States or anything remotely near this. Education teaches us to be mediocrities. It is dedicated to selling the child short from the first day he walks through a school door. Now this is *not* pure romanticism, for the key to Maslow's argument is the fact that none of his students wanted to be the best of *anything*; they would be happy to settle for mediocrity within the system. It's not that no one wanted to be the next President, just that nobody had the courage to proclaim that they wanted to be *great* at anything – and great in the sense of being *worthy*, and not in the sense of 'having it all', that hideous American sickness of worshipping appearances and denying the substance of merit inside a person.

There is a strong attraction to a theory which says that the desires for justice, fairness, equity, compassion and kinship with our fellows are needs which can be liberated within us, and which – if realized – become our most gratifying needs when they are satisfied. Moreover, Maslow is a realist. He acknowledges the frequently greater power of lower needs and the adverse effects of poverty, insecurity and helplessness on our personalities. Human nature has been sold short, Maslow proclaims. We are better creatures than we give ourselves credit for, and better than we often allow ourselves (and others) to become. Yet, our cultural institutions frequently deny us access to our better selves, both as systems (like education) and as approved ways for gaining knowledge (like science). Maslow always considered science a valuable tool for human understanding, and used scientific methods (such as his perceptual experiments we noted earlier) to test his theory. But he also sharply criticized science for its inhibiting worship of orthodoxy, and its refusal to admit to the value-laden, subjective philosophy buried behind the facade of 'objectivity'. In particular, the ruthless drive to reductionism, pulling everything into its component parts, denied the value of looking at human beings as wholes, as complete people.

If science denied full humanity, George Kelly turned the picture upside-down by considering man as scientist. Maslow asserted that science inhibited much of human nature; for Kelly, human nature in some strange sense *is* science. This provocative theory is our last subject for inquiry.

George Kelly: Constructing the World

George Kelly, an American psychologist who also worked with the mentally ill, considered that man could be viewed as a scientist in the way he dealt with his world. We construct internal, mental 'patterns' to perceive the world – Kelly terms these *constructs*. The key to understanding personality is examining how we perceive the world in terms of our inner constructs, and how they grow and develop and determine our actions. Literally, we are in the business of constructing the world! Some constructs are publicly shared, and others are private, idiosyncratic affairs. For Kelly, the fundamental thing about human beings is that they attempt to *anticipate* events. This, as in Rogers and Maslow, is a dynamic affair – we are always testing the world, changing our constructs to achieve better predictions of future events. Our unique ability to anticipate the future is reflected in this overriding desire for prediction and thus for control. Prediction and control would certainly be two keywords for science and, Kelly argues, they are the ultimate goals for humans.

This desire for prediction and control is Kelly's one fundamental claim about human nature. His other suggestions are developed in a number of what he terms 'corollary arguments', embellishing the details. Some of these follow fairly obviously, for example, Kelly argues that people anticipate future events by considering possible re-occurrences of events which are fundamentally similar in kind. Then again, it's likely that no single construct will be able to deal with any future event of any real complexity so, Kelly argues, we employ a number of constructs together to do this, and we also use these in an orderly way. We *don't* use combinations of constructs which are contradictory and disconnected; we use a 'construction system' involving logical linkage of different constructs. This isn't a need to be consistent within oneself so much as a seeking to anticipate as much of the future as is possible, and relating ourselves to that world of events. We try to predict all we can and place ourselves within that range of events so that we can operate most efficiently. We dislike contradictions, paradoxes, and disorderedness. We are really quite logical creatures!

Another of Kelly's claims gives us a clearer idea of what he means by 'constructs'. These constructs are dichotomies: things are either-or, this-or-that. We use binary classifications, at the elementary level. A construct is a way in which some things are construed as being alike, and different from other things. So we classify and construct events as black-white, painful-painless, public-private, and so on. This doesn't mean that we can't use more sophisticated ways of looking at things. We can, but the building blocks are this 'binary coding' and more complex constructions are built of several simple ones operating together (think of adding strong-weak to pain-pleasure and you already have a 4-point scale. Add in transient-enduring and arguably you have an 8-point scale. One can see how subtler constructs evolve. This 'binary code' has a strong affinity with the Tarot, with its use of dark-light, above-below, masculine-feminine, and similar elements; but more of this shortly.

Constructs vary greatly in how far we apply them. This is not unlike scientific theories; some have very general application, some much more limited application. And every theory has an area where it is especially suited; the general and special theories of relativity are useful in most areas of physics, but totally useless to a psychologist, even if in some sense those theories remain 'true' in the social science. So it is with constructs. We are logical, and logical in a very pragmatic way. Cold-hot is a useful construct to deploy when approaching food, but not much use when dealing with books. Constructs, like theories, are tools. Consider an analogy. What is the more useful tool, a hammer or a screwdriver? Answer: it obviously depends on what you want to do. Faced with a need to drive a nail into wood, the hammer; faced with a need to screw in a wall-bracket, obviously the screwdriver. No tool is useful for everything but is best suited for particular kinds of tasks.

Constructs are altered by experience; if we employ constructs to predict events and the predictions don't turn out to be accurate, we may modify our construction system, try out new predictors, and update our bank of constructs to achieve better prediction in the future. We may even devise entirely new constructs to deal with novel problems, but there can be difficulties. Kelly argues that certain constructs may not be very permeable, that is, they are resistant to change. The reasons for this may include perceived threats, a preoccupation with old material, a failure to reach out to the new and an inability to test any new ideas. When Kelly addresses the social life of people, what may seem so far to be a strange idea about personality seems less implausible and a trifle more interesting. For instance, Kelly claims that we understand each other through shared systems of constructs. Shared constructs are shared social processes, things we have in common, how we relate to each other. An extreme case may bring this point home. Schizophrenics have been described by many psychiatrists as being the one type of mentally ill person where there is a profound sense of *strangeness* about the person, an inability to achieve any kind of rapport. In Kelly's terms, this would be explicable, because the constructs of schizophrenics are so different from those used by other people that the discrepancy creates an inability on our part to understand them and their behaviour. Again, Kelly notes that one reason for not altering faulty constructs may be that the person lacks opportunities to do so. For example, a social isolate – without friends – has no chance to alter his disliked behaviours, because he cannot test any of his constructs in a social setting and compare his predictions (as it were) with the reactions which actually occur. These examples hopefully show that Kelly's ideas aren't some wholly abstract and irrelevant notion.

We can gain a better understanding of Kelly's ideas by considering how he measured personal constructs. A typical procedure is to take a group of names of people we know well; mother, father, brother, sister, best friend, spouse or boy/girlfriend, trusted workmate, and so on, and then to set up triads (groups of three) of these people and ask the person to specify one *important* way in which two of them are alike and different from the third. For example, mother and girl-friend might be seen as *kind* while father is *harsh*. By repeating this exercise with different groupings – which can be applied to imagined or idealized people as well as real ones – the nature of the bipolar constructs which form the basis of how a person classifies and interprets his world can become clarified. The results of this type of procedure can be put through a statistical mincing machine of some complexity (we needn't consider this here) and interesting factors may emerge. It may be surprising to us to find that we use certain constructs much more often than we realize, and it is also possible to examine the relationships between constructs, so that the independence (or lack of it) between different constructs can be examined. These relationships can be quite complex – thus *idealism-realism* and *practical-impractical* might be much the same thing for one person, but another might see realism as always being practical, while accepting that practicality can be allied with idealism too. This second person might construe that realism is practical, and idealism may be practical or impractical.

For Kelly, mental ill-health is always attributable to an inability to carry on this business of attempting to predict the events of the world around oneself. This may be due to highly idiosyncratic individual constructs, which don't mesh with those of others and lead to our becoming social isolates with entirely false theories about the world, unable to alter those defective constructs; excessively 'impermeable' constructs (which can generate anxiety and neurosis due to an increasing inability to predict anything of significance to us); failing to understand the constructs of others, and so on. In particular, 'dilated' and 'constricted' constructs will present problems. Dilated constructs are ones so general and over-extended that many judgements are made in terms of them which are completely inappropriate (for the task of prediction). The construct of *threatening-safe* is one which paranoids, for example, deploy in inappropriate situations. Excessive constriction of constructs forces the person into obsessional patterns of behaviour, adhering to rigid behaviour patterns, forced into stereotyped actions because no higher level constructs with any flexibility within them permit the possibility of changing behaviour. There are, I think, some real problems with this way of looking at things. It does not explain different forms of mental ill-health sufficiently well, and the origins of such things as the 'impermeability' of constructs are really not explained in any convincing manner. While some emotions – notably anxiety – can be understood very well in Kelly's terms, others are not so plausibly accounted for. Consider the peak experience Maslow writes about. One *could* perhaps argue that the upshot of this is that one will update some high-level construct systems (the 'superordinate constructs' Kelly discusses) and one could even claim that the person will feel a stronger sense of the intelligibility of things afterwards, which will certainly go hand-in-glove with the drive to make things predictable (knowledge is power, after all). But, on the other hand, such a formulation surely misses what is the most important aspect of this experience – the fact that it is transcendental, that it actually *dissolves* certain constructs (like objective-subjective), and that self-actualized people will frequently have a taste for the paradoxical. Kelly could give an account of the experience, but would it aid our understanding of it?

However, this seeming put-down of Kelly brings us to a crucial point which is lifted straight out of the theory. Recall that constructs, like theories and tools, have limited areas of usefulness. If this is so (and who can deny it?) then it is clear that *different theories of personality are useful to us in understanding different things about ourselves*. This point will be at the heart of our summing-up all these writings about personality in due course. Further, some of Kelly's ways of viewing matters reveal interesting new slants on old problems. Kelly discusses 'submerged' and 'lopsided' constructs, constructs which we are not aware of deploying in our ordinary lives, or where one pole of the bipolar constructs is badly defined and we have difficulty in explaining exactly what we mean by it. (This reminds us strongly of Jung's suggestion that typically the thinking function is dominant in the conscious; if the 'submerged' pole is unconscious, no wonder we may find it hard to describe in words.) Kelly also allows for the possibility of nonverbal constructs, although these present obvious problems for measurement and description. And if Kelly's theory doesn't deal with some areas of our personality, the way in which he looks at things has value in others. It is not so much the specifics of Kelly's writings which are important to us here as the *nature of the enquiry he makes, and the arguments he uses*. Let me illustrate what I mean in a related area.

Depression is an illness which afflicts a fair percentage of the population at some time or other – figures vary, but a five per cent lifetime risk would be among the lower end of the estimates. I'm not considering just feeling blue, or a couple of days of feeling really low, but an illness which is debilitating enough for the affected person to seek some kind of professional help for the problem. The usual treatment, of course, is drugs, especially if the sufferer happens to be a woman; usually one of the minor tranquillizers, Librium or Valium, and if that doesn't work then a tricyclic or MAO anti-depressant may be trotted out. Now, the major anti-depressant drugs are really rather unpleasant, their unpleasant effects, of course, being dismissed by that convenient lie of medicine as 'side effects'. There are no such things, only effects which are undesirable. If some psychotherapy could be found to be of real value, then life would be rather improved for depressed people although the huge majority will get better with time anyway. This may not be much consolation for someone going through a severe depression, but it happens to be true. Recent clinical trials suggest that there is such a therapy. To understand it, we need to go back to some research on the causes of depression.

Martin Seligman, a behaviourist, initially claimed that depression could be produced by what he termed *learned helplessness*. Simply, if one could not avoid unpleasant things happening by taking evasive (or any other) actions, one became helpless, lethargic and depressed. In fact, Seligman claimed that this helplessness resulted from being unable to control any significant external events, positive or negative, but no evidence supporting the role of positive uncontrolled events has ever been forthcoming. In animal experiments, dogs given inescapable electric shocks proved less able to learn to avoid avoidable ones in later learning tests than dogs who hadn't been subjected to the inescapable ones, and they tended to become lethargic and suffer the now-avoidable shocks without making any effort to avoid them. Now this is hardly enough for us to claim that the dogs are depressed in any meaningful sense; as a good behaviourist, Seligman effectively appears to equate depression with simple retardation in actions, and anyone who has ever suffered from it knows that there is a bit more to it than that. Seligman suggested that childhood experience of being unable to control aversive events would predispose the person to later adult depression, a speculative suggestion which was never supported by evidence (although trying to do that would be fiendishly hard anyway).

The theory of learned helplessness was shot full of holes from the start. In addition to certain problems with the experiments, almost all of the dogs given the unavoidable shocks did learn to escape the later ones – they just took slightly longer than the other dogs. Analogous experiments with human volunteers also showed similar, rather weak, effects. The most telling fact was that in any group of creatures – rats, dogs, or people – put through these experiments, quite a few would actually show no evidence of any kind of learned helplessness or depression at all. Even genetically identical litter-mates would not behave in the same way. On the other hand, experiments with depressed people had shown that they did respond especially negatively to failures in experiments and appeared to give up trying to master problems in the face of failure, earlier than other people. The latest formulations in the learned helplessness story, which have shot the behaviourist origins of the idea to shreds, invoke differences in individual *attributions* of adverse events as the explanation for why some people react to failure and inability to control events by becoming depressed while others do not.

One of these important attributional factors is referred to as the *locus of control* – how people construct the causes of things which happen to them (the use of Kelly's term is not accidental here). People with an external locus tend to invoke good luck (or bad luck), and chance events, or the benign (or malign) intentions of other people as major reasons for many external events; those with an internal locus do the reverse. Thus, consider two people who have both just lost a good sum of money at poker. The man with the external locus of control says, 'I just got bad hands of cards,' and the man with the internal locus of control says, 'I played badly.' Since poker is a game of luck *and* skill, there is room for both views. It is those with an internal locus of control who tend to get depressed when faced with many adverse events which they cannot influence as much as they would like, for they are more likely to construe such events as reflecting a failure of their own competence.

A second element is whether attributions are made *globally* or in a much more limited way. A student flunking a mathematics exam may feel that he is stupid (a global attribution), or that he just isn't that good at the subject (a more limited one). Feeling that one isn't that good at maths (but not stupid) *and* that the paper was a very tough one anyway (external locus of control) would be a combined attribution. Again, having generalized attributions will be more likely to generate depression, since failures and adversity affect the whole of one's self-esteem rather than an isolated part or a minor part of one's personality and competence. It seems fairly obvious that this has a strong affinity with Kelly's notion of a dilated construct, at a very high superordinate level.

There is a clear affinity between these 'attributional styles', Kelly's arguments about constructs and their breadth of application. Where matters get interesting is that attempts have been made, successfully, to treat depressed people by altering these attributional styles. Therapists isolate 'irrational' attributional styles (such as considering that a single, specific failure means that one is *generally* and *completely* worthless) and point out their illogical nature to the sufferer. Then, the therapist and client work through alternative attributions, of a more 'logical' sort, and work through exercises of interpreting (constructing) the same events which precipitated the depression according to these alternative attributions. It appears that the therapy is successful, but it has *not* been shown that the specific reason for this is the changes in cognitive style being taught to people. It *could* just be that having the chance to talk with an interested and sympathetic therapist for hours on end (this is a time-consuming therapy) is good for depressed people.

With this caveat, we can say that this 'cognitive' approach to our behaviour has paid off in the case of this form of mental illness. The tool has applicability here, and it has obvious affinity, as noted, with Kelly's language; construing and attributing are very similar constructs! Indeed, Kelly's theory is the forerunner of a whole gamut of cognitive approaches to human thought and action, although his work is rarely acknowledged as such; one reason for including it here. Another is that one would not exactly pick on this type of theory as an obviously likely one for being successfully related to the Tarot, so it presents a challenge; a challenge to be taken up later. The cognitive view is a limited one – but one with value, nonetheless.

Putting It All Together

The important idea we must take from these different theories has already been mooted. Each one is a tool, a way of understanding some part of our total personality. Freudian theory is valuable in understanding neurosis, much of our instinctual lives, sexuality, dreams, and the like, but in dealing with higher drives and aspirations, art and creativity, it is valueless, possibly even pernicious. Jung has much to say about the adult development of personality, much about areas of psychology (alchemy, myth and legend, stories and folklore) no one else has addressed, and his view of the conscious and unconscious minds standing in a complementary relationship is intriguing, but of childhood development we can learn little here, and many of our day-to-day concerns seem almost ignored. Maslow is a powerful theorist of neglected and undervalued human needs, an inspirational writer about personality development and the inhibiting effects of culture, but there is little here about the unconscious and quite deliberately Maslow wanted to get away from a basis of neurosis as a framework for understanding personality. Kelly and the cognitive theorists deal with how we solve puzzles, explore the world, and construct our world, but again there is little on the unconscious, little that is persuasive about our emotions and an unsatisfying theory of development. Each theory has its shortcomings; each tool is only useful for some tasks. Yet, we shall find that the Tarot is a toolbox containing almost all the useful things which these theories have shown to us. We must open the lid and take a first look at the contents.

3
The Major Arcana

3

The Major Arcana

The Twenty-Two Trumps of the Major Arcana

Introduction

The twenty-two cards of the Major Arcana are easily summarized: these cards show us our journey through life, our early development and our individuation, or self-actualization, as adults. They reveal to us the key wisdom of the theories of Jung and Maslow, and also essential elements of Freudian theory. They are the deepest and most numinous of the Tarot images, possessing great emotional force, and when they appear in a Tarot reading (Chapter 5 details the use of the Tarot) they always point to something of major importance in our lives.

Card zero, 0, the Fool, is unclassifiable; he is singular, the most beautiful and indescribable of all Tarot images. Understand the Fool and all wisdom will be revealed for you, one writer claims, and I would have to agree with this. Cards 1–5 show us stages of our early development fused with archetypal content. Cards 6–7 show us more of our early development in childhood and as young adults. Cards 8–14 show us our adult lives, growing towards greater individuation and the development of our higher needs. Cards 15–21 take us beyond ourselves, from the realm of the Shadow Devil of Card 15 to the timelessness of the World, the last of the Major Arcana images. These divisions are not absolute; thus card 13, Death, is a harbinger of our highest development and growth, while the Devil points both back to our personal Shadow and forward to our collective Shadow and our fear of our own powers and creativity. This is a more profound insight into our 'selling ourselves short', as Maslow might have agreed had he ever written about the Tarot; he was concerned with our devaluation and fear of what is 'best' in us, but the imagery of the Devil as a Shadow-figure shows that we also lose if we cannot accept what may appear to be negative within our natures. There are no true divisions, only the divisions of convenience I have imposed here. The Major Arcana cards (or trumps) are a continuous line, a path of progress and development. In discussing each of them, I'll deal first with the images on each card, what they portray, how they relate to the theories of personality we have examined and lastly their meaning when a Tarot reading is being carried out. Each card may refer to either (or both) internal or external events, as Chapter 5 details, and the suggested interpretation reflects this dual aspect of each card. Further, for each card a positive (+) or negative (−) meaning is given. Again, this will be explained in Chapter 5, but at this stage we might note that the *divinational* nature of a card will always be very similar to, but not necessarily identical to, the way in which the card has been explained and tied in to the Tarot's theory of personality. This is because, even with the Major Arcana, in addition to the profound insights within the symbols, there are slightly more mundane qualities to, and attributions for, the cards which are also included in the description of their divinational meaning.

0   The Fool

LE·MAT

The Fool has no number; he is wholly unrestricted and free. The Fool wanders as he wishes, accompanied only by his little dog, and the staff and the wand (bearing a small bag) which he carries. In many Tarot decks, although this is not obvious in the Marseilles deck, he stands close to a cliff-face, to an abyss, seemingly uncaring of the danger the fall presents. He is the eternal wanderer, the free spirit, the unchained and unchainable. He combines folly, wisdom, and madness; he is a figure of paradox. In some decks he is a young man; in some, an old one. This is his paradox; as a youth, he is a child, the child before experience, virginal and utterly innocent and naive. As an old man he is the Wise Fool, his experiences carried within his bag, not burdening him but carried with a seeming carelessness and ease. They do not encumber him, any more than a clear path directs his journey; external constraints have no role for the Fool. The Fool wanders where he wills; he is the anarchic, the unpredictable, that which is uncontrollable within ourselves.

We cannot possibly exclude the Fool. The medieval custom of the 'Feast of Fools', the time when justice and authority were turned upside-down and openly mocked, is perhaps the most open acknowledgement of this. As St Paul wrote, 'Let us be fools, for Christ's sake.' The Fool has a wisdom we can never truly understand or evaluate. After all, the Fool has foregone human company; all he has is his own inner guidance and the dog which travels with him. He stands alone, impervious to and beyond our petty customs and dictates, and he smiles as he stares beyond himself to the roads and pathways and lands beyond. And the Fool walks on, as the road ever beckons to him. . . .

Psychologically, the duality of the Fool is crucial. On the one hand he is the child, the original balance within ourselves before we became the imbalanced, pressurized, unhappy adults which most of us are. As such he possesses a primal naivety which might seem enviable, but which has its dangers; we cannot regress (to use a Freudian term) to that stage in our development again. This would be the inferior foolishness of the Fool. The Fool's wisdom, rather, consists in his other facet: his *childlike* qualities, rather than his childish ones. As the Fool looks back, he ever looks forward, to when we are so complete that we are *as* children again. Only if we are as children shall we enter the Kingdom of God; only as childlike creatures will we fulfil ourselves. This is the Jungian notion of recreating that original balance at a higher level, of the supreme balance of the Self after everything within ourselves has been differentiated and individuated. The mythology of the Fool also shows his Maslovian qualities; just as the Fool is purely himself, his presence is essential for the well-being of society as a whole. The urge to anarchy cannot be denied, and the place given to the Fool accepts this and makes this chaotic tendency part of the structure of society. The selfish and the selfless are not opposed; they are one and the same, as Maslow claimed. We can go further. The Fool is a perfect symbol for the self-actualizer, he who registers and communes with the peak experience, for he rejects nothing and all experiences are open to him. He accepts things as they are; and his dreaming, creative nature is ready, even eager, to accept the experience which takes him beyond himself.

The Fool most beautifully proclaims one of Jung's central claims: a symbol can never be fully understood. One can write down every association one has wtih him, but something ever-elusive about his essence remains unaccounted for. This is appropriate, because he speaks to us of freedom and the endless possibilities of all things. He could never be fully explained or his potentialities fully exhausted, so long as we understand that his possibilities include madness, self-deception and foolishness.

The divinatory meanings of the Fool in a Tarot reading are these:

+ All things are possible to you, both in terms of your own development and in terms of outside opportunities. This is a time to let imagination run free and trust in your instincts. External developments may bring great luck and good fortune. An entirely unexpected influence is of major importance.

− Reckless or impulsive actions will be disastrous; your dreams and fantasies are delusions. This at least you can control; simply *don't* act on impulse or instinct. Check your ideas with others and be cautious. Be careful of those around you who suggest inspired schemes or have sudden insights. If in doubt, *don't do it*.

1   The Magician

The Magician stands, magic wand in his left hand, behind a table bearing a jumble of items. He is a complex and tricky figure, a mass of contradictions we need to tease apart.

On the one hand, the Magician is a serious professional, a dedicated artist and craftsman. On the other, he's a conjurer, using sleight of hand to deceive us. This is a familiar ambiguity. But there is a second duality to his nature, which Jung explains for us in his writings on alchemy. The Magician is both a *transforming* agent – the alchemist with his array of techniques for transmuting material things – and also *that which is to be transformed*. This is the psychological theme of alchemy, and it brings us closer to the essence of this complex figure.

On the one hand, the Magician is a very powerful, archetypal figure; an aspect of the Wise Old Man, herald of, and guide to, the deepest mysteries of individuation. He directs us to our unconscious, and he is infused with its power: the magic wand, as noted, is in his *left* hand. He links the conscious with the unconscious; he draws down power from above (consciousness) through the medium of his wand to cast light upon what is below (the unconscious). For Jung, such a connection is the essence of the spiritual principle, embodied in the Wise Old Man archetype.

But on the other, the Magician is a figure much less sure of himself. Look carefully at his face; there is a childlike quality to him, and he does not look like a man in certain control of what he is doing. Look at the clutter before him! In some decks, he is shown with the four Minor Arcana symbols – a wand, a sword, a cup, and a coin – laid out with a neat symmetry before him. The Marseilles deck shows us a different, and much more chaotic, picture. There is a feeling of a figure struggling to make sense of, and inject order into, the jumble of what is below (unconscious). In this aspect, the Magician stands for the young child, the developing consciousness, struggling to gain power over the unconscious. The early consciousness of the Freudian theory is shown here; insecure, uncertain, still emergent and largely at the mercy of the powerful unconscious forces. Keep in mind here that the left-handed wand shows us that the origins of consciousness lie in the unconscious, as Freud and others realized – this unconscious is still a major source of the Magician's power. In this view, the figure is the little individual Magician of our personal, early lives, rather than the Great Magus of the collective unconscious. He can either be a very young figure just beginning his struggle for control, or an old figure filled with knowledge and understanding.

The negative side of the Magician, likewise, is very different depending on which aspect we are dealing with.

The childish young Magician can lose nerve, be timid and afraid, retreating into a refusal to face reality, an inability to develop the conscious mind. The archetypal Magician is a liar, a weaver of illusions concerned with power over others rather than inner understanding.

Thus, giving interpretative meanings for the Magician is clearly difficult – it depends which aspect of the Magician is relevant to the spread of the cards and the story they tell as a whole. Again, Chapter 5 takes up this matter.

+ A positive strength of will, a sense of mastery over problems. A time of expansion – developing new skills, new talents, taking on new ventures. Risk-taking is likely to work out well. Adaptability and versatility are emphasized.

– Mental weakness, a refusal to accept and face hard realities. Timidity, hesitation, an inability to grasp opportunities. Inability to concentrate, distractedness, mental disquiet and anxiety, particularly anxiety about strong emotions and emotional reactions. In some cases, an abuse of power, manipulating others by force of will, or by deceptions.

2   The High Priestess

A middle-aged (or older) woman sits, robed, on a throne, looking out beyond the book which she holds on her lap. In many decks, she sits between two pillars – one black, one white – emphasizing her role as a guardian of some kind, a keeper of some mysteries. Unlike the Magician, who is an active figure, the High Priestess is quite passive, almost rooted in place, and her book emphasizes her contemplative nature. Much about the High Priestess is concealed. Only her face and hands are uncovered. Even her hair is completely bound up within her head-dress. She is obviously a woman of authority, and her authority comes from her wisdom, not just by virtue of her position in the scheme of things.

Just as the Magician links the conscious and the unconscious, so too the High Priestess, but in a different way. The Magician is an active link, using the abilities of consciousness – especially the thinking function – to illuminate the unconscious. The High Priestess is the passive counterpart; through the feeling or intuitive functions, insights from the unconscious enrich our consciousness.

The High Priestess is a strongly archetypal figure, and relates to more than one archetype. For men, she is partly an anima figure; for women, she has the qualities of the slightly darker side of the Magna Mater, while her counterpart, the Empress, is usually taken to represent the lighter, more joyful qualities, the earthy, rather than the spiritual. The High Priestess is a somewhat frightening figure; she radiates a strong power, the power of unconscious forces, and the deep blue of her robes indicate an affinity with water, with its endless depths and the seeming stillness of the deep unconscious (some packs show her robes almost dissolving into watery patterns at the hems). And yet, the fact that she is clothed in an almost confining set of garments suggests that there is a quality of unwillingness about her, that she is a guardian of secrets but unready to reveal them. Although these coverings have often been seen to reflect the mysterious nature of the (unconscious) secrets she understands, I consider that there is more to it than that. This helps us understand the different faces of the High Priestess as an archetypal figure and in early development. Although she represents the wisdom of the unconscious, she also represents the dangers of the unconscious and is a protective figure, denying access until the time is right. In the latter aspect, she has a repressive quality, and it is tempting to link her with the role of the mother in the child's early life as the one who teaches the child restraint, socialization, renunciation of instinctual demands. As the conscious mind grows and develops and gains mastery over the unconscious, the mother is a key figure in strengthening the child's developing consciousness. Part of the High Priestess's wisdom of the unconscious is the wisdom of *renunciation*. This seems paradoxical, but the energies of the conscious mind develop from the unconscious, and taming the early furies of instinctual demands is one of the first tasks of consciousness. Hence the twin aspects are not so different after all: the High Priestess is a card which shows the unconscious in a harmonious state, either stirring us to individuation (as the anima or Magna Mater) or helping us to attend, rather, to the tasks of differentiation (in early life, the mother symbolism predominating).

+ Insights, glimpses of hidden meanings, intuitive understandings which are to be trusted. Solving problems through intuitions and hunches which are strongly felt. Externally, the card may show some female figure who is a wise adviser.

− In men, the negative aspects of the anima; either a woman, or the internal anima, which is emotionally compelling and exerts an unbalancing and negative effect. More generally, emotional instability, a failure to act rationally and with caution; emotional impulsivity with bad consequences.

3 The Empress

Another female figure commands our attention: seated on her throne, bearing a sceptre and shield which are symbols of her worldly dominion, the Empress looks out towards us. She seems, clearly, to be a figure of the material and temporal worlds, rather than the spiritual world of the High Priestess, and thus naturally appears as an image of the Earth Mother. But the Empress also appears to have wings in the Marseilles deck, and this shows that she is not without spiritual qualities: she has the ability to ascend to the heavens as well as being an earthly ruler. Likewise, the eagle on her shield (a symbol of spirit) has his wings unfurled and is also seemingly ready to ascend to the heavens as he wishes. The division between spirit (High Priestess) and matter (the Empress) is not as clear-cut as it seems. This echoes a point I made earlier, about the Jungian Great Mother archetype; although the feminine principle is material-passive, it is wrong to construe 'material' as implying a lack of spirituality. These two early Tarot cards show this very clearly. Although the Empress is a part of the material-passive feminine, she is clearly a more active figure than the High Priestess, despite her sitting quietly on her throne.

The role of Empress as an Earth Mother is shown, again, in the orb and cross of her sceptre, the symbol for Venus and for the female, and in her pose; her arms are opened, her hair falls luxuriant and freely, unlike that of the High Priestess. As such a figure, she stands for the creative (spiritual) made real (material), creative drives made fruitful and useful. She is a symbol of doing, and especially *becoming*, rather than the more passive *being* quality of her sister the High Priestess. Her archetypal quality as a reflection of the Great Mother (and, again, the anima of men) is clear. In our early development, this is the beneficent face of the mother: the protective, nurturing mother. The child gains a sense of the goodness of the world around him from this source, and in the Maslovian scheme of things here is someone who attends to our basic and safety needs, in her role as feeder and protectress. Naturally, this leads on to our belongingness and love needs, the next step in the hierarchy. The Freudian concept of incestuous, libidinal attraction to a mother-figure is too narrow to illuminate this figure, although one could obviously relate it to the Empress. Indeed, in many versions of this card the Empress sits within a very luxuriant garden, and is clearly a libidinal figure; all material pleasures, including sex, are associated with this card.

This powerful figure, so clearly rooted in the material world but capable of leading beyond it, forms a pairing with her sister card, the High Priestess; this shows us much of what different personality theorists have had to say both about early development and the role of the feminine, and higher needs, in our lives.

+ Satisfaction in the material world; satiety, safety, being protected and/or protective, fertility, fruitfulness, an abundance of things pleasurably enjoyed. Comfort, reassurance, and a sense of security. The Empress can also be a symbol of growth in an important way: material needs are satisfied, and other, creative, needs may come into play, our freedom to develop them guaranteed by a sense of material security.

− Extravagance, an excessive absorption in material things, hedonism, over-indulgence; or sterility, material insecurity, an inability to grow beyond the material and consequent stulting effects.

4 The Emperor

The Emperor is the consort of the Empress, but his principle is a different one. Not love, but power! The number of this card is important and is emphasized in the symbolism of the card: the number 4 is shown even in the way that the Emperor has crossed his legs, so that they form a figure 4. Four is, traditionally, the number of practicality and balance: 'four-square', different principles and functions brought into a balance, the number of practicality in the material and temporal world. He sits, not facing us as the Empress was, but gazing to one side, looking out over his dominion, the realms over which his authority extends. He is clearly in part an archetypal figure, an aspect of the Wise Old Man. Primarily, though, he is an embodiment of the rational, the practical here-and-now. He stands for an orderliness, an organization of energies, and a practical Law by which he rules his empire.

Look also at the eagle of his shield; while the wings on the Empress's eagle were unfolded, raised to heaven (just as she had wings), those of the eagle the Emperor's shield bears are tucked in. This eagle is clearly not intending to soar to the heavens just at the moment; it is perched on the ground, at one with the material world. This again stresses the Emperor's primary role as an earthly ruler.

But there is another side to him. Like the Empress, he holds a sceptre which bears above it the orb and cross of Venus, and the way he holds this before him leaves us in no doubt that this sceptre is a key part of his authority and rulership. The Emperor is a man, in his better aspect, who rules through love and peace, for all that he is so practical, a man who denotes the force of will and reason. This again underscores his Wise Old Man aspect, uniting the material-temporal with the spiritual. He is also a powerful animus figure, an embodiment of the rule of law and logic, and a physically strong and decisive man. He has shortcomings, certainly, and these become clearer to us when we look at the next Major Arcana trump.

In our early development, the Emperor is obviously a father-figure. He clearly stands for our developing consciousness, our acquisition of logical and rational thought (the 'secondary process' thinking of the conscious mind which Freud described – rational, verbal, evaluative) and moving away from the unconscious. Modelling ourselves upon him (*identifying* with him, as Freud would say) is a crucial step in leaving behind the dominance of the unconscious, and also in taking our first steps towards asserting our independence. We still must obey his Laws, but we explore new ways of controlling our lives and understanding the world around us, and, as our minds begin to develop and differentiate (to borrow Jung's term), this gives us greater freedom to choose. He is also obviously a protector as is the Empress, particularly so far as our safety needs are concerned. Recall how Maslow emphasized our need for security, a sense of structure and lawfulness, and even Kelly's point about our desiring an orderly and *predictable* world, but his darker side is also obvious: the tyrant, the bullying and feared father. This is an ever-present danger with him, for despite his sceptre he is still strongly a figure of the material world, not easily able to cope with the creativity of the unconscious.

+ Self-control and strong willpower. Authority, rulership, being in a position of responsibility and command. Vigour and strength, a sense of natural dominance and control over what one is doing.

− Bullying, tyranny, lording it over others and being unresponsive to their feelings and desires; stressing the letter of the Law rather than the spirit of it; harshness and justice placed above and over mercy. Also, negative reactions and attitudes from those in authority, possibly leading to one's own loss of prestige or position.

5   The Hierophant

Seated on his throne, bearing the triple-tiered cross and other symbols of his authority, the Hierophant (or Pope) appears to be giving his blessing to the two young acolytes who kneel before him. He is an old man, clearly older than the Emperor (just as the High Priestess was clearly older than the Empress), and his face carries a benevolent, almost a serene, expression. This is a beautiful card, and the Pope has a function which does justice to this; he makes accessible to us the spiritual world, he is a guide and a revealer of our higher selves. The Latin word *pontifex* is the origin of the word Pontiff (one of the Pope's names), and this literally means 'bridge-builder'. The Pope bridges our ordinary lives with the eternal and spiritual which are his timeless realm of authority. If the Emperor helped us grow and develop within the material world, the Pope reminds us of the spiritual, and even an Emperor has to kneel before a Pope.

The Pope is often known as 'Papa', and his role as a father-figure is obvious; it is even shown in the card by the youth of the priests kneeling before him (even though we cannot see their faces, they are obviously very young). They are weak, small figures, but the blessings the Pope dispenses with his *right* hand will – and we intuitively grasp this – be a source of comfort and strength to them. That the Pope uses his right hand – traditionally the hand of rationality and 'rightness' as well as Light and 'righteousness' – is interesting, for it shows that the spiritual and the rational are not separated in this figure. The Pope's spiritual commands are given in a way which shows his awareness of practical realities. This is rather like the material-practical Emperor nonetheless bearing a sceptre of Venus. But, as the Emperor is clearly primarily of the material world, the Pope is still clearly primarily of the spiritual one.

The Pope is clearly an aspect of the Wise Old Man, perhaps the purest symbolization of this within the Tarot, together with the Hermit we shall meet later. But he, again, is an animus figure, a man transcending the material world, a potent force. His role as a figure in early development is more complex than his archetypal role, and needs some explaining.

We need to expand on part of Freudian theory here. Freud argued that we carry inside us an internal moral arbiter, the 'superego', which is formed from the moral strictures of our parents (especially our fathers) being in some sense internalized within us. The superego, for Freud, is a harsh and unbending agent, bullying the conscious mind (the ego) into repressing and inhibiting our unconscious needs. The immaturity of our childish minds is reflected in the intolerance of the superego, formed during childhood. The superego comes into being when we renounce libidinal desire for the cross-sex parent (the Pope follows the Empress and Emperor in the Tarot sequence; these two earlier cards are the parental symbols *par excellence*).

The Tarot shows us a different aspect: the Pope as a kind and wise man, the nurturer of our moral *consciences*, rather than our cruel and repressive superegos. As such, it shows us the rightness of the Maslovian view that we have a natural, inner morality, which is well-disposed towards others. As Maslow claims that selflessness and selfishness are not opposites at all in the highest stages of our development, so the Pope teaches us that his natural Law – a higher Law than the one the Emperor held out to us – frees us and liberates others also. The Pope stands for the earliest development of our consciences, and our growing ability to understand the needs and desires of others. Our own development as individuals is intimately linked with this

latter ability – the notion of *myself* logically involves sepa-
rating myself from other people. The Pope shows us that it
is in the growth of our moral sense that this individuality is
nurtured and grows. This is a powerful card, and a useful
symbol for meditational purposes.

+ Viewing problems and acting in a moral way, good
counsel and helpful advice, rectitude and decency, fairness.
Sometimes, a revelation of a hidden element of a problem.
Authority by virtue of *who* someone is, rather than *what* they
are.

– Distortions of the truth, deceptions, unfairness, cheating,
slander and propaganda. Denial of the needs of others. Bad
advice, someone telling us what to do to serve their own
immediate needs.

Major Arcana: Cards 1–5

At this stage, it is worth drawing our conclusions about these
first five trumps together. They point both forwards and
backwards in our lives; they are dual-aspected.

As symbols of early development, the Magician shows our
struggle to develop consciousness and a sense of control over
our lives, and the High Priestess and the Empress represent
the influence of the mother in protecting and nurturing the
child, helping the child to be trusting of the world and
drawing him out into the external, 'extravert', social universe
beyond himself. The Empress is the more satisfying of the
two cards in standing for these qualities. The Emperor and
the Pope show the paternal influence, the father as the
embodiment of Law and masculine reason, and the fostering
of the child's recognition of the rights of others through a
growing moral awareness. The father-figure is protective of
the development of consciousness and reason, the external
reassurer of the internal struggles the Magician represents.
Of these two symbols, the Emperor is the more obviously

satisfying. The more obviously 'appropriate' feel of the Emperor and Empress reflects their more earthy, material, natures: our parents are real others, external agents, and the rootedness of the material rulers within this external, material world gives them greater potency as symbols for this early development than the others.

The High Priestess and the Pope have greater 'face validity' as more archetypal, inner forms, but they also stand for important early inner developments in the child. It is unusual to interpret the High Priestess as a figure who shows the mother's role in *renouncing* unconscious desires, but I consider that her secrecy and concealed nature shows us that there are times when it is important to *counter* the unconscious. This is still very hard for the young child, but essential: the energies of the conscious mind grow out of the unconscious, after all. The Pope shows the growing natural sense of morality in the sense of recognition of others and their desires and wishes, an important developmental milestone, in addition to his archetypal role as an aspect of the Wise Old Man.

There is also a clear sense of developing series of needs at work in this sequence, with basic needs, then safety needs, and then belongingness and love needs entering the picture. The Pope shows the first appearance of higher needs, those involved with a desire for justice and rightfulness and fairness. This progression is a clear portrayal of Maslow's arguments about the hierarchical structure of needs and the fact that higher needs are later developments.

So, these first powerful, cards show clearly both early development and late archetypal qualities; they can be analysed at both levels and they have a completeness about them, as a grouping, which is deeply satisfying. The next two trumps in the Major Arcana are concerned much more clearly with the development of the older child and the young adult only, although there are some archetypal elements buried within them. We can take a look at how these two continue the story which the picture-book is now beginning to unfold for us.

6   The Lover

Sometimes (and quite wrongly, I think) labelled in the plural, the card of the Lover shows us a man, standing between two women, while Cupid aims his arrow at him. The woman to the left of him (on his right-hand side) is darker and older; the woman to the right of him is young and fair-haired. It is obvious that both of them have a hold over him; while his body is inclined to the younger woman, and his hands point towards her, he is facing the older woman. The older one has her hand on his shoulder, as if to emphasize some claim upon the young man, but the younger woman stands closer by him, and on his left side, close to his heart. For the first time we are shown an ordinary mortal figure at the heart of the action, not an archetype or a figure with some great authority who appears distant. This is just a confused callow youth, an ordinary person.

It is obvious that the young man is faced with some important choice here. More than being merely *important*, it is a *fateful* one, for Cupid is about to fire an arrow at the hapless youth. Cupid is an important figure: while the potency of his love-darts are well known, Cupid was also an angelic creature concerned with fate and destiny, not just trivial love affairs. Moreover, in the card Cupid is seen (as it were) *within the Sun*, and the Sun is a powerful image of Selfhood, as we will see later. Thus, it is clear that the decision to be made here will be of fateful consequence along the path to the distant future Selfhood. It is pretty obvious which way Cupid wants matters to go. We don't need to be told that Cupid will certainly smite the young man with love for the youthful blonde who stands close to his heart. But what may not be so obvious is that Cupid's involvement tells us that this is an *essential* decision for the young man, which can't be evaded. Trying not to have to make it will only frustrate further growth.

The two female figures almost cry out their nature to us; the older woman is the mother of the young man, the blonde woman is his sweetheart or his potential lover. The youth has to renounce his mother to be at one with his lover.

This should not be understood in too concrete a way. At a more general level, the card speaks to both men and women, and its developmental message is that we must detach ourselves from our parents in order to become independent people. Since our first sweetheart is a crucial figure in our growth as young adults, the difficulty and painfulness of the necessary choice in detaching ourselves from those who have protected, loved and instructed us for so many years is emphasized in the conflict shown in the card. But this is our destiny: destiny is Cupid's realm. Detach and grow up we must. If we fail to do this, neurosis and a total inability to develop will be the price paid. Most of us know that rather pathetic figure, the middle-aged man who still lives with his mother. We understand the neurotic pathology of this inability to grow up.

The young woman also reminds us of the Empress, and she seems obviously associated with the material world, with earthiness, pleasure and sexuality. More generally, she stands for the outer world: the world of others, of developing in a social world, of the extravert attitude, of a disinclination to deal with inner, unconscious events, and this is the appropriate development for the young adult. Much has to be learned, much done and achieved, friends and lovers found and good times enjoyed. This card is obviously bound up with Maslow's belongingness and love needs, with sex and love and affection and affiliation with others, and with growth of our personalities through experience in these areas.

+ Love and affection, friendship and companionship. Enjoyment of good times with others. Also, an important choice, one which will affect our lives and personality greatly. The right choice will be made intuitively, by feeling and not by reason, by the heart rather than the head.

− An inability to make an important choice, caused by immaturity, neurotic fears and apprehensions, emotional cowardice. Also, making an erroneous choice, a moral lapse of some kind, succumbing to temptations, indiscretions.

7 The Chariot

A powerful and confident figure faces us here; his sceptre and crown are symbols of his attainments, and the solidity of the chariot within which he rides shows us the security of his material foundation in life. His chariot is obviously the vehicle of battle and conquest, in which the young man rides forth to gain his victories. This seems a straightforward representation of what we need to attain in young adulthood: power, wealth, a sense of security and competence. In more concrete terms, a job, enough money to feel secure, a vehicle for satisfying our career ambitions, and so on. But this is a very complex card and there is a lot more to it than just these aspects.

For a start, there is unquestionably something completely *wrong* with this chariot. For a start, the wheels seem to be aligned not with it but at 90 degrees to it! Further, the horses are very peculiar indeed. For one thing, they are not even reined to the chariot, and they appear to be growing out of it. This is no accidental slip of design: the horse is a potent symbol for the unconscious, and has been recognized as so frequently (by Freud in psychoanalysis, by Ibsen in literature, and by many others). The fact that the horses clearly don't *need* reining shows us that obviously they must move as the charioteer wills: *they are his own unconscious* and their fusion with the chariot (the force of the charioteer's conscious mind and his attainments) again underlines this point.

So, matters are not so simple here. The Chariot is a symbol of conscious attainments, and in particular it shows us that mastery of the challenges which face this hardy young hero is a way we develop and learn about ourselves. But the charioteer is still young, and relatively inexperienced in life. That he is virtually walled-in within the chariot shows us that he is blinded in an important sense; he thinks that conscious struggle and material acquisitions are all that the world contains. His vision does not extend to the horses of his own unconscious which he has set before and below him, and he gazes out over their heads, not seeing them. He is too busy as a young adult finding his place in the scheme of things in the material world, through interactions with others, through developing a sense of position and prestige and power. In Maslovian terms, this is partly the concern for belongingness which the Lover showed us, but also involves the basic and security needs, and there is a slight fore-shadowing of esteem needs. The charioteer does want respect and admiration, but has no developed sense of wanting *earned* respect. Certainly he wants to be competent and develop his powers, but the attainment is perhaps more important to him than an inner sense of worthiness at this stage of his development. After all, he is the supreme extra-vert symbol in the Jungian sense, living almost wholly in the external, material world. Why, is he not a King as well as a hero, is he not crowned? Here is the danger of this card, which otherwise shows us a *necessary* imbalance in our young lives: *hubris*, the arrogance which brings the wrath of the gods. The hero thinks that his conscious will can achieve all things, and that it is all that he needs.

+ Triumph! Success in the material world, conquest, ambitions which are satisfied, ventures rewarded with gain, progress achieved through personal effort and striving. Good fortune and the efforts of others have, respectively, nothing and very little to do with it.

– Bullying and exploitation, ruthless treatment of others, overweening pride and ambition. Obsessive concern with material gain and temporal power, denial of all sentiment and feeling, riding rough-shod over the legitimate wishes and needs of others.

8 Justice

(Note: this card is, in some decks, numbered 11 and exchanges places with the card Strength.)

Gazing impassively, the figure of Justice holds a sword in her right hand and the scales in her left. Again, her number is significant: by numerologists and others, the 8-sided figure, the octagon, was considered to stand between the 4-sided square (symbol of the worldly and material and practical) and the circle, the Self symbol. This point is well made by Alfred Douglas in his book on the Tarot. As such, Justice occupies a pivotal point between our conscious, worldly concerns and our calling to higher development.

Justice is the symbol for the development of our natural conscience, linked with the Pope, and there are inner and outer aspects of this. The card shows a time when we have become more mature adults, and the first stirrings of the unconscious begin to trouble us (we are prone to construe things in this fashion, given the reliance on consciousness we have developed in our Chariot-stage). Maslow homes in on this by emphasizing that our esteem needs include the aspect of *earned* esteem, that we should have achieved success and wealth and competence in ways which are *rightful* and fair, and gaining success by underhand means is something which many of us do not like. Our conscience nags away at us. Likewise, the unconscious as described by Jung calls for justice: we live entirely in the external world, we have given over our energies to consciousness, and the unconscious is neglected and unused and it begins to claim a share of our attentions, concerns and time. The *balancing* scales of Justice show this developing need within us, and the sword of Justice is clearly not there for beheading or smiting the wicked. The figure surely does not seem to us as if this is what she intends.

Rather, Justice is the equilibrator, that which seeks to regulate emotional tensions caused by our neglect of our inner lives. She does not judge by intellect alone; the natural morality by which she judges (and this is surely a harbinger of the self-actualization needs Maslow discusses) is far less narrowly based than this. The notion of *poetic* justice would come closer to the truth. Nonetheless, Justice is not a symbol for the fully developed process of individuation, or self-actualization; we would not expect this as she is too early in the sequence of Major Arcana cards. She bears no symbols or signs showing us the four mental functions in balance, and there is no balance of light and dark which might reflect even the full beginnings of higher development. Rather, she is *the call* to us of our need to develop further; the conscience which nags away and will not be stilled. Her scales, and her clear equilibrating role, show that if we heed her, there is the promise of a better balance within our lives and personalities.

+ Formal judgements, contracts, agreements, arbitration, negotiations. Integrity and fairness, fair judgements and equitable treatment. This, of course, may involve punishment if the person for whom a question is being asked has behaved in some wrongful manner; 'just deserts'.

− Injustice and bias, prejudice and ill-treatment, unfairness and extreme views which are harmful and damaging. Also, red tape, bureaucracy, time-wasting, inhibiting regulations and rules.

9   The Hermit

An old man walks along a path, bare-headed, carrying only his staff and a small lantern to light his way. He is clearly alone, and it seems to us as if alone-ness is a natural and rightful quality for the old man – he is a Hermit, after all.

If Justice called to us of the dangers of not attending to our inner personality and the unconscious, the Hermit is a friendly helper, for with the light of his lamp he can cast light upon the inner darkness. He is an obviously introvert figure, one who is embarked upon a long, possibly endless, journey, exploring the depths. He also has a function allied with that of Justice; he is the enemy of the conscious sense of futility and meaninglessness the conscious mind may develop in mid-life, when the demands of external life and career have been at least initially met and one is left to ask, 'Is this all?' Clearly not, the Hermit reveals to us. As one writer has delightfully put it, he 'warms hearts empty of hope and meaning'. His lamp is a symbol of the inner insight with which he explores the deeper recesses, and he keeps it shuttered, for its light is very precious and the flickering flame must be protected from the elements.

At an archetypal level, the Hermit is clearly an aspect of the Wise Old Man, part of the archetype of the Spirit. More precisely within this sequence of cards, the Hermit stands for our first hesitating and tricky encounters with the unconscious in later life. It would have been nice, perhaps, if the card had shown him faced with a road leading far into the distance, leading into a cave mouth (where the later card Strength is often depicted). But even as he stands, some further elements of this picture are crucial to our understanding of what he portrays within us.

His aloneness has two important lessons for us. It is *obviously* different from the singularity of the charioteer in Card 7, for example. In that card, there was only one figure, but as a hero and conqueror the King in that card was obviously a man living and striving in a social world. Not so the Hermit. His introversion, the fact that his light is covered for his own use, is crucial. They show us that he is an aspect of our inner selves, and can only be reached by a positive *turning away from the world*. This has a corollary, the second point: it is always an error to project the Hermit onto the outside world, a mistake which can lead us to worship some external guru-figure. If we do this, we misunderstand wholly the nature of the Hermit's little lamp and the source of its illumination. There are no short-cuts to the development the Tarot lays out for us. This does not mean that an external wise helper can be of no value to us, but it does mean that we have to tread the Hermit's path for ourselves, using our own lamp to light the way.

The Hermit is also a caller for us to return to being individuals again, away from the cultivation of the persona in the social world. The path of aloneness is not an easy one to take, but the Hermit shows us that there is no other way. He does not ask us to run or follow blindly; his own tread is a measured and slow one (isn't this obvious from his appearance?) and he shows us that we too have our own lamps to begin the journey. The meagreness of the possessions he has – only the essentials of clothes, a staff to lean on, and his lamp – show us that obsessions with material wealth, status, power and the other qualities and possessions the charioteer found so valuable are not going to help us to follow this path. We have lived in the material world and this was rightful; now our attentions must slowly turn elsewhere if we are to grow and develop any further.

+ A need for solitude, choosing oneself rather than accepting the advice of others, being slow and cautious, avoiding precipitate action and impulsivity. Discretion, tact, keeping secrets, keeping to one's own counsel. A temporary withdrawal from society, but not from humanity. Sometimes, wise and helpful counsel, often from an older person.

− A pathological introversion, self-absorption, obsessive secrecy and distrust of others, obstinacy and refusal to listen to others. Childishness, a refusal to grow beyond the immediate here-and-now, denial of spiritual concerns.

10   The Wheel

This is surely an extraordinary card! For the first time there are no human figures at all. Rather, we see two monkeys, one ascending the wheel and one falling upon it, and a winged and crowned sword-bearing sphinx atop the wheel. These creatures are slightly different in some packs – the sphinx may be a dragon, the monkeys may be asses or jackal-like creatures. In some, also, the wheel is being turned by a monkey which sits on the ground. As we might expect, this is a card riddled with complex symbolisms.

The basic nature of the wheel is obviously that of circular motion, bringing what once was atop it (the monkey on the left side of the card) to the bottom, and exalting that which was once below it. In the Wheel there is an obvious promise of retribution for the hubris of the charioteer, if he has developed that sin. Further, everything about the Wheel pronounces the similarity of what appear as opposites: the rulers (the monkey once atop the wheel) will be brought down and the meek (the rising monkey) shall inherit. The old formula of 'that which is up is like that which is down' seems to force itself on us, save that the Wheel says to us that *shall be* would be a better formula, stressing the unity of inner and outer and that our divorce between the two in the process of differentiation is, at this stage in our lives, an error to be corrected. Further, the sphinx (or dragon) atop the wheel is a creature which is possessed of cunning, and speaks in riddles; the function of intellect and thinking won't do us any good here.

The cyclical motion of the Wheel also says to us, 'Well, it's been a nice linear development so far – school, apprenticeship or higher education, a career, a marriage, perhaps children, promotions, the accumulation of money and position. All this linear development stuff is at an end if you want to go any further rather than stagnating.' This dovetails with the point Jung, Maslow and Rogers made in rebuttal of Freud – one can *never* fully satisfy the drives of personality for they are ever-dynamic, and as soon as one is satisfied another clamours for action. There is an endless cycle of need-satisfaction-re-emergent need. Maslow's needs could almost be seen as a series of loosely coupled Wheels . . . but this is perhaps too fanciful. What *is* certain is that the Wheel shows us the essential *process* which dominates our later development, and the fact that it is a process being revealed and not some definite archetype which is part of that which is being shown in the Wheel, is skilfully reflected in the fact that *no human figure is shown here*. This is not so much a part of personality, as a process governing development.

The Wheel is often considered as the Wheel of Fortune, a 'benevolent' card in the days when Tarot cards were classified as evil or benign. Don't believe it. The Wheel can give a tremendous jolt and it can bring the high low; it can bring the man of material wealth and power to bankruptcy or (more hopefully) suddenly make him feel that all he possesses is as worthless as grains of sand which could slip through his fingers and leave him holding nothing. Another negative quality is shown by considering what happens when a wheel turns over endlessly in the same place; a rut is created. One remains stuck, unable to progress, unable to harness the dynamisms shown in the Wheel.

+ A new cycle of affairs in life, even a process of destiny, over which one has relatively little control. A time to swim with the tide; the current of life runs favourably. Good fortune, fair rewards for past enterprises, achievements, merited by what one has done previously.

− Ill-luck, or the past catching up with one: deserved retributions for past errors and wrongful actions. The inability to progress, being stuck in a rut, a sense of being unable to affect stagnating or bad states of affairs, ill fortune which makes directed actions fruitless.

11 Strength

No Daniel stands in the lion's den, but a powerful young woman who holds the jaws of a lion open with her bare hands. In this card, for the first time, an ordinary mortal woman is the central figure, rather as the Lover was the first ordinary mortal man to appear in Card 6. Well, perhaps she is not so ordinary − she is mastering a lion, after all!

In cards 8–10, the Tarot images showed us the problems of having developed our conscious minds in the material world and having shunned the unconscious, placing an emphasis on our lower needs. Justice showed the call of the unconscious and the first higher need feelings, the Hermit offered to light our way on a journey and the Wheel showed us the very real change which the nature of our future development would mean in our lives − from a linear path to a dynamic process. In this card, we are faced with the first of the archetypes we will meet on the journey, the feared Shadow. And here is the Shadow, the beast, being mastered by a woman. This is no accident. So far, we have developed a masculine part of our personality because this is what the world demands of us. We became the dominant, powerful, possibly wealthy, person within the chariot. Now, Strength shows us that it is feminine qualities which are associated with the unconscious, and that they will be our saving grace for the next part of the journey. Our previously revered reason, logic, and masculine Law will not bring us further at this point. It is the strength of the woman shown in this card which leads us on.

What, *exactly*, is this woman doing? It seems clear that she is mastering the lion. She is exerting her power over him, and that she is doing this bare-handed shows that it is her inner, personal strength which allows her to do this. She needs no props such as the wand of the Magician or a badge of authority like the shield of the Emperor and Empress to subdue this fierce beast. Now, if this were all there were to it, the image would not fit with our arguments at all. To progress, it is necessary to *accept* the Shadow, not to subdue it.

Well, on the one hand, we are still dealing with an early stage of individuation and the development of higher needs here, and we could not expect to find a figure openly accepting the beast within at this stage. There is clearly a frightening quality to this lion; we fear being engulfed by that hungry pair of jaws, we fear being swallowed up into the darkness of the Shadow. The woman stands away from the lion, where he cannot see her, she does not take him on face-to-face.

On the other hand, the symbolism of the lion is important in seeing that the perception of what the Shadow means is beginning to change. This is not just some wild, ravening animal; this is the King of beasts. His nobility is accepted, just as the Tarot crowned the King within his chariot in Card 7. The Shadow is not demeaned, but is accepted and the term 'mastery' needs considering carefully. It does not mean total control, forcing something to do what is against its nature; not here, surely. For what the woman seems to be doing is *exercising her Strength* over the lion; perhaps she is even mastering a fear of him. The 'defeat' of the lion is surely the reconciliation of the conscious and unconscious, the loss of the power of the Shadow to terrify and frighten which comes with its acceptance. This echoes Maslow's point that self-acceptance is a key quality of highly developed people. Maslow stated that without accepting oneself one cannot accept others; the Tarot card shows this process of self-acceptance in the first struggle to accept the Shadow. The strength gained here is not the strength of domination, but the strength gained by that acceptance and by not rejecting the Shadow. It is as if the strength of the woman partly derives from the nature of the creature she is mastering.

Seeing the lion in this picture surely brings to mind another story which has many variants in folklore, the story of the lion driven almost to a madness by the pain of a thorn in his paw which was extracted by the hero (the journeyer, in the Tarot cards). This is not exactly in accord with what is going on here, but it has relevance. It is not that the Shadow is driven to violence and rage (and is thus frightening) by any such wound; there is no psychic equivalent of the thorn in the paw which is involved here. But what the hero (here, the heroine) does is to approach the lion, without fear or the desire to hurt him, but rather with a sense of *pity*. Now this definitely *is* relevant to the approach our heroine takes to the beast, and to the psychology of this card. Accepting the Shadow in some sense involves a pity for the rejection the Shadow has suffered; the döppelganger is a lonely creature, outcast and alone, and the scapegoat (the projected Shadow) is a figure to be pitied. The Shadow has suffered through our neglect, its primitive and childish nature and its 'badness' are a result of our imbalance and denial of its needs, of our failure to accept our Shadow side and our ostracism of it.

+ Being able to face difficult problems, especially emotional ones, with fortitude; inner strength and resourcefulness; passions felt strongly which do not carry one away; persistence, in adversity if necessary, and taking a courageous risk for something one believes in.

— Weakness, pessimism, inner torments and disquiet, passion felt as destructive and uncontrolled, failure of nerve and opportunities lost.

12 The Hanged Man

A young man hangs from a bough, tied to it by one foot, hands tied behind his back. His left leg is crooked behind his right one, and his face seems serene enough, even slightly smiling. His head is close to the ground; there is even a ditch of some kind in which it hangs.

This is an extraordinary and very beautiful card. We may be familiar with other Tarot images from other sources (after all, Strength, Justice, Temperance and Prudence are the four cardinal virtues, and Death and the Devil are familiar enough!) but this is unique. A first question is: why is this man hanging? It might be that he is a criminal. Indeed, in Italy being hung by the feet is a traditional method for executing traitors (recall Mussolini) and in some packs the Hanged Man is even labelled as 'Il Traditore' ('The Traitor'). In some sense this is his crime. The Hanged Man has followed his own conscience and he spurns the approved ways of society when these do not accord with the inner voice which guides him. As Maslow says, most self-actualized people have strong inner convictions which make them critical of the ways of most others. Not that the Hanged Man is this far along the road to development; he is not even certain where he is going, but he feels that he knows how he might get there.

The struggle with the Shadow which we saw in the last

card has disturbed our journeyer as we see this person now portrayed. He had hints from Justice and the Hermit of what was necessary, and the Wheel may have shown him the inevitability of the need for change, but in confronting the dark and feared side the struggle has been enjoined in earnest. He knows from his personal experience, in his guts and emotions, that he is not the man he thought he was, and that his conscious mind is but part of a far greater whole. He can't go back and become the self-assured young man riding the Chariot. Neither can he submit to the Shadow, and he knows that he must find a way of reconciling the two. Further, he knows that passivity and contemplation are the only ways of knowing which he can use to become free of the tyranny of the external world on the one hand and the Shadow on the other. He has rejected reason and intellect as guides; his head, the proud crown of reason, is brought low, down to the ground. He has learned the necessity of this not least from the Wheel.

In doing this, he has brought his intellect closer to his unconscious (the subterranean). This begins the rapprochement he longs for. Inside the Hanged Man, the energies and abilities shown in earlier cards are being drawn down into the unconscious to be deepened and expanded. The return to the world of his here-and-now, practical-rational ego-consciousness is impossible. The Hanged Man has the wisdom to know this; this is why he has placed *himself* where he is, hanging in contemplation, and this is the nature of his sacrifice. He knows, as the Norse God Odin did when he hung from the great World-tree to gain the wisdom of runic lore, that only by such a sacrifice can he grow any further. But he knows that he will grow; this is why he smiles, and why his legs seem almost to be describing a dance. The key to this image is that the Hanged Man has *chosen* his fate, and by this active choice he has liberated himself from the dilemmas of his life. He can only hope, and retain a naive trust, concerning the success of his venture. He has only his own inner guidance to trust, after all.

+ Accepting one's inner guidance, ignoring external demands and dictates and the advice of others. Doing what feels right even (*especially*) if others think this is wrong, impractical, strange. Good results, greater inner peace, resulting from such actions. A necessary self-sacrifice, voluntarily foregoing something (especially material objects).

— Inability to escape social pressure; fighting one's inner self and nature; over-reliance on the linear, the logical, the easily demonstrated; an inability to make a jump of faith or belief which would bring advantages and peace of mind. An inner struggle which exhausts one, and/or ends in some sense of defeat.

13   Death

The Grim Reaper strides out over a black field, reaping his never-ending harvest with the scythe he carries before him. Severed heads and limbs lie strewn upon the ground, and the face of Death is a mask of horror and inhumanity. So this card may appear, and most people recoil instinctively from Death when he appears in a reading. But Death is in one sense our greatest friend and ally within the Tarot. Without Death, there would be no growth at all, and Death is the *only* thing which can help us in the darkest days. The key to this card is that Death and Rebirth are but two faces of the same coin.

Consider Death's taking of life: he is governed by a Law, the Law which says that there is always an appointed time for Death's actions. He is in this sense impersonal. If you wish, *there is never a wrongful death*. This may seem a crazy or even callous statement. But it is powerfully true in the psychological sense at least. Look, also, at the heads which lie on the ground. One is crowned (showing us again that Death is no respecter of aristocrats and that the young man in the Chariot, like everyone else, had better watch out for his approach!) but both are clearly *alive*, even smiling. The hands in the ground are almost waving to us, as if they are also alive, and they grow beside the abundance of plants shown. Below Death's scythe everything in this picture is *bursting* with life, new life, the life of Rebirth, and, crucially, this life grows from the dark ground – from the unconscious, from within ourselves.

This is the nature of Death: he is the destroyer of the outmoded and outworn parts of our personalities. Because of the very radical nature of his operations, one could even see him in another language as destroying an entire network of 'constricted constructs' that we have built up over the years. He is the key to revitalization, renewal, growing into an entirely new person. Well, not *entirely* new perhaps, but revitalized all the same. As the crowned figure in the bottom right-hand part of the picture proclaims to us, 'The King is dead – long live the King.'

The symbol of Death also contains an important lesson; as a skeleton, he is comprised of bone, and bone is the most durable thing about us. Our bones remain long after the rest of us is gone. But the process of Death is endless; all things must change, all things must be revitalized and reborn as Death's scythe sweeps to and fro. Thus, this single figure teaches us the lesson that what is most enduring and what is most dynamic are one and the same. The persona-mask, our social roles, the possessions we gained – these are the real illusions; the true eternal substance is the stuff of change. Death portrays a time when we realize this, when we feel it deeply – in our bones, if you like.

Death is the irrevocable step. The Hanged Man chose to hang in the wind, and now the Grim Reaper has come for him, and the processes of change have been set into irreversible motion. This may, most definitely, be a painful process. Part of the natural cycle of Death's domain is mourning, even if a rebirth is implicit; a mourning for what is lost and gone. Preparing for that mourning and the pain of it was part of the Hanged Man's preparations as he renounced his past, but no amount of preparation can obviate all of the pain and sorrow Death trails in his wake.

This reminds us of Jung's and Maslow's repeated insistence that self-actualization (or individuation) is hardly an easy process and that it demands much of the person determined to grow and develop. What makes it worthwhile is the promise of greater joys to come, and a keen sense of the inevitability of it; and Death is the card which brings this inevitability home to us very forcefully. If we have come this far, there can be no possibility of turning back. The Hanged Man understood this, and Death brings the point home with complete finality. Death's changes are painful, radical, complete and lasting, and there is an appointed time for them when they cannot be evaded any longer.

+ A drastic and probably unexpected change. This change is nonetheless the 'logical' outcome of past events, and while it may be painful in the short-term the ultimate results will be good. Getting rid of that which is superfluous, outmoded, useless, especially in our personal lives.

− Being stuck in old habits and ways, a complete inability to adjust to new demands, lethargy and defence against the awareness of a need for change. Fear of change and physical death itself, a major loss of some kind.

14 Temperance

The winged female angel of Temperance is clearly absorbed in her task of pouring a liquid from one (blue) vessel to another (red) one. In most packs, she is shown standing by a pool of water, with one foot on the water, dipping below the surface, and one on dry land. She is thus obviously a figure who brings opposites together; land and water, the contents of different vessels. Incidentally, whatever she's doing, it's clearly impossible. Since the red vessel is not directly below the blue one, it's obvious that the liquid can't pour out like that. Neither can you stand on water as if it were solid ground. This doesn't bother Temperance too much; she just gets on with the task. Perhaps what she is doing *is* impossible, for the conscious-logical mind, but then she is absorbed in something too profound to be apprehended by such limited means.

In the Marseilles deck, Temperance wears a single blossom on her brow and plants grow on either side of her; in some decks, these are irises growing by the pool, and many writers have compared this angel with the Greek goddess Iris, whose symbol was the rainbow. The rainbow, indeed, appears in some versions of this card, and it would be a fitting one for Temperance; after Death's black thunderclouds of ill-omen, the promise of the rainbow illuminates the sky. There is peace after the turmoil Death caused, and Temperance calmly goes about her task. She practises the technique which will produce new life; synthesizing opposites, bringing the duality of conscious and unconscious together. As such, she is a potent symbol of the individuation process which Jung described. In other guises, she is an alchemist or an artist, sublimating baser energies, to use the Freudian term. As an anima figure, she shows that this process is not a consciously

controlled one. It is a natural development after the renunci-
ations and self-sacrifice of the Hanged Man and the changes
Death brought.

In addition to this general function, Temperance has a
more specific and pressing task. The peacefulness and sense
of inner calm she brings is essential for coping with the
powerful collective-unconscious archetypal forms we will
soon have to deal with, most notably the Devil. By
connecting the conscious and unconscious in an effortless,
easy way, she makes confronting these deepest unconscious
energies less effortful than they would otherwise be. She has
a quality of an inner knowing (as befits her role as an anima
image), and she is a vital stage in development.

At this stage, the opposition of the conscious ego and the
Shadow (specifically the personal Shadow) has been rejected
by the Hanged Man, the necessity of further development
brought home by Death, and now Temperance symbolizes
the tool we need for the last stages of self-development, the
harmonious interchange and exchange of opposing energies,
the individuation function. But, importantly, for all this the
person still has but the seed, a hope of new life and greater
development. What the personality was has been finally
discarded, but now the person is in a state of passivity,
quiescence and stillness despite the motion of the waters in
this card. One is ready to progress, but there is still much to
do.

Many writers consider this a weak card, but I think this is
erroneous; Temperance *does* show a state of passivity and
apparent lack of any kind of action, but this is necessary, for
what she is doing is largely internal, achieving a state of
peace within the person rather than acting externally.

+ Blending opposites harmoniously, an inner peacefulness.
A need for quietness, solitude, getting away from external
distractions and demands in so far as this is possible.
Balancing different areas of one's life.

— Inability to balance things; sliding from one extreme to another; volatile situations (and people, sometimes) one cannot control and which are disruptive. A need for rest and peace which is thwarted.

15   The Devil

This card probably causes more fear in many viewers than any other, save for Death itself. This is doubtless due to the associations this card has for religious teachings many have learned. So, the Devil is seen as the Prince of Darkness, evil and cruel, sadistic and dwelling in eternal darkness. But the Tarot Devil is a much more complex creature than this. He needs a detailed discussion to do him justice, for the Devil is a crucial figure in the Tarot.

For one thing, he is a mass of contradictions. One of them is well known to us: although he dwells in hell, he is an Angel (like Temperance), but a fallen one. Originally, he was radiant with Light – Lucifer the Light-bringer. Other paradoxes are obvious in the card. He appears to be a male figure; he has male genitals, it seems, and he also has phallic horns although – another contradiction – they almost look as if they have been stuck onto him, rather than being natural growths. On the other hand, he is heavy-breasted, a distinctly female quality and, although apparently human in appearance, he has stag's antlers, clawed talons like some bird of prey and bat's wings! What a jumble he is!

Further, we know the Devil's power and ability to use black magic, and to teach it to witches and other minions of his evil. Perhaps he has even used such magic to ensnare the two slaves who stand before him. In the Marseilles deck, these look like lesser devils, but in most decks they are shown as two people, a man and a woman, and the ropes around their necks are *very loose*. This is crucial; they seem to be *willing* slaves, for they could surely free themselves from their physical bonds easily enough. But, in comparison with this feared magical power of his, look at the Devil's sword, traditionally the instrument of masculine *Logos* and power. He doesn't seem to be holding it in a way which suggests that he knows how to use it! It seems to be being held for the sake of appearance, to frighten us, rather than being readied for any actual *usefulness* it might have as a weapon. Hmmm. Quite a difficult fellow, the Devil.

The Devil is a Shadow figure; this seems clear enough. He may also be an animus figure, the feared rapacious masculine. Certainly, in his Shadow aspect he is a deeper version of the Shadow seen earlier in the form of the lion in the Strength card. He is strongly charged with the archetypal power of the *collective* shadow *as well as* the personal-unconscious shadow. This distinction is obvious, as he has greater power than the lion, and it is in accord with Jung's distinction between the two. Struggle is now enjoined in earnest with this collective archetypal power. How we will triumph over him once again involves the same mastery we developed over the lion; *acceptance* of the Devil. This is very tricky, for the Devil is a talented weaver of illusions, and he wants to seduce us into staying in his lair and being slaves like those before him. Perhaps, after all, they are willing slaves in the sense that *they do not realize that they could slip off their bonds and be free of him*. This is our fate if the Devil succeeds in his aims. Not the least of his blandishments is the whispered insinuation that his world is all there is, and usually this is the material world, the here-and-now, materialistic, hedonistic world of possessions, sex, money and power. After all, Satan offered Christ dominion over the *material world* when he sought to tempt him; Satan is not in the business of offering spiritual awareness or self-development, but *power*. He does this with all the seductive power of our collective and personal Shadows. Dealing with him is clearly going to be a dangerous business. Our early steps along the way have prepared us to some extent, but with this powerful archetypal figure we are faced with a wily and cunning adversary.

His sexual nature needs further discussion, too. Clearly, Jung's suggestion that many of the sexually-based conflicts which Freud studied were Shadow elements seem borne out by the repressiveness and sexual confusions of this Shadow-Devil. He is traditionally a sexually rapacious figure, and his subterranean abode symbolizes the repression of sexual energies (this is one of the reasons why we need to liberate the energies shown in this card). His appearance of possible bisexuality may symbolize the damage to these energies which repression brings. Freud had a difficult time with bisexuality: although he recognized that 'active-masculine' and 'passive-feminine' sexual inclinations were part of libidinal nature, he considered that homosexuality and bisexuality were a form of pathology engendered by repression. The Devil may be symbolizing this with his bisexuality and confusion of gender identity. This latter point is crucial: while views may differ on homo- and bi-sexuality as pathology, very few people would consider confused gender identity (trans-sexualism) as anything but pathology. Freud's problem was in being unable to distinguish between our sense of being male/female, masculine/feminine, and homo-/hetero-sexual; he conflated these, reducing complex psychological processes (which, for the record, seem to be largely independent of each other) to the same thing, which is simply wrong. Perhaps Freud never could understand the Devil; his excessive absorption in his realm suggests this. But, at any rate, it is crazy to regard the sexual confusion of the Devil as symbolizing some kind of basic inner bisexuality within us; this is a trendy myth perpetrated by some people who ought to know better. Rather, he symbolizes sexual pathology, the pathology caused by repression. The trick is to realize that repression causes the problems, and that the Devil must be accepted, without falling prey to the pathologically confused desires with which he seeks to seduce us.

If he were just evil, as Jung says about the Shadow, then

there wouldn't be a problem. Well, maybe there would. After all, if evil is not even available to us as an option then moral choice no longer exists. You cannot choose to be good, moral, a better person, if the option of being a real swine is not meaningfully open to you. Without Eve and Satan there would be no possibility of an *informed* morality. If we can't confront the Devil then we can't be fully human.

What's more, we have to acknowledge the undoubted attractions of the Devil. If he is purely an evil and destructive agency, how come he wears antlers, symbols of growth and regeneration? And his role as a Light-bringer needs reinterpreting; this function of his has been lost, but he can still be a spur to our attaining the light. Understanding his darkness directs us upwards to that light. Standing as he does for the split-off parts of ourselves, Shadow impulses and images, if we cannot accept him then we can never make ourselves whole and emerge into the light of the Sun as we hope to later.

Again, as Maslow stressed, self-actualized people aren't perfect. They can, for example, be ruthless; but if they didn't have that quality, they would not be unambivalent, and without *that* quality they would not be capable of the unconditional love and regard which they can feel for others. Perfection may be a quality of God but it isn't part of the human condition. The trick is in denying the Devil his power to seduce us, to bind us round with illusions, and in accepting the dark side of ourselves without identifying with it or being overwhelmed by it. Accepting him can mean the release of still-repressed energies, unifying split-off parts of the Shadow with the rest of ourselves, and beginning the final stages of the journey after the trauma of what card 16, the Tower, may bring.

+ The need, and ability, to face baser impulses within ourselves. The operation of hidden forces, a revelation of some 'dark secret' which brings relief and release. The release of repressed energy in a constructive manner. Self-acceptance, confronting and mastering disturbing inner desires and fantasies.

– Either an excessive repression of instincts by the intellect, or an erupting-forth of destructive instinctual energy: aggression, even violence, sexual license, manipulating and scheming deceitfulness. Bondage to some powerful (perhaps secret) instinctual desire. Compelling obsessions, sadism, cruelty.

16 The Tower

A lightning bolt has struck the crown of a tall tower, knocking it off, and two human figures (who clearly must have been at the top of the Tower before the lightning struck) have been thrown down, falling to the ground. There is obviously a cautionary element about this card, to say the least!

The people who built the tower and lived in it were clearly arrogant – they even put a crown atop it, obviously believing that it was their rightful place to take such a symbol of authority for their own creation. Now they have been cast down, but matters are not so bad as they might seem. For one thing, that lightning bolt isn't as unpleasant as it looks at first glimpse – why, it appears almost feathery and light, it almost has a *friendly* texture to it, despite what it has done (actually, to some extent *because* of what it has done, but this will become clearer later). While the people look surprised and even dazed or shocked, clearly no permanent damage seems to have been done. They do not lie dead, or bleeding.

What has happened, clearly, is that these people have been *liberated* from their home. Look how narrow and confining it was! Their self-enforced imprisonment is over, but their pride is certainly going to be hurt and their prized building toppled. It is obvious what the crown was: at the head of the building, it was the arrogance of the rationality of the conscious mind, believing that they could understand all things through the powers of logic and intellect (and possibly their scientific experiments. Remember Frankenstein's tower?). Why, their stupidity was so great that their Tower even had no door – they were walled in by their own beliefs, unable to grow or develop. From the blue has come a bolt of divine energy – perhaps one of Jupiter's thunderbolts – to free them.

The Tower is clearly strongly linked with general themes which every card since Card 8 has been developing, and specifically with the Devil. In the Devil, we had to face the need to confront the most-feared archetypal material within ourselves, the demonic energies of the collective and personal Shadow. Within that card there were hints that the powers of that figure were in part dependent on illusions; there were symbols of our potential freedom from the Devil's enslavement there. In the Tower, the blinding light of the bolt shows us more obviously the nature of our liberation; the light of Selfhood beckons, the powerful energies of the unconscious have gained access to the realms of the Light now that the Devil has been understood and dealt with, and they strike down the last vestiges of our unbalanced ego-consciousness. This is indeed liberation. The key to this card is that *the lightning is not aimed at the person within, but at the Tower itself.* Freedom from the Devil meant freedom from being enslaved by our instincts (shown symbolically by the nakedness of the figures and their abode in hell as the Devil's slaves); freedom from the Tower means freedom from being enslaved from our hellish reason (shown symbolically by the clothed figures, and the struck-down crown). The full name of this card is the Tower of Destruction, forcing us to face the fact that our reason can destroy us as finally and completely as ever our instincts can. This is a symbolism impossible to deny when scientists have developed a very large number of ways of destroying the entire planet and everything which lives on it by exercising the power of intellect. It is not that we are destroyed by the hellishness of the Tower. The links between this card and what Jung and Maslow, in particular, have had to say about the limits of human 'reason' are too obvious to need explaining.

Coping with the Devil was no simple matter. Neither is coping with the difficulties the Tower, as a symbol, portrays for us; as with Death, events indicated here may be painful and hard to accept but, unlike Death, Light was involved in this apparent disaster, and we have been given a surer omen for future hope.

+ Violent upheaval and change which has positive consequences (eventually); the destruction of long-established situations, break-ups in relationships, new interests in the occult, the inspirational and creative; a sudden moment of enlightenment. Even in positive aspect, suffering is associated with this card, even if it is only pride which suffers.

− A disaster which could have been avoided if one had had the courage to face up to it, lessening the negative effects; unnecessary suffering, a sudden loss of prestige and position, self-undoing, an inability to find positive factors in adversity.

17   The Star

A naked girl kneels beside a stream, holding two pitchers of water, which she is pouring out. Trees grow behind her, and a small bird nests in one of them. Above her, eight stars twinkle in the heavens, the central one of these being geometric and eight-pointed, the others arrayed around it. The Star is in many ways the most perfect and beautiful of all the Tarot's images. Her meaning obviously leads on from that shown in the Tower.

For a start, this is the first naked human figure we have seen, save for the devils in card 15 – but their humanity was somewhat questionable, and they aren't humans in this deck (they are in others). The Star-maiden is thus the first human being to be seen lacking any artifice or clothing of her basic Self. Her clothes (persona) stripped away, she reveals her basic nature.

The blinding Light which struck from the heavens in the last card is now the soft glow of the stars above her. What was too bright to be a source of enlightenment before (unless we were very lucky) is now clearly a guide: soft starlight rather than the brilliance of lightning. The eight-pointed central star is a symbol of the Selfhood so close at hand; the octagon stands between four-square material 'reality' and the circle of the Sun, only two cards away, and the final circle of the World. The central star is undoubtedly an image of wholeness, of things in balance. The smaller stars around it correspond to the parts of our personalities, the 'sub-systems', the ego and the Shadow and the other archetypes, but the central star is a Self-image. But its light is still weak. This is not yet the radiance of the Sun.

The Star obviously reminds us of Temperance with her urns, but she is doing something very different. For a start, she is not an angel, but a mortal woman, and being naked her link with nature is obvious and direct. What's more, she is pouring some of her water onto the ground and some into the stream. Perhaps the water she is returning to its source stands for the part of unconsciousness which, as Jung says, can *never* be known, which is too deep and collective to be raised into the star-lit consciousness at all. That which she is pouring onto the ground shows that she is a creature belonging both to the spiritual (watery) and practical (earthy) worlds. She has brought the task of Temperance closer to fruition. Her obvious anima-nature again shows that this could not have been achieved by any conscious process alone.

It is also clear that the Star's mystery is a private one. She is carrying out her own personal ceremony under the night-time sky, and in this respect she is unlike the Devil (with his slaves) or the two people within the tower. The symbol stresses again what Jung nd Maslow claim about higher self-development being something which always involves trusting to an inner sense of morality and rightfulness. The Hermit told us that this was so, the Hanged Man accepted his advice and the girl in the Star card is joyfully absorbed in her own, inner-directed task.

+ Hopefulness, optimism, peace after difficult times. Resting, not doing too much, developing insight into future problems and possibilities.

− Insecurity, fear of failure, possibly reflected in a compensatory arrogance; dark pessimism, an inability to look beyond present adversity and to see future opportunities.

18   The Moon

After the hopefulness and joy of the Star, what a cruel blow this card deals us; although we may have hope (from the Star) that this is but the last 'dark night of the soul', weariness and fear dog our footsteps. The Moon is the mistress of madness and illusions, and all Moon goddesses have violently cruel and destructive aspects. It almost seems as if we shall never get through at all, and yet, all Moon goddesses are guardians of secret knowledge and wisdom, and many are skilled in the ways of magic. Perhaps not everything will be so bleak after all. But the path before us still winds ever on, and the landscape is only bleakly lit. If no help can be found within the symbols of this card, the adversity may be too great.

We know that beyond the twin towers lies a new land, and the rise of the Sun, but our way is barred by the deep water before us and the dogs which howl at the Moon beyond. And yet these barriers are truly just illusion; this is what the Moon is testing us with.

Within the deep water (the unconscious) there is a crayfish, close by the surface. As a creature, the crayfish is armoured, immutable, wholly unchanging for millions of years; he endures in his watery abode, and his solidity is reassuring. He even looks like a stepping-stone; we feel we could reach out a foot and he would help us across, if we trusted in him to help us. It is that trust which will get us across; this little creature stands for our own unconscious, hidden in the depths, but now a helper to us, once a feared part of ourselves but now accepted and befriended.

Once we are across, those dogs need hold no fear for us. Indeed, in a sense they are like us; they seem more in thrall to the Moon than we are, baying and crying. They don't seem to have any choice in the matter, unlike us as we travel along this path. Anyway, aren't dogs man's best friend? Unlike the savage lion of Strength, these animals (again symbols of our own unconscious: the 'Underworld' is usually guarded by such creatures) could obviously be friends. It depends on our reactions. It is often thought that dogs 'smell fear', and that once mastered they will not attack. If we have mastered the fear of our own unconscious then we have nothing to fear from these dogs. On the contrary, the journeyer needs their companionship. They are, after all, part of his very nature, and if they travel within him then they will have been released from their bondage to the Moon and her illusions. By accepting our unconscious we transform and liberate it, just as unconsciousness transforms our conscious minds and liberates us from the crippling inhibitions we have developed there.

The twinning of the symbols in this card – two dogs, two towers, two golden small plants which stand beyond our apparent obstacles and have the colour of the Sun within them – show that the Moon is, after all, a card which symbolizes the union of opposites. The realms of heaven and earth, buildings and nature, animal and human (the journeyer through the card), the water of the unconscious (below) and the Moon's gentle dewy tears, falling to refresh us, are all shown here. Liberation from the madness and illusions of the Moon comes in realizing the unity of these many dualities, of finally accepting the equipotency of consciousness and unconsciousness. On this last journey through difficult times, and facing the darkness of the moonlit night, we have only our inner light to guide us, only the wisdom we have gained through experience and our individuation so far.

In the sequence of Jungian archetypes, if the Devil is a collective Shadow and (for women) a dangerous animus figure (rather too limited a view, but as an aspect of this, the interpretation is possible), and the Star the best qualities of the anima figure, then the Moon would surely have to contain some element of the Wise Old Man or Magna Mater figures to continue the sequence. Although this isn't a prime aspect, the Magna Mater as Moon goddess is one symbolization behind this card, and the Moon's threat of insanity and obsession with illusion surely gives weight to Jung's warning that individuation can be especially dangerous if the deep collective archetypes are contacted, for they have such *mana* power that they can overwhelm, almost possess, us. Our intuitive judgement about following the right path will never have been so tested.

+ A test of faith and belief, powerful unconsciously-generated events; dreams, daydreams, fantasies, even hallucinations. Fertile imagination, artistic creativity, moodiness, strange emotional states. Having to depend on one's own emotional judgement about significant events.

− Deception and self-deception, crankiness and strange imaginings; or else a fear of going beyond oneself, failure of nerve and inability to transcend boundaries, a crippling of the imagination.

19   The Sun

The golden, warming rays of the risen Sun shine out over the world after the long Moon-lit night. In a walled garden, two children play under his benevolent gaze. At last the night of self-doubt is over, and we rest and bask in the warmth of the source of all life.

This walled garden is the world of innocents at play, children happy and harmonious, an inner harmony within them paralleling the warmth and light of the Sun. The fact that these children are clothed, unlike the girl in the Star, is significant. It is as if the artist wishes to say, 'These are not just children. Rather, children are a symbol for a *childlike* state; but to show that the growing personality of an adult is shown here, the figures are clothed.' Such a complexity was not necessary for the girl in the Star, for she was obviously adult anyway. So, the children stand for adults who have discovered the childlike state, who have regained the original balance of childhood at a higher level. The Sun is obviously a straightforward representation of the Jungian individuated Self, especially since children are often used as symbols of the undeveloped, the 'inferior function' and the other previously underused unconscious abilities and powers. Further, the use of the child as a symbol reflects the fact that the Self is still young; newly emergent, happy and delighted below the Sun, but young nonetheless.

Tarot writers have often stressed also that the development of this childlike state is the development of a *new way of experiencing* life; most specifically, a regaining of the freshness and spontaneity of the child, only at a higher level. This is echoed by Jung, and quite explicitly by Maslow in his writings on perception. He claims that self-actualized people have superior perceptual powers and that they perceive things in a fundamentally different way, neither purely subjectively nor purely in a rational-analytic way but in a manner which fuses the two. In a provocative way one could say they have a very *moral* way of perceiving the world, and that their perceptions transcend those of others. There is also the peak experience Maslow stressed; increasingly, the ability to experience in this way is shown to us in the development from the Sun, to Judgement, to the World. There is an *obvious* sense both of the timelessness (the rebirth element of Judgement) and great subjective significance (shown at least in part here, in the Sun) which Maslow demarcates as part of this way of experiencing in these final trumps.

Even the rays of the Sun proclaim the final uniting of opposites into the Self, for they are alternately straight and crooked, as if to proclaim a uniting of the linear-rational and crooked-irrational, and not just in terms of rational and irrational Jungian functions, although that's one way of seeing the dichotomy. What a perfect symbol this card is!

Why do we not stay here, then? Isn't this the end of the whole business? Not quite. The wall around the garden shows that this new Self is still in need of some protection. It is a newly emergent structure. There are still risks; perhaps we will be stuck here, playing in the Sun, too absorbed in ourselves to develop further. And there *is* further work to be done, although it is better to see the last cards as united with the Sun in a crowning triad, with the World at the apex, rather than as a linear progression. For Maslow stressed that self-actualized people valued their privacy and had strong internal senses of morality, but that they were no ivory-tower dwellers and very much concerned themselves with the affairs of others and the world in general, motivated by a keen sense of injustice and unfairness when they came across it and felt that they could do something about it. That quality is reflected, with others, in the last two cards.

+ Great attainment, happiness, joy and pleasure, a profound experience of beauty, seeing everything afresh, enthusiasm and wonderment, optimism and boundless energy. 'A place in the sun' – good fortune and inner harmony.

– Happiness which is vitiated in some way; possible fantasies about great achievements which deny or delay true success; infantile reactions, childishness, laziness, complacency.

20 Judgement

In the sky, a winged angel blows his trumpet, as he resides within what seems to be a circular halo of cloud from which the solar rays fan out. Below, two mature adults welcome a young person from subterranean confinement. At last, the journeyer is *facing* the source of illumination, unlike the children in the card of the Sun, who had their backs to him. This is a mature Self, able to face the Light. This is clearly a time for rejoicing. Perhaps the adults are welcoming back to life he who was lost below, in the unconscious, in the last long night below the Moon. The protectiveness of the Sun dispensed with, the person can face Judgement happily.

Surely the two mature adults – indeed, the man seems very old – are, after all, the Magna Mater and the Wise Old Man. This conclusion is reinforced by reflecting again on the fact that they seem to be the parents of the person emerging from the gloom, and as such there are echoes of the earlier trumps, 2–5, which stood for both the parents of the child and the deepest archetypes within the collective unconscious. In particular, the more earthy of the mother-figures, the Empress, and the more spiritual of the father figures, the Pope, have a very close affinity with the Magna Mater and the Wise Old Man, and there are echoes of them here, in these parental figures which greet the emergent new person. Crucially, these are *not* in any sense our real parents. Look how much older the man is than the woman; the Magna Mater may be old or young or inbetween, but the Wise Old Man is almost always as venerable as the man shown in the picture, for his wisdom is in part acquired by his many years of reflection and experience. Thus, the symbolisms of the

Tarot ever seem to return unto themselves. This is, after all, how the journey will 'end'.

It may seem surprising that these deepest archetypes are shown in a card *after* the Self has been shown (in the Sun): not so. The coming into being of the Self has been a nascent process indicated in much earlier cards, after all, and full Selfhood is still to be shown in the mandala of the World. As I said, it is best to see the Sun, Judgement, and the World as a triad, with the World at the apex, rather than as a linear sequence.

The notion of Judgement has only a slight affinity with any notion of the Day of Judgement. To be sure, there is a powerful element of rebirth about this card, but its key is surely that our judgement at this stage *comes from within*. This is Maslow's natural morality, and the card also shows the commitment to external affairs he stresses. The person has entered back into a social world; in the Waite-Rider deck, Waite and Smith added three extra human figures, and one of the standard commentaries on this deck emphasizes that this is to illustrate that the salvation which is shown in Judgement is not an individual matter; that our salvation, in the sense of being liberated as new people, is always bound up with that of other people. So indeed it is within the Tarot, echoing Maslow's stressing that self-actualized people are never dwellers in ivory towers, some navel-contemplating bunch of self-congratulating pseudo-mystics. The Tarot symbolism is in clear agreement. Are we not, after all, about to enter the World?

+ An inner sense that some judgement must be made, and some change effected, often with respect to important matters. A challenge to expand one's powers, a need to acknowledge and recognize that a new state of affairs exists.

− Often, trying to evade a judgement, out of fear or uncertainty as to what to do. A quality of moral cowardice or evasion, punishment for some failure, making excuses for oneself.

21   The World

The World-dancer, an androgynous figure partaking of male and female nature (and thus the most complete symbol of the reconciliation of opposites), is within a garland of flowers – a mandala or, more strictly, an elliptical mandorla (although the card as a whole is a mandala shape). Around the dancer are the whole of creation, it seems; the angel, the lion, the eagle, and the bull. This is the 'anima mundi' of the alchemists, the longed-for goal of their work, the World-Spirit, a force in the whole of nature from the furthest stars in the firmament to the animals, plants, and the very waters and rocks of earth. This is the archetype of the Self transcendent, shown in the human dancer and in the whole of creation, and it shows that by this commonality we are indeed made in the image of God, and we have the spark of divine radiance within. There is no Star, no Moon, no Sun, to give light for none is needed; the dancer's path is lit by his/her own inner light, the light which the Hermit first showed to us, and which now burns brightly from within. Everything here is in balance (the four symbols could readily be related to the four functions of Jung, for example), the balance of perpetual and measured motion, the ultimate Law of all things, as the Wheel and Death revealed to us earlier.

That emphasis on motion as the eternal unchanging principle brings us back once more to the stress which Jung and Maslow placed on the irreducibly dynamic and, in some sense, unsatisfiable nature of the motivations which are our personalities. We will never stop desiring and wishing, for this is not possible for us. But, in the World, there is a Zen-like quality of absorption within the endless dance and a simultaneous detachment from it, something which Maslow emphasized as a prime quality of self-actualized people. One is apart from and yet absorbed into this dance at the same time. *Of course* this is a paradox. *Of course* people obsessed with making things logical and rational and predictable will not comprehend this or will denounce it as nonsense. We have grown far beyond the petulant arrogance of this by now. Being detached from, and part of, are no more contradictory and opposed than are selfishness and selflessness. Maslow explained the resolution of that polarity within the higher awareness of the self-actualized man.

Let us turn to the central figure for a final view. S/he is an androgynous figure, yet clearly predominantly feminine, as befits her role as the *anima mundi* liberated from the prison of the unconscious. Perhaps this is fitting, with the many male figures used earlier in the Tarot to portray the journeyer through life – beginning with the male figure of the Lover. Importantly, s/he is partly clothed; the genitals are hidden by clothing, as was the case for the children in the card of the Sun. It is as if the figure wishes not to deny something about his/her Self by such concealment, but is simply saying (in effect) that some mysteries remain irreducible, just as Jung argued that some parts of the unconscious can never be made conscious. Therein lies their (particularly strong) power, and the mystery of procreation and life itself is protected, hidden, and kept intimate by the World-dancer.

This final, haunting image is a state of perfection which perhaps few of us will ever know. The important thing lies not in getting this far, but in knowing where one is headed. While the Hermit's little lamp has now grown into a complete inner illumination for the World-dancer, his inner light has been growing all the time, and it is the journey which matters, not the destination. Even when we have arrived, the Tarot will soon turn back upon itself. . . .

+ A final, complete lasting achievement. The ending of a cycle of affairs, culminations and conclusions. Unity between internal desires and the external world, flowing with the current, ease of motion through life.

— Stagnation and the cessation of growth, being unable to respond with flexibility to changing circumstances. A loss of momentum and energy, one's energies getting stuck in obsessive or fixed patterns.

0 The Fool

The World is not our 'destination'. This should be obvious, given the endless dynamism of the card. To stress the endless dynamic of the Tarot, let us place the Fool at the end of the sequence, linking the first with the last of the numbered cards, but this time seen in a different guise. We have already acknowledged that the Fool is a card for whom duality is the key, but now the Fool leads ever on to another plane of existence.

Now the Fool has passed through the world, and his own spirit has changed it as he has changed himself. At the beginning, the Fool was filled by, intoxicated with, the possibilities of all things. Nothing could deter him from his journey, for he understood that his travels were the essence of life itself Now the Fool is full of his sense of possibilities *and* actualities, and he is more joyful than ever in his wandering. The young fool may have been ignoring the precipice because he didn't see it. The mature Fool ignores it because he knows that he is immortal; he no longer feels that his physical body, nor even his earthly personality, is *him*. He is part of the Eternal Dance, absorbed into the transcendental, grown far beyond the constraints of his earthly life.

I wrote earlier that the Fool looked forward to a time when his original childish nature would become the childlike quality of the young Self, but in his position at this stage of the cycle the Fool has gone beyond even this. He is indeed part of the mind of God, and the understanding and experiences he carries in his bag are priceless and timeless. He could not explain them to us, and we could not understand him; the wisdom of the Wise Fool is beyond our comprehension. I don't think we could even understand where he is going, where he is now travelling, into what kinds of lands and places his steps will take him. He seems to walk on a different ground, to breathe a different air, he is almost lost to us. But still he accepts the companionship of his best friend, his little dog, although he seems oblivious to the animal's playful jumping up at him (it even seems as if it is taking a playful nip at him). We still have this much in common with him – that we both accept the friendship and companionship of such a creature. But this Fool is eager to leave us, to disappear into another world and another plane, and who can say how we shall see him again?

The Major Arcana: Reflections and Conclusions

We have come to the end of the journey, although we see that the journey shown by the Major Arcana is a never-ending one. How well supported is my claim that the Tarot is some super-theory of personality, containing the key insights of the personality theories we have considered earlier?

The affinity with Jungian theory is blindingly obvious, and it is no coincidence that writers on the Tarot have often turned to Jung when discussing their presentation of the Tarot. The development of personality which Jung discusses as individuation is obviously portrayed in the Tarot's later cards. The shift from reliance on consciousness to the rapprochement with the unconscious is common to the Tarot and to Jung. Many of the Major Arcana cards show obvious archetypal forms, and others even show the *processes* Jung described in symbolic form. The Wheel is almost a pictorial description of what Jung termed 'enantiodromia' – returning to the opposite, beginning to turn to the unconscious and its opposite qualities, although the Wheel signifies more than this. The Tower shows the sudden flash of enlightenment which is replete with danger, both in the card (the figures may not be dead but they are dazed and confused) and in the process of individuation. The parallels are so many, and so obvious, that they hardly require further comment.

Because the Tarot deals with archetypal forms and adult growth to a large extent, we would not expect to find a rich representation of the kernel of Freudian theory here. Freud's conception of human personality and growth is too limited for this. However, there are many allusions in the Major Arcana to the processes discussed and pondered over by Freud. Cards 2–5 show, clearly, parental figures in differing roles; the ambivalence the child has towards its parents is reflected in the different attributes of the figures and in the fact that each is also split, the mother-figure into the High Priestess and Empress, and the father-figure into the Emperor and the Pope. The Pope, coming last in this sequence, also stands in direct correspondence with the development of the superego as described by Freud, a development which occurs late in childhood and which is created by an internalization of the strictures of the father. But the Pope shows us also a natural conscience, a burgeoning awareness of the morality of life, which corresponds more to an awakening of the inner moral sense Maslow and other humanistic psychologists have described. We would have to go deep into Freudian writings to get to grips with all the details of this. Freud does not only discuss the superego, he also refers in some more obscure writings to what he terms the conscience, although he sees this as something based on the fear of loss of love and care from the mother, a primitive thing linked directly to bodily needs rather than any moral sense. Later Freudian writers have further complicated the issue. What we can extract from this is that the Freudian view relating to how our moral sense is formed is complex, confused, and utilitarian. There is no accepting any inner moral sense for Freud, there is no 'natural morality' save that based on some form of self-interest. The Pope shows us that, while the Freudian superego may be formed through the (father) figure, which Freud suggests, and while this may occur at the time Freud says it does (the Pope is the last of these four 'parental' cards), there is more to matters than this.

The early Major Arcana cards around these four also show early happenings discussed by Freud. The Magician is clearly the early conscious mind, the ego, struggling to inject order and form into a confusing and chaotic world. In the card it is the confusion of the items laid out before the Magician, in the Freudian story it is the confusion of external impressions and the inner signals and demands of instincts and unconscious needs and desires. The Lover shows what Freud described as the turning away from the mother, which he saw as being triggered by the fear of the father and his punishment for desiring the mother. The Tarot shows us the same choice, but this is brought into being not least by the need to grow, develop, and become an individual freed from parental restrictions and strictures.

Freud's major concern with our adult lives, repressed sexuality and its effects on our mental health, is most obviously addressed in the Devil. This card, as we saw, has a confusion all of its own which has a parallel in Freud's own confusion about this problem. Freud never could find a satisfactory formula for how conflicts developed about sexuality. As we saw before, at first he thought libido might be in conflict with self-preservation. The idea isn't so far-fetched; one could, for example, imagine a necessary affinity between self-preservation and the conscious mind, and the logical-analytic 'secondary process' thinking that system possesses. On the other hand, sexual desire has a strong fantasizing element and one could see how it might more easily align with the unconscious and the fantasizing-hallucinatory 'primary process' of the unconscious realms. Sexuality is more clearly allied with the famous pleasure principle of Freud also. But Freud rejected this because certain forms of mental ill-health – masochism being a compelling example – just could not be explained in terms of this polarity. Indeed, in this original sex-versus-self-preservation idea, one cannot see the *opposition* involved. Rather, one would be better off thinking of the two in terms of their simply being *different* systems without the necessity for much direct conflict. In this case one would be edging uncomfortably closer to the Jungian view of matters so far as the avoidability of conflict between the conscious and unconscious goes. Small wonder Freud eschewed this option.

So Freud ended up with the idea of life and death instincts, of sex and self-preservation being allied (Eros) against self-destructive drives and desires (Thanatos). The latter Freud sees as some kind of mental entropy, the desire for peace and finality in ending the struggle of existence. This formula allowed him to deal with such issues as sexual sadism and masochism quite satisfactorily. It is a formula which manifestly does not deal with many other problems, which Freud got around by simply ignoring them and not writing about them.

So: there is much confusion within Freudian writing, over the decades, about the problems of sexuality. It is difficult to evade the conclusion that Freud was simply obsessed with this instinctual need to the exclusion of others. The Devil reflects this obsessiveness and confusion perfectly. In looking at the confusion of sexual identity in the card, and its quality of repressiveness through self-inflicted bondage, it tells us the same story Freud did, but in a clearer way. The confusions, self-deception, inability to release oneself through powerful obsessions, are all present in the card. The Tarot has the same saving message which Freud had: if this can be made conscious, then the personality can be saved from sickness. For Freud, this was the free-association method and the process of catharsis; in the Tarot (and for Jung) this was acceptance of the Shadow-figure and bringing up the unconscious into the light of the conscious mind. The darkness of the Devil shows us just how tricky this is going to be. Indeed, this very darkness shows us how badly we want to shove the Devil out of our minds, to project him outside and scapegoat him, and how much we *need* to accept the energies he has. Given that this Tarot card shows us the extremity of this need, is it any wonder that Freud should have stressed this need so much to the exclusion of others? The Tarot would have predicted that this would be so.

Many of the defences (defence mechanisms) Freud describes are also obvious within the structure of the Major Arcana. The Pope we have already noted; since he is obviously imparting a blessing and knowledge to his acolytes, this is a clear representation of the internalizing of external strictures in superego formation which Freud describes (although, as we've seen, the Pope shows us more than this). The High Priestess as guardian, as a figure who forbids us access to the unconscious when this is right for us (which it is in the early stages of development when consciousness needs to grow) could show a form of repression, but this is rather the process of using the energies of the unconscious to develop and build the strength of the conscious mind. She is the ally of the Magician in this aspect of her wisdom. The use of projection in denying the Devil is clear – the human (in the Marseilles deck, little demon) figures who are slaves to this externalized figure, the looseness of their bonds showing how they have in effect inflicted their own slavery upon themselves. The acolytes turned to the Pope, but these two have their back to the Devil; they cannot see what they have made 'out there', which is the whole point about projection. The repressed is made external and rejected from one's conscious mind. One could also see sublimation in the work of Temperance – this card is actually named Art in Aleister Crowley's Thoth Tarot; but this would be only a superficial description of the card. There is much more to Temperance than this.

Given that the Tarot is more concerned with adult growth, a process wholly undescribed by Freud save as (in effect) a recapitulation of the past, it is remarkable that so many striking parallels with Freudian theory can be found. I could go further even than we have already. 'The ego is first and foremost a bodily ego,' says Freud, and the Lover and Chariot cards show this very clearly. And so on, but the point should be taken by now!

Because there is an affinity between Jung's writings and those of the humanistic psychologists, one would expect to find some agreement between the Tarot and the latter. This would obviously be true for the process of self-actualization, which has many similarities with individuation, and, as we've seen, the Major Arcana has a powerful story to show us about this kind of development. However, there are closer parallels than this. The early cards in the Major Arcana show us the hierarchy of needs which Maslow describes. They show us the developing concern from basic needs to safety needs (the Emperor being a powerful representative of our need for security and lawfulness and a feeling for the order of things), then to esteem needs (Chariot and then Justice, the latter showing us the growing need for a feeling that we have *deserved* what we have) and on to the development of self-actualization needs. This is a powerful progression, and one which stands outside the Jungian parallels, so it is an additional wealth of detail within the Tarot. It adds extra understanding to our interpretation of the Major Arcana. Just as the Devil was an important card for Freudian concerns, the case of Justice is a nice one for examining the links with Maslow in greater detail. Traditionally, Justice has been interpreted by writers versed in Jungian theory as the need for inner balance, an inner sense of the unbalanced state of affairs shown by the Chariot. This is indeed one aspect of what Justice stands for. But this powerful figure stands a little early in the sequence to be just this factor; and, instead, there is the additional point that she develops what the Charioteer has built up for himself. The Charioteer was much concerned with security and also belongingness; a material man in a material world, finding a place for himself within the social order of things. Justice shows us the same man now feeling that what he has should be earned *rightfully*, that a sense of integrity about what one does is natural and a growing development. So, Justice is both a growth from the Chariot stage (Maslow) and a reaction against its excesses (Jung). It seems clear that a richer understanding of what this card clearly shows is to be had when we look at both these personality theories.

What is particularly delightful about the self-actualization process and the later Tarot cards is Maslow's insistence that many conflicts and many apparent oppositions disappear for the self-actualized person. The most important example is the selfish-selfless dichotomy; Maslows urges us to consider that, for a person with the natural morality of the self-actualized person, these two are no longer opposites. What is good for the Self is good for others, too. Maslow gives another example we haven't considered yet; developing the theme that, for such people, work is play and duty is pleasure because these things are rooted in the natural morality of the self-actualized person, he laconically notes that the most ethical and moral people will be the most lustful and libidinal as well. The division between physicality and spirituality is a false one when the Self is fully developed. This is obviously just what the Tarot says to us also.

Further, the role of the Sun card here is a special case for illuminating our understanding. Maslow described how the very perceptions of self-actualized people change. The analytic-concrete dichotomy disappears as many other falsities do. They do not see things in their concrete aspects as children do, they do not have the analytical, thinking perceptions of adults, they see *both* the concrete and the abstract *together* in a single act of perception. One can add to this an immediate awareness, as the object of perception is brought into focus, of the potentialities of the object. Perception is fused with imagination. Now, in case all of this sounds too wonderful to be true, if not too abstract to be believable, let me give a concrete example of what I mean, and return to the Tarot Sun.

Some years ago, a friend of mine who would have to be considered pretty high on any measure of self-actualization, visited me in Cambridge, not having been there in many years. In the course of wandering along the small back streets around some of the University buildings, he stopped to look up at one particular building, hesitated for a moment, and then continued to walk along with me. I asked him what he had stopped for. In a quite offhand way, he simply said that he had been looking at the brickwork of the wall which he had been standing next to. The weathering of the brickwork, and the chipping of the mortar between the bricks and the little moss growths there, had given him a strong sense of the enduring quality of the place, and he had had fun with a little imaginative fantasy about the generations of scholars who had worked there, Rutherford splitting the atom, Newton wandering the city. . . .

All this from what you and I would see as a few bricks. After all, whoever notices, at a casual glance, the moss on mortar work on a stroll around some dirty old buildings? This is a perfect example of what Maslow describes when he says the perceptual world changes for such a person, that we can have powerfully imaginative perceptions (a whole trail of history is set off as a daydream) and powerfully accurate ones (moss on mortar work) fused together. Daydreaming and accurate perception is another opposition which goes to the wall (no pun intended) for the self-actualized person.

This is just what the Sun shows us. Tarot authors have always said that what is shown in this card is an *entirely new way of perceiving the world* which is shown as the children, the child*like* (not child*ish*) qualities of the new Self. To our analytical, adult way of perceiving the world, the ability to see things in fresh immediacy, the concrete perceptions of the child, return to us and a new whole is created. Perhaps the journey we made under the Moon's baneful eye has given us the ability to fuse the imaginings and fantasies of her realm with the perceptual world as Maslow describes. Certainly, as is clear when the Fool returns, our changes have transformed the world, just as Maslow says.

The strongest link between Kelly's construct theory and the Tarot is the basic structure: the bipolar construct for Kelly, the endless dualities of the Tarot (the dualities of the Moon, the two pillars behind the High Priestess, and so many others). Kelly's writings about lopsided constructs and the like show him revealing a simple basic postulate of the Tarot: everything, no matter how linear and one-sided it seems, has an opposite quality. Further, in such cases there is an *implicit* opposite quality which we may not appreciate and utilize, and this may make our judgements and (for Kelly) attempts at prediction less accurate. The Tarot expresses this by showing the necessity of reconciling opposites, and in this it goes into the realm of transcendent constructs. Kelly *might* have considered these superordinate constructs. Analysing the Tarot in Kellian terms reveals surprising new ways of looking at the cards. The Charioteer is easily seen as the man in the world of impermeable constructs; he knows his realm, he operates within the limits of the material world, he is single-minded and purposive within his *self-delimited* realm. The imprisoning nature of these constructs is symbolized as the four-square solidity of the chariot itself. Beginning with this example, we can ram home a point which Kelly and the Tarot share at a higher level: this is an unusual way of looking at the chariot. It may even seem an odd language to describe this card. But this is simply because we are used to other ways of looking at the Tarot; we tend to construe it as occult/ arcane/symbolic and not concrete/practical. To reject a Kellian perspective on it shows that we are simply suffering from not being able to re-construe it in a different mental framework of constructs. This is a slightly awkward way of describing the process; at a more platitudinous level, one could say that it all depends on how you look at it . . . Kelly's point entirely.

What we could call the pathologies of construction are also shown in the Tarot: the impermeable constructs of the Chariot, the general theme of lopsided constructs and the development of implicit, hidden, unconscious opposites (the other pole of the bipolar construct). There will be more to consider about this general approach when we examine the Minor Arcana, but for now we should understand that the Tarot shows us a greater scope than the Kellian approach could take. Consider the Wheel as an example. To be sure, this card shows the endless dynamism which Kelly postulates (and Jung and Maslow also), but while Kelly sees this as a movement towards ever-superior control and prediction the Wheel takes us beyond this. The later cards take us into the realms of the transcendent; the World and the return of the Fool take us into realms which we cannot even comprehend if we have not been there. Kelly's theory is not, I think, capable of dealing with this level of development, for it is one in which the thinking function has been fused with the others and has taken off into another world entirely.

Finally, we can return to where we began, with the Jungian theory, and take on a final problem with the Tarot within the context of this. For Jung, it is simply the case that in early development in our adult life we begin *differentiation* and the conscious mind develops one of the attitudes (extraversion-introversion), and one of the functions (thinking-feeling-sensation-intuition) becomes superior. Now, it is clear that the Tarot shows one set of such differentiations; it shows the early adult as a thinking-extravert, for the most part, and we might wonder whether this really fits with Jungian theory at all. I consider that it does, for the Tarot is clearly showing the *general* Jungian principle by a concrete example from within the range of possibilities (it would be impossible to show several at the same time, after all). I think that it also shows the possibility which is most likely to be the one in accordance with what society expects of us, both today and clearly for centuries in the past, by showing the thinking-extraverted-'masculine' path as the typical one of early adult development. This does not mean that the Tarot cannot accept the case of an intuitive-introvert differentiation; it could do so. This, in turn, brings me to a final point about the Tarot which most obviously affects the Major Arcana.

The journeyer in the path of the Major Arcana is clearly male, and has the qualities noted above. He is shown as an extravert and, I consider, as a thinking type (but not over-differentiated). Now, obviously, the Tarot had to show *either* a male or a female figure, since the whole point about the final Selfhood of the World is the fusion in the androgyne figure there (the maleness of the original figure is reflected in the predominant femininity of that World-dancer). I think that bleating about a sexist Tarot, and asserting that it is alienating for women when the journeyer is a male figure, is missing the point entirely. One can, instead, consider that the journeyer is shown as someone developing the 'masculine' concerns of early adulthood – activity, dominance, wealth, possessions, external objects – and learning to grow through embracing the 'feminine' within – passivity, compassion, contemplation, inner resources. Both attributes, the masculine and feminine, have virtues and vices, both have their dark, destructive sides and both their positive, constructive qualities. The Tarot's final World-dancer, about to re-enter the eternal world of the returning Fool, has understood this and has fused into an entirely new way of perceiving – the Sun's brightness – moving far beyond the original antipathies of the masculine and feminine.

But our journey now takes us away from that final strange and mysterious disappearance, back to the mundane world of the Minor Arcana and its story about our more everyday lives and tasks.

4
The Minor Arcana

4

The Minor Arcana

The Major Arcana tells us a story, in picture form, about the course of our lives from cradle to grave, about our fateful choices and the major influences upon us. The Minor Arcana is a much less ambitious project. In each suit, there are the court cards and the ten numbered cards (taking the Ace as having a value of 1). The sequence 1–10 shows stages of development of a problem of some kind and our best options for dealing with it. The term 'problem' shouldn't be taken in too negative a sense; it may mean a task, a job or project we enjoy being involved with. Neither should the term be taken in too intellectual a sense; it may relate to money, career, or to our relationships and emotional life. The court cards, Knave, Knight, Queen and King, show something slightly different, in that they simply portray certain problem areas which exist which may be difficult for us, or certain opportunities which may arise, alerting us to their existence. They have a somewhat more abstract quality about them than the ten other cards in each suit. Finally, while the cards of the Minor Arcana seem more clearly to relate to day-to-day problems than the grand themes of the Major Arcana, the problems many of the Minor Arcana cards show are important ones, and our actions with respect to them may affect much of our personal future for some time!

We have two things to consider initially. Firstly, the four suits of cards; in what way do these differ? Basically, they show different realms of problems, different involvements of intellectual, emotional, internal and external problems, as we will soon see. The second factor we need to consider is the exact nature of the 1–10 sequence, and what each number within a suit shows in the way of developments and diffi-

127

culties a problem faces us with. At the end of considering the Minor Arcana, I'll come back to perspectives on it from personality theories, rather than beginning such a discussion now and returning to it later (although there will be one or two isolated points to make as we go along). Let's take the Minor Arcana on its own terms first.

The suits of the Minor Arcana

The suit of swords has been identified with Jung's function of thinking by some writers. The problem areas here are primarily intellectual, concerned with reasoning and analysis, verbal communication, and the like. Likewise, cards from the swords suit show the resources we have for using such thinking and logic in constructive ways. Many packs which have individually illustrated Minor Arcana cards (as opposed to the simple representations in the Marseilles deck) and show figures and symbols on each of them portray swords as a grim suit indeed, culminating in the utter defeat and destruction of the 9 and 10 denominations. This seems to be an excessive reaction, rather like the sinister representations of the Devil or Tower in many Tarot decks and the over-idealization of certain other cards. Nonetheless, many problems relating to harshness, cruelty and wilful hurtfulness relate to the swords suit. That simply reiterates the double-edged nature of the sword. On the other hand, many issues pertaining to communication and how one expresses oneself to others are associated with this suit too; *style* as well as content.

If swords have been harshly treated by many, the suit of cups is often romanticized. Not surprising, since cups are often considered as being involved with the Jungian feeling function, with compassion, sympathy, romance, and love. One would sometimes not imagine that emotion had any pathology to match with that of intellect, save for the laziness and over-indulgence certain cards of this suit suggest. Nonetheless, the suit also deals with finer qualities.

The suit of coins or pentacles is traditionally thought to represent the material world, physical pleasures, goods, commerce and practicalities. Sensation would be the Jungian function allied with this suit – the immediate here-and-now. This is not a suit associated with fast thinking or smartness, but with qualities of persistence and durability, and practical solutions.

The suit of wands is the one which really does not fit with the Jungian function model; intuition seems too passive a function to be identified with the fiery energies and dominance of wands. Nonetheless, there is a link. Intuition is the most *unlimited* of the four functions, for it is always concerned with projecting beyond what is known and given into the realm of possibilities. The energy of wands has an affinity with this, in that wands symbolize powerful energies which can be directed almost anywhere. Wands also have an affinity with what is termed 'willpower' in the vernacular sense, and also with one's self (in the vernacular; not in the Jungian sense), how one *projects* oneself to others. There is no simple formula for summing up the basic meaning of Wands as there is for the other suits, but matters should be clearer when we consider the individual cards in the suit later.

Ace to 10: the unfolding problem

Aces in any suit signify a *beginning*. This is usually some new opportunity opening up, some new area of interest, a fresh orientation to the area of life the suit is concerned with. Usually this is a positive card, a fresh start, a time when anything seems possible and the energies of the suit are liberated within oneself.

The 2 is the card of *developing*. After the energy of the Ace (1) has started something new, the 2 develops that interest and begins to accumulate more information about it. This is the initial stage of grappling with the problem, extracting more information about it.

The 3 is a card of *planning*. Traditionally, this number

stands for some synthesis of (two) opposites, and an extension beyond that point. This is the stage of looking ahead beyond the immediacies of the problem, and making plans for – and beginning – to do things about it. When other people are involved in the problem to hand, the 3 suggests some balancing act with respect to their interests, so that one has managed to reconcile their different roles and interests in the further developing of the problem, or at least taken their viewpoints into account.

The 4 is a card of *practical attainment* of some kind. It isn't easy to find a one-word formula for the 4, since it has more than one meaning. It can show some practical, useful, or satisfying solution to a problem, although this is in some limited form. However, it is likely that this practical solution is one which will do for the time being but certainly not permanently. It is something to fall back on, or some kind of compromise. The problem with this is that developing beyond 4 four is important, but we may prefer not to do so!

The 5 card in the pack shows a further test in our ability to handle problems, for It represents *coping*; specifically, coping with some fairly sudden change or alteration in the state of affairs, something which has thrown a spanner in the works. It may also represent the kick-start which we need with the possibility of stagnating in the 4. It may further show some new development of a problem, in that it is extended further, enters a new cycle of complexity, or some such.

The 6 is a card which, we can say, stands for a *steadying*; after the tricky times the 5 gave us, here we accept the extra difficulty and manage to keep going, taking the extra complexity into our lives. Perhaps the most important thing about the 6 is the acceptance of problems as dynamic; the 4 showed us moving towards stable, secure solutions, but the 6 shows us learning the lessons of the 5, that such stability is illusory. The only reliable thing is unreliability, and the only unchanging thing is that everything changes. The 6 is the card of swimming with the current rather than struggling against it, although this can lead to laziness and lack of effort in negative situations.

The 7 shows a time of complex and important choice. Although the element of choice is present in all cards and right throughout the Tarot, we could still fairly call these cards ones of *choosing* for the choices here are particularly important. Correct choices bring matters towards the successful conclusions shown in later cards in the sequence; incorrect ones lose us much time or bring sad disappointments. Sevens always deal with having many options, and can bring much zest and diverse interest, in addition to presenting us with tricky choices to be made.

The 8 is a card of *ordering*. It shows a time for organizing and getting priorities right, rather than for swift action or getting on with things. This card stands for assimilating what has been learned so far after making the choice the 7 faced us with, and simplifying matters after the complexity of the 7. Decisions associated with an 8 are frequently those concerned with isolating what is most important in some problem area and dealing with this as a matter of priority when the time is right. Frequently, there is also an element of abandoning something from the past; since priorities must be established, it is necessary to let go of earlier involvements in order to concentrate on what are now the most important elements of the problem. The role of past events may be particularly important since the 8 may show that some past attainment provides the basis for some new success which is built upon that past, but needs to develop beyond it.

The 9 is the card of successful final choice. It is a card of *concluding* business at hand, a time when not too much needs to be done for success to be had. Simply going along as one has been will lead to a positive outcome. Nines are good news in a Tarot reading! Even the more negative readings of 9 suggest that one is not getting as much out of some state of affairs as one might (typically), so that one is under-rewarded. This is clearly not the worst of messages to get from the Tarot!

The 10 might seem to be logically the card of successful outcome par excellence, but it is actually a dual-aspected card. On the one hand the 10 does reflect a state of affairs when some problem has been dealt with satisfactorily but, on the other, it also shows the need to begin something new, returning to the Ace as a symbol which shows that something new is beginning; the Tarot again shows the endless dynamism of human personality and motivation which so many personality theorists have stressed. It is time to grow beyond the problem area now, so the 10 might be termed a card of *anticipating*. The negative side of this, obviously, would be hanging on to something after its usefulness and value has gone, lingering in some outmoded pattern of behaviour or feeling which is no longer helpful.

For the forty numbered cards of the Minor Arcana, the positive (+) and negative (−) divinational meanings of the cards are given; the nature of the problem-area covered by the card is clear from these descriptions of the divinational meanings.

The Suit of Swords

The Ace of Swords

(+) Some new thought or idea, the opening-up of some new intellectual challenge, a new way in which one can use one's rational thinking to good effect. This may involve the breakdown of some old problem, or some blockage which prevented one from making a break-through into a new problem area before. Intellectual energy, mental speed, fast thinking, an excellent time to begin new intellectual pursuits of almost any kind, from a university course to doodling with a crossword!

(−) There may be two possible meanings. The first is simply that one has *too many* ideas buzzing around in one's head; one lacks the ability to concentrate, to sit down and sort out which ideas should be worked on and which not. Distractions, trivial pursuits which waste time. Or the card may suggest intellectual stagnation, an inability to develop some insight into a problem which would lead to new beginnings, spin-offs into a new area of thought, and the like; getting stuck in stereotyped thinking and being unable to progress further.

The 2 of Swords

(+) The new thought or idea has been accepted, agreed with and affirmed. Now one is acquiring information relevant to it, learning how to use the idea, playing around with it. This 'idea' may be a new philosophy, a new way of communicating with others or something more mundane, but at this stage it is still in the development stage even though it is something one is happy with and accepts.

(−) Frustration at some block on intellectual creativity which is annoyingly early, at the first stages of trying to build and develop an idea. An inability to *play* with an idea, to toss it around in one's mind, due to distractions or lack of imagination or more mundane things such as a lack of time to do it. Wanting to do something in the intellectual sphere and not being able to get it off the ground at the stage of beginning to acquire information about it or apply it. Alternatively, wasting time with some new idea or range of interests for which one simply isn't ready or which are not appropriate to one's life.

The 3 of Swords

(+) Some problem is being understood better and different strands of the problem reconciled and brought together. A good time for obtaining agreements between people with divergent viewpoints, using one's ability to communicate to balance competing interests and different ways of thinking and styles of approach to almost any difficulty. Smoothing over or avoiding arguments. Finally, the growing ability to express some idea effectively to others.

(−) Quarrels and arguments, different views which cannot be reconciled or where reconciliation seems to be beyond one's power to achieve. Discord with a frequent aspect of mental cruelty and strife. Harsh words which may be regretted later. Also, disorder; an inability to pull arguments together and achieve a synthesis, being unable to resolve intellectual problems in any way.

The 4 of Swords

(+) An agreement or compromise, some balancing of different ideas in a way which may be only a temporary expedient but which serves its function. Putting an idea into some practical form which has a limited usefulness, but usefulness nonetheless. Possibly, some form of written contract or agreement which provides a firm basis for further progress. Relief from some mental conflict, a time for taking some rest from struggling with a problem (including those of others), the end to some argument or conflict of ideas with (or between) others which has been upsetting, although this may not be lasting.

(−) A cop-out through compromise, yielding to the ideas and views of others because this is the easiest thing to do, often motivated by being tired or anxious. Lacking the strength to argue for one's viewpoint when this is necessary. Thinking that one has achieved some balance and agreement which is durable and secure when this is, in fact, only a temporary compromise or step along the path. A problem with carrying out a plan, or expressing one's view, in a practical and concrete way; being unrealistic or unable to tailor one's plans to the circumstances, or to communicate effectively with others to get something done.

The 5 of Swords

(+) Some new twist to a problem makes an unexpected demand on one's ability to think and communicate effectively. This may be a trigger to a new insight into a problem, bringing forth some new creativity or resource from within oneself. This is not an easy state of affairs or a card which brings a state of peace or ease, but the difficulty which arises can be clearly seen in retrospect as a stimulus to breaking some deadlock or other.

(−) An unexpected twist in a problem which throws one's plans out of focus and with which one cannot cope. An inability to respond to changes in circumstance in practical ways, being unable to change one's ideas or communications with others to take these changes of the environment into account. A lack of mental flexibility, the fear of change and challenge, retreat into stereotyped ways of thinking and communicating as a defence against the changing challenges the world presents.

The 6 of Swords

(+) Accepting and mastering some fresh element of a problem and solving an immediately pressing problem by careful thought and communicating with others. Some nasty, tricky obstacle has been overcome and further progress can be made in the near future. A feeling of ease and comfort which is more securely rooted than that shown in the 4.

Feeling that one is moving along comfortably, being able to handle small day-to-day difficulties which crop up with a minimum of tension. This card suggests that there are no major conflicts to be expected in the short term.

(−) There are two possible meanings. This card may indicate laziness, a feeling that one has dealt with some difficult problem and one is now entitled to do nothing at all for a while. On the other hand, the card may suggest that the ease following the solution of a nasty twist to a problem may be very short-lived and that further difficulties can be expected very shortly, so that the promise of relief the card has in its positive aspect is denied to the person.

The 7 of Swords

(+) Some major choice has to be made: there is a range of possible ways to go and ideas to pursue, many people with whom one might communicate one's ideas and concerns. Only one of these choices is correct and it must be made with careful thought and by taking as much time as one can over the decision. An incorrect choice will be a perilous and possibly disastrous one. One is dependent on one's own powers of thought for the answer; the advice of others is not of much value at this time. At best, the challenge of some decisive choice which stimulates the person into activity and thought which reveals the best course of action. Caution and foresight are called for and one may face powerful opposition in some form (notably from others in positions of authority).

(−) An erroneous choice when some important decision has to be made, a confusion of possibilities which makes sound reflection and wise choice almost impossible. Opposition from others who make their case and communicate their ideas, which are in conflict with one's own, more effectively. This card always suggests some loss of possibilities and opportunity which are due to an inability to think a problem out clearly, or making the wrong choice because one does not (or cannot) concentrate effectively on the matter in hand. In negative aspect, the loss suggested here cannot be avoided; in some cases, one may meet with secret opposition one does not anticipate.

The 8 of Swords

(+) Isolating the most important ideas in one's life and organizing oneself and one's activities around these. Giving priority to what one judges to be most important; this may be the most pressing, or the most valued in the long term, depending on the circumstances. Choosing some strategy and sticking with it; this brings positive results. A colourful term for the positive aspect of this card would be 'cut the crap!', ignoring peripheral concerns and trivia and dealing only with what is most important, especially in dealing with others. A time when such a priority will bring the best results.

(−) An inability to see what is the most important part of some problem, being over-concerned with trivia and the details of everything. An inability to get below surface appearance and isolate the key areas of some problem, to 'get down to bedrock'. There is also the possibility that one may over-analyse everything, having a head so full of rational analysis that one is not living one's life so much as thinking endlessly about it in a way which is not productive or helpful.

The 9 of Swords

(+) A time when ideas flow smoothly and one can communicate well with others. Little needs to be done to keep things going; the correct choices have been made, one knows what is important and what is trivial, and this has communicated itself to others. A peak time for mental ability and thinking; an ability to cope with problems effectively and usefully.

Some problem is solved in a final and satisfying way through careful thought and communication with others.

(−) The problem here is that in some sense things *do* seem to be going quite well; others are reasonably responsive to one's views and one has a clear flow of ideas and all seems well enough on the surface. However, some error has been made, most likely at the level of the 8; a false priority has been selected and one is not using one's energies and abilities in the most useful way. A time when full attainment is being lost, when second- or third-best solutions are being accepted without stopping to think about this, because there is little tension or anxiety and the failure may not be obvious.

The 10 of Swords

(+) Now that a problem has been solved and matters dealt with by careful thinking and sorting-out, it's time to be looking for something else to be worthy of one's time. The Ace is the card which brings this about, but the lesson of the 10 is that there is a need to look for the new, and one should do things which make this more likely. This can be reading something one normally wouldn't bother with, socializing with others who might discuss some new idea which can trigger the energy of the Ace, most generally just exposing oneself to inputs and interactions which stimulate one's thinking. There may be a tendency not to do this because of laziness and satisfaction in a job well done; if one does, this is not likely to be a major mistake, although it may delay the appearance of further rewarding opportunities to use one's mental abilities.

(−) Stagnation. Smugness and self-satisfaction, patting oneself on the back because one has solved some problem or other, denying the need to use one's talents and skills at the present time. An inability to open oneself up to any kind of mental stimulation or challenge, or at least the complete disinclination to do this. Staying with some kind of problem area which has exhausted one's mental abilities and where no more can be achieved, simply out of habit.

The Suit of Cups

The Ace of Cups

(+) Some major new feeling or emotional relationship is awakening in one's life. This may be something one has never felt before, or it can be some major event such as marriage on the horizon or pregnancy or motherhood, or simply a crush on someone. The wider meaning of Cups as a suit may be reflected in this card, referring to artistic creativity of almost any kind. In any event, this is a time when emotional possibilities are opening up (or about to open up) in an exciting way, a way through which one grows and develops. A good time to forge some new affectional and loving relationship.

(−) There are multiple possible meanings. On the one hand, one may simply not be ready for some emotional involvement which the card suggests may be on the way. A second meaning is the possibility of some hidden, or secret, emotional involvement or feelings which may be inappropriate or even destructive in some way. The card may also mean barrenness, infertility, an inability to feel, the inability to experience life joyfully or in a loving way. Which meaning is appropriate will depend on the circumstances which apply when a Tarot reading is made.

The 2 of Cups

(+) An emotional affinity or relationship which has started off on the right foot. A better understanding of some positive emotion; a growing knowledge of the other person involved in a relationship, a superior awareness of the nature and needs of some other person of whom one is very fond. Harmony between people in close relationship (or even workmates who are friendly to each other, for example), reconciling opposites and different feelings in a harmonious atmosphere. Understanding and sympathy, helpfulness and fellow-feeling. A powerfully positive card.

(−) On the one hand, a false dawn of some kind in the emotional sphere of life; something which looked good turned (or turns) out not to be happy and good when one learns more about it. Separation and alienation of the affections, possibly the betrayal of some emotional trust or confidences, the loss of something cherished and valued. Dissent and argument, hurtful exchanges with someone close, even separation or divorce in a very few cases. Perhaps the hallmark of this card is disillusionment, learning that the things or people in which one had invested a naive trust and joyfulness were not worthy of this.

The 3 of Cups

(+) A better understanding of what one feels and quite possibly making plans for a loving or affectional relationship. One has a clear sense now of what one wants oneself and what the other person also wants in a relationship. One has an awareness of one's own feelings; this may be a new development if a relationship has been long-lasting, but now one knows what one wants and why and can face one's own feelings and discuss them with others more freely. Getting one's own feelings *clear*. In its most positive aspect this card may even signify a great happiness arising from the union shown in the 2; marriage or childbirth, or a time of great joyfulness for two people in emotional union.

(−) Confusion about what one really *does* feel. An inability to reconcile one's own feelings with those of others, exacerbated by this confusion on one's own part. A time when one is vulnerable to the emotional influences of others which are not helpful and may cause conflict and stress. Being unable to make any kind of plans for a relationship, perhaps because one tells oneself one cannot think clearly about such emotional matters (in this case this is merely an excuse). Rejecting the legitimate needs of others so far as such plans go.

The 4 of Cups

(+) This card conveys the notion of some emotional attainment or satisfaction, some fulfilment, which has been as great an achievement as was possible. The pleasure and satisfaction which has been obtained is as much as could have been had, given the other person(s) and the circumstances. The card certainly suggests peace and relaxation, but it also suggests a growing need for something more which can manifest as a restlessness. This may very well take the form of 'I want something but I don't know what' (even though one feels an emotional dissatisfaction and not an intellectual one). Some fulfilment has been obtained, but what more can be had? Is this all there is? However, this card may also suggest a state of emotional relief after some struggle, which is agreeable and a welcome rest; but dissatisfaction still lurks around the corner.

(−) There are two possible meanings. On the one hand, the card can simply mean emotional stagnation, an acceptance of the fulfilments obtained so far and the belief that these are indeed all that one can hope for. There is a loss of emotional spontaneity, a deadening of the heart, as love turns into familiarity and comfortableness. The card may, however, also show a chronic emotional restlessness as a reaction to this, without one's feeling able to change things without taking unacceptable risks. Lastly, in a few cases the card may suggest excessive absorption in transient emotional or sexual pleasures.

The 5 of Cups

(+) Even the positive aspect of this card is not easy. Some emotional shock or disappointment which comes unexpectedly (in most cases) challenges one and throws feelings into flux. The sadness, even melancholy, this card suggests are unavoidable even in positive aspect, but there is the opportunity to examine one's emotional life and feelings, and to change those aspects of one's feelings which may have been negative or destructive in the past. The card suggests a positive coping with some event which is not easy to bear, but the re-appraisal of one's feelings and relationships which may be called for may be quite deep and extensive. It also suggests that when this is done old emotional problems which have not been adequately dealt with in the past may then be successfully faced anew. A difficult card which still holds out much hope for better times to come.

(−) A painful and traumatic time. An unavoidable emotional trauma seems almost too much to bear and makes one anxious, depressed, unable to think clearly or deal with others. The pressure of external events generates stress which makes one less capable of dealing with any further adverse events, and this vicious circle is draining of one's emotional strength. A very difficult card which promises disappointments and heartache which can only be dissolved by the passage of time. Other people, and one's own efforts, are not helpful.

The 6 of Cups

(+) Happiness which comes after a difficult and tense time, emotional relief and a strong sense of wellbeing. Moving with the flow of things emotionally, a natural harmony with the world and the people one cares about. Moods and feelings ebb and flow in a fairly effortless way with which one feels at ease. This may be a time when emotionally significant events or people from the past are re-appraised in some less effortful and difficult way, and past events and emotions somehow affect the present, but not in a disruptive manner.

(−) This card may have more than one possible meaning. First, it may suggest that the painfulness and difficulties of the 5 do not disappear, that some emotional upset persists after one thought it had lost the power to be so affecting. Second, the card may suggest some quality of nostalgia, an absorption in the past, some sentimental fantasizing which cuts one off from reality and real emotional support. Lastly, emotional laziness and a disinclination to share with others and express affection and concern may be part of the negative aspect of this card.

The 7 of Cups

(+) A good time for wider experience and enjoying new emotions after a time of relative emotional calm. One is ready for some excitement, new friendships and affections. This card suggests that firm commitments will not initially be called for, but eventually some choice will have to be made, and this will be an important one, affecting much of one's emotional life. The card also has the traditional association of the possibility of some new form of emotional experience; specifically, a mystical one of some kind.

(−) A difficult time when many emotional entanglements are indicated. Too many demands are made, and it is very hard

to cope with them all. Disappointment – some of the relationships involved turning out poorly – and self-deception
(seeing some of the relationships involved as being more
helpful and rewarding than they are) are also suggested. An
emotional choice of some kind will be wrongly made, unless
one examines one's goals and motives very carefully. It is
necessary to get some peace and quiet and reflect carefully
on emotions and relationships.

The 8 of Cups

(+) Successfully working out what is really important
emotionally, the people and feelings which really matter.
This card also emphasizes the abandonment of some past
affiliation which needs to be outgrown and left behind;
moving away from a relationship which has lost its value in
order to concentrate on something which leads to deeper and
more satisfying emotional rewards. Disillusionment with the
past leads to a better emotional future.

(−) There are two possible meanings for this card. First, one
may be preoccupied with over-analysing emotions, chasing
one's tail in trying to sort out what is most important, being
unable to make a successful choice and analysing rather than
feeling and acting. Second, a wrong emotional choice,
particularly the rejection of some valuable long-standing
relationship in favour of some illusory new involvement.
Loss of something enduring because one is pursuing some
foolish new goal or relationship; self-deception.

The 9 of Cups

(+) Emotional harmony, contentedness, a positive flow of
emotional energies. Relationships which work well and are
beneficial and developing. An inner feeling of security which
enables one to be generous and good-willed; emotional satis-
factions of many kinds. Successful creative endeavours;

aesthetic pleasure and enjoyment. A very favourable card in any reading!

(−) Self-satisfaction and complacency in the emotional life. Vanity and sentimentality may both be involved. Everything feels right, but in truth there is a quality of stagnation and satisfaction with an unproductive and time-wasting state of affairs. An inability, or disinclination, to act in emotional matters which may lead to one being unhelpful to others and unable to grow and progress oneself.

The 10 of Cups

(+) A harmonious blend of two feelings which might normally be in opposition. On the one hand, emotional satis-faction, complete contentment, emotional pleasure and satisfying relationships; a security of emotion which is delightful and pleasing. On the other, an awareness that what has been (and still is) giving great emotional reward is no longer growing and developing, and that one needs something more. This card, in positive aspect, suggests that one can wait for the possibility of change and growth to come along in the form of someone or some new interest which will stimulate that growth and development, that one may enjoy what one has, nonetheless, and need not be too active in finding that possibility for further growth.

(−) A difficult time when one experiences a secure, stable and rewarding emotional environment but is restless, wanting something more, and probably not knowing what that might be. A dissatisfaction which may lead to guilt as one wonders why what is a good thing (and may be envied by others) isn't enough somehow. Further, it is difficult to make any choice to develop anything new; one is strangely reluctant to do so for reasons one does not understand. It is necessary to face up to matters and try to figure out what one does want, specifically what one feels is missing, and how this could be obtained without being too selfish or demanding.

The Suit of Coins

The Ace of Coins

(+): A new opportunity opens up, on the basis of some existing secure foundation. This may be a chance for promotion in one's career, some financial dealing, moving to a new house, anything which is in the sphere of the world of material objects and rewards. An excellent time for almost any new venture which promises rewards of these kinds. Enterprise and hard work will be called for, but one can summon the energies to carry out a plan effectively and grab the opportunity. Possibly, a time when one is blessed with particularly good health, or when one can change diet or exercise for benefit.

(−) One may be tempted into some new project of the type noted above too early, possibly motivated by greed or overly selfish concerns. The card warns that the planned involvement is premature or that one is planning to commit too many resources to this. The venture will not turn out well. A time to re-examine one's priorities and motivations carefully and seek the advice of others who know more about the matters involved.

The 2 of Coins

(+) A stimulating and fruitful time for developing some practical project and building on beginnings. Finding out more about what is involved, getting more information which is helpful and enables one to plan more carefully for what one will need to do. Checking the details – pay scales, a surveyor's report for a possible new home, this kind of thing. Energies which naturally flow into such practical planning and building a secure plan upon the beginnings of some enterprise. A good time to develop any practical enterprise one has begun and perhaps not fully developed, or put to one side for a time.

(−) Not so much building castles in the air as assembling the bricks with an eye to doing this! One is involved in some foolhardy or impractical project and there is self-deception; one thinks that by attention to detail one can ensure the success of what one is doing. In fact, the basic idea is wrong, the blueprint is flawed. A time to step back from examining the details, working with minutiae, and re-examine the basic idea one is developing.

The 3 of Coins

(+) A very good time for developing practical plans, for career, money, home. In particular, a time when the attitudes of others who are important to what you are trying to do are helpful, and such people can offer constructive advice. There are no major conflicts of interests blocking one's path. Also, a good time to persuade others to lend their support; a time when one's influence is successful and others respond in positive ways. Smoothing out minor practical problems and steaming ahead. Notably, a time when using one's own skills and working hard is noticed by others (a good time to impress the boss!). A very positive card for achievement in practical projects of all kinds.

(-) A conflict of interests which delays, or leads to the aban-donment of, some practical project. Disagreements between people involved, criticism of what one is trying to do which leads to fruitless arguments. Obstinacy and procrastination from others, and stubbornness on one's own part. A time when discussions and attempts to persuade others are pointless. At the very least it is necessary to delay the project until a better atmosphere develops, and one *must* desist from attempts to force through what one wishes to do.

The 4 of Coins

(+) An important practical accomplishment. While this is not the end point, some satisfying and concrete realization of practical plans is indicated. Something is built, a move is made, a contract signed. A good base of material security, finding oneself in a position of authority, overcoming obstacles and getting a concrete reward for one's efforts. A powerfully positive card.

(−) While some practical goal is attained, this is in some way a disappointment or may even be a block to a further development. The disappointing aspect may be that the success is a compromise, one has settled for something below the level of one's abilities and competence. If this is not immediately apparent, then the potential in the project may be less than one considered – for example, one may have got the job, but the promotion prospects are soon seen to be notably poorer than one thought (or was led to believe). Also, the gain may be one which leads to stagnation – holding on to something for fear of insecurity, an obstinate clinging-on to something safe which actually leads to one's being too blinkered to see the chance of having something better when a suitable opportunity arises. A card of partial attainment and disappointing limitations.

The 5 of Coins

(+) A time when one is unsure about one's material security and the foundations of one's practical efforts. A sudden change which shows that all is not as stable as one thought; some financial misfortune, for example. Certainly, an upsetting and unsettling change. The card suggests that there is the promise of better things to come, but this may not be seen for a while, since one is too fretful and anxious to look for positive trends. The company and support of others with similar concerns may be helpful in getting through the difficulty and in giving one the resources to find the better future prospects the card promises.

(−) A time of drastic and negative change in one's material circumstances, some major setback which affects one very badly. Severe financial loss may be indicated by this card. The problems are either unavoidable, or else one's own limitations make them so; lack of imagination, inflexibility, being unable to cope with changing circumstances may turn a difficult state of affairs into a possibly disastrous one. A very difficult card with a strong negative implication in any reading.

The 6 of Coins

(+) Recovery and/or stability in material circumstances. Frequently, this card suggests that some difficulty (the preceding 5) has been overcome (or will be overcome) and that things settle down to a quieter phase. In particular, since an ease of the ebb and flow of things is suggested by a 6, this card may imply that difficulties with regard to some expected, regular payments (or some such) may be resolved, or that there is an addition to such inflow of resources. A time when managing one's financial affairs over an extended period of time is easy and fluent, rather than (for example) a sudden windfall.

(−) Two possible meanings apply here. First, one may be bogged down in some monotonous and tedious dealings in the material sphere: red tape, hours spent accounting, recurring and irritating financial/material planning which is tiresome and drains one's energies. On the other, an established cycle of financial affairs which is unhelpful and shows no sign of change; an inability to gain new resources, being stuck at some level of under-achievement which threatens to continue for some time. A stability which is disappointing and limiting.

The 7 of Coins

(+) One is faced with many choices and a variety of options concerning what to do with one's material resources; there may be several ventures or possibilities opening up. This card suggests that one of these possibilities may lead to great rewards, but it is not easy to see which one this is. Failure to take advice from others, and one's own inertia and inability to act decisively after careful contemplation, are the problems which will need to be overcome if a decision is to be taken successfully. Despite the positive aspect of this card, this correct decision is not easily come by, and it may be best to hedge one's bets (if possible) if one is not able to commit oneself enthusiastically to any one particular option after taking advice and planning carefully oneself.

(−) A time when material security may be threatened by one's own inability to sort out a complexity of competing interests and possible choices. There is too much going on, and one may over-extend oneself getting involved with too many things. Choices made at this time are most unlikely to be the correct ones and one runs the risk of self-produced material loss. It is necessary to pull in one's horns and minimize risks. The key message is to simplify matters and, if in doubt, don't do it!

The 8 of Coins

(+) An important time for getting financial priorities straight. The card promises that this can be achieved if careful thought is given to financial and material matters. Sort out where resources most need to go, and where one needs to use most of one's energies. The card also implies that past involvements and efforts are not so much abandoned here, but rather they may form a secure base from which further efforts and striving can be made with success. One may end up developing something well away from those original involvements, but they are grown beyond rather than abandoned as such. A time when thought and hard work may produce a lasting and satisfying reward in the future; a good, positive card.

(−) Material stability and security is attained by some choice, and an establishment of priorities, but the choice made is not the best one. In particular, it may be that a choice is based on short-term goals and rewards rather than with an eye to enduring achievements which reap rewards into the future. There may be a possibility that some dishonesty in business or financial affairs is beneficial in the short term and has been indulged in by someone (not necessarily the person for whom the reading is being given!). Even in negative aspect this card is hardly disastrous, but it does suggest the need for looking beyond the immediate.

The 9 of Coins

(+) Excellent material success, an enduring and satisfying achievement of objectives. The card suggests particular skill at a managerial/executive level, although this shouldn't be taken too narrowly – it may simply mean an excellent overall management of one's own affairs. Balancing different goals and perspectives, and producing an outstanding solution which solves almost all problems. A very powerfully positive card which promises great material rewards for dedicated effort and security of achievement also.

(−) Two possible meanings are implied here. There is the possibility that while things are currently stable, and one does not have to make too much of an effort to keep things on an even keel, this will not persist for much longer. One must be aware of the imminence of change and prepare for it. On the other hand, the stability may be real and persisting but matters are not really to one's advantage although they may appear so. For example, some apparently successful financial or business involvement may be of notably greater benefit to others involved than to oneself.

The 10 of Coins

(+) Material security which is satisfying and enduring, but which still leaves one hankering for more. A state of affairs which may be constricting, forcing one to use one's energies in a stereotyped way, and feeling an inner dissatisfaction with the value of what one is doing. Stagnation, and an inability to take on new goals and projects. One may have a feeling of smugness or complacency which makes it very difficult to redeploy one's energies in new, adaptive ways. However, the card at least shows a stable and secure state of external affairs!

(−) The meaning of the card in negative aspect is similar to its meaning in positive aspect, save that the element of stagnation is stronger, as may be one's inner sense of frustrating limitations. This combination can produce a powerful sense of confusion and inability to act to change anything. It may be that small-scale experimenting (e.g., with small sums of money) in a few speculative areas may help to kindle some interest and energy which leads to new involvements, dispelling the feeling of frustration and opening up satisfying projects of some kind.

The Suit of Wands

(Note: the Marseilles deck terms these *clubs*, but almost all decks use the older name, and I shall term them wands also.)

The Ace of Wands

(+) An important creative beginning of some kind, a new avenue for one to use one's energies. The meaning of this card is necessarily very vague, for Aces indicate the opening up of new possibilities and the suit of Wands shows energies which can be used for almost any purpose. All that one can be sure of is that the card indicates an exciting time when one's energy level is high, almost anything seems possible, and it is a good time to begin almost any new venture or project!

(−) There are two possible meanings. On the one hand, one may simply feel a complete lack of energy and willpower, so that one cannot begin anything new nor even develop what one is doing. A card of lethargy, exhaustion, world-weariness. On the other hand, the card may indicate someone shooting off in all directions, pursuing far too many enthusiasms and objectives without making discriminative choices between them, and being a Jack of all trades, master of none. The card warns that the person concerned will need to become better informed about what he/she is doing and settle down to concentrate on rather fewer involvements.

The 2 of Wands

(+) Energy is being put into building something up, at the level of finding out the details, laying foundations, getting the early stages right. Again, the nature of this project can be almost anything, but this card emphasizes *social* ends and means. One gains information and useful help by talking with others, and one can understand one's own goals and thoughts more clearly by contrasting them with those of other people. One's energy is now committed to some particular goal, and the ramifications of that need to be worked out.

(−) The inability to get some cherished new idea or venture off the ground, early obstacles put in the way of making something work, disagreements with others or a lack of support for one's ideas and projects. Bad initial planning, an inability to grasp the details of what may be done, possibly slapdash and devil-may-care attitudes towards those details, treating them (wrongly) as unimportant.

The 3 of Wands

(+) Successfully getting something off the ground – a card of inspiration turned into a practical plan, a dream made into reality. The ability to communicate effectively with others, get their support, and make progress. The card indicates that while one's own inspiration is the key drive which leads to success, communication with others – including discussions and taking advice – is a crucial means for furthering one's own ends. Decide what you want to do and make efforts to persuade others, and success will be forthcoming. This is a particularly favourable card for developing almost any goal which is close to one's heart, or which has proved tricky to achieve in the past.

(−) Disagreements and quarrels with others which prevent one using one's energies in useful ways. Conflicts and arguments, and lack of support in crucial quarters, make it impossible or very difficult to make further progress. At the very least, a considerable delay is indicated, and one will need all one's persuasive skills to get anywhere. The best course of action is probably to stop banging one's head against a brick wall and back away from arguments and conflicts which are non-productive and simply sap one's energies.

The 4 of Wands

(+) This is a particularly powerful card, for it brings together the ideas and energies of Wands with the practical attainments of the 4. The plan of the 3 has been made into something concrete and durable; this may be the first practical and useful outcome for some plan after all the work of thinking, planning, and discussion. A very favourable card for professional people, inventors, artists, writers, anyone who works at expressing ideas in concrete forms, for it promises the successful realization of some idea or goal. While the achievement is not some great, final, success, it is a satisfying and secure one.

(−) A conflict between ideals and energy on the one hand and the practical world on the other. The card may suggest an inability to think and plan in practical ways, fantasizing about achievements rather than doing anything constructive, a refusal to accept necessary pragmatic limitations on what one hopes to do. Another meaning is that the inspiration and energy within one is deadened by practical constraints, one's creativity is destroyed by narrow-mindedness, hidebound tradition, people without any imagination. Not a good card.

The 5 of Wands

(+) A tricky and difficult time. This card suggests that one will meet opposition which will need cunning and resourcefulness to overcome. This opposition takes the form of some competing interest, a talented person (or powerful group of people) who do not accept one's plans, goals and attitudes, and may even scheme against one. It is possible to advance, but this will take much energy and a lot of careful thinking, even plotting and deviousness in certain circumstances. Secret oppositions and dislikes may be indicated by this card; even in positive aspect, this is not a well-omened card.

(−) Opposition from others which is overpowering. Their actions may very possibly be deceitful, dishonest, even illegal. One is outwitted and beaten by resourceful and unscrupulous opponents whose actions may in large part be covert and secretive, so that one cannot anticipate and plan for their behaviour. A very tricky card indeed.

The 6 of Wands

(+) A card which promises both relief and success. After a difficult time, one's plans and hopes move closer to being realized. Tension, and external obstacles, are overcome and one is able to use one's energies efficiently and usefully. There is a decrease in anxiety, an ability to work with less tension and greater efficiency. The card also promises the possibility of some important success which has been earned through hard work and careful planning, a reward for past efforts which one has made in a time of adversity or difficulty. However, the nature of this success is vague; the card can indicate almost any kind of achievement and its likely nature must be inferred from other cards in the reading.

(−) A dangerous time, for it seems that things are going fairly well and that one's life is on an even keel. There are no obvious sources of conflict and anxiety. However, below the surface there are tricky undercurrents; one is unaware of developments which may undermine one's efforts. Again, this card suggests covert and deceitful actions, and while one is unaware of what these might be, the card suggests that a rising apprehension which one cannot rationally account for may be a recognition of such actions.

The 7 of Wands

(+) A powerful and potent card. This suggests a time fraught with difficulty, even danger, in which one is faced with many options concerning how to concentrate one's energies. There is also opposition from competing interests and people. A highly successful choice is possible from the many options one could pursue, and this choice may very well be correctly made on the basis of one's own judgement. However, even so, considerable courage and single-mindedness will be needed, and scrupulous honesty. The card promises that if such virtues are adhered to, one may triumph over powerful competition and attain some major success.

(−) Many choices are available for how to use one's energies, and only one of these is profitable and helpful; the odds are that this choice will not be correctly made and that the nature of the error will not be too long in being perceived. Both one's own judgement and the advice of others are equally flawed so far as this choice is concerned. It may even be that the choice one does make is a very bad one, even potentially disastrous. It would be prudent to delay choices, and/or not commit too much to any particular goal or interest right now. Keep your eggs in a variety of baskets!

The 8 of Wands

(+) The selecting-a-priority element which an 8 always indi-cates has a particular meaning here. This card shows a time when the priority which must be established is a fundamental one; the energy of Wands must be committed to some defi-nite and clarified *role* of some kind. People who are doing many things must establish clear priorities among them, but even more importantly people who play several roles (e.g., mother/spouse/housewife/part-time worker) have to make a commitment as to which of these roles is most important at the present time. It need not be the case that such a choice must be made for all time, but the card suggests that it is important that a choice must be made for the time being and for the foreseeable future. The necessity of the choice is balanced by the fact that, in positive aspect, this card suggests the correctness of the choice made, and that it is a satisfying and rewarding one.

(−) There are two possible meanings, although the important choice and establishment of a priority as needs right now remain. It may be that such a choice is wrongly made, that one establishes a priority which is not the right one at this time. Or one may fail to make a necessary choice, possibly for fear of limiting oneself (the reverse is true: it is the inability to establish a priority and make a commitment which is limiting at the present time!). Finally, it may be that some choice is forced on one by others or by circumstance, so that one *has* to be limited to one role or task in a way which is undesirable.

The 9 of Wands

(+) Great inner strength and determination. This card indicates a time when one's energies are almost unbounded and one's willpower dominates others (without irritating them) and circumstance. At best, one may be in a virtually undefeatable and unassailable position, doing exactly what one wishes to do. A sense of wholeness within oneself, of having the energy and ability to achieve what one wishes. There seems to be almost nothing one cannot do. A very powerful and positive card in any reading.

(−) Strength and energy are indicated by the card, but one may be missing out in some way, obtaining a reward which is not quite what one deserves. Not a time of restrictions or adverse circumstance, but a disappointment even if one cannot see this. There is an element of settling for second best with this card, although the second best involved may be no poor thing!

The 10 of Wands

(+) A time when one's energies begin to move away from the activities and roles one has been engaged in for some time. A natural restlessness which seeks new avenues of exploration; curiosity which leads one away from what is established in one's life. The card indicates the need to recognize that this restlessness is an important signal and that it is time to find new challenges and activities, despite the securities and comforts one has already obtained.

(−) There are multiple possible meanings, although the unifying theme is the conflict between some established security and the need to develop one's energies into some new field. This conflict may be troubling and anxiety-arousing, and one's fears of possible insecurity may lead one to deny the need to develop any further, creating chronic frustration and irritability. One may repress the energy, leading to lethargy, conservatism, inability to adjust, inflexibility. At worst the card suggests that the thwarted energy may turn in upon oneself and even get projected, so that one becomes an oppressor of others, inhibiting them by using the dead weight of tradition and the realm of the established order of things to suppress their creativity and efforts.

The Sixteen Court Cards of the Minor Arcana

These cards exist almost as a bridge between the archetypal forms of the Major Arcana and the forty numbered cards of the Minor Arcana suits. They are certainly part of the Minor Arcana, but they show figures upon them, as do the Major Arcana. It is necessary to consider the psychology which underpins them before detailing their divinational meanings.

We have already considered that the four suits might stand

in relation to the four Jungian functions, with swords=
thinking, cups=feeling, coins=sensation and the less
convincing link of wands=intuition. Now, matters become
more complex, for the four court card types have also been
linked with these four functions: King=thinking, Queen=
feeling, Knight=intuition, Knave=sensation. So the court
cards are, in a way, a kernel of the fourfold functions within
each individual suit, as if to emphasize that the four functions
are not isolated and wholly separated but can be associated.
There is a problem with this; using this idea all sixteen
matches (including duplications) are possible, whereas Jung
was insistent that opposed functions (thought-feeling, intuition-sensation) could not be allied and combined. However,
this conflict is less apparent than real if we consider that these
opposite pairings are given negative meanings by almost all
Tarot writers, the unnaturalness of the bonding being
reflected in the generally inauspicious meaning ascribed to
the card. This is not reflected in the meanings given here for
the cards. I don't consider that thinking-feeling and intuition-
sensation necessarily *must* be in conflict; obviously, Jung
would agree for the individuated person. Hence, both positive and negative meanings will be given in the usual way.

The divinational meanings of these cards are almost always
rather abstract, certainly more so than the other forty Minor
Arcana cards. Each one shows a fusion of two psychological
functions (save for the four which show only one) and it is
the general *theme* they show, rather than specific meanings
so far as external events are concerned, which is important.
When they appear in a reading their interpretation will
frequently depend in large part on the cards around them.
Hopefully the following descriptions will make them not *too*
abstract for the reader!

The Suit of Swords

The King of Swords

A fairly beneficent monarch looks out from this card, sword held in his *right* hand (the power of thinking is conscious), wearing some intriguing-looking robes. The robes on his shoulders almost seem to have the face of the Moon designed upon them! Surely this must be to remind us that to place all our faith in the power of reason is an illusion as certain as any which the Moon creates for us. This delightful little symbolism is rarely commented on. Both his kingly nature and the suit of Swords show that he is the power of pure reason.

(+) Mental prowess, mental speed and flexibility, the primacy of reason and intellect. Seeking authority so as to be able to use one's mental powers and put plans into operation. Stripping away tradition, useless and outdated regulations and rules, relying on thinking alone. However, even in positive aspect there may be an ignoring of values which are not 'rationally' based so that the desires and needs of others may be misinterpreted or pushed aside.

(−) Denial of feeling and emotion, a cold and cruel impersonality bordering on the sadistic. A calculating and shrewd person, who knows what he wants and how to get it; at worst, a quality of elemental evil backed by brutally efficient planning. Arguably the worst-aspected card in the entire pack.

The Queen of Swords

REYNE ·D'ÉPÉE

A somewhat forbidding (although possibly kindly) woman is seated on a throne, sword in her right hand, with her left hand raised as if in warning. Unlike the King, she is unarmoured, but she is clearly a strong figure, not someone to be trifled with. The Queen brings together the functions of thinking and feeling, a powerful combination which can – in harmony – produce ethically-imbued thinking and emotional balance.

(+) Thoughts and feelings flow together; ethical and aesthetic thought, so that problems are not seen merely in the abstract but with an inner feeling for their moral and ethical dimensions. A regularity of flow, and balance, of the emotions As a warner or guardian, the Queen may be refusing to countenance actions which are immoral or which harm others.

(−) The card may indicate thinking and feeling at war with each other, so that one knows one should do one thing but feels one should do something else. A difficult and troubling conflict of this kind. However, the card may also show a malign alliance of the two functions, a vituperative and emotionally fired-up slanderer and abuser, a shrewish and vicious person.

The Knight of Swords

CAVALIER·D'EPÉE

Fully armoured and mounted, the Knight bears a sword in his *left* hand, as if to emphasize that his knightly function (intuition) is an *irrational* one in Jungian terms, unlike the rationality of the King and Queen (who both held their swords in their right hands). His horse is rearing up a little, and in many decks he looks even more martial and determined than he is in the Marseilles deck. He also has a moon-face on his robes on the left side only, perhaps to show that the blend of rational and irrational functions leaves him prone to illusions and self-deceptions. Bringing together thinking and intuition, the Knight is a young man going everywhere in a hurry.

(+) Great energy and mental speed; forming many plans and ideas (but not putting them into effect). An abundance of ideas; 'brainstorming', creativity. This is the stage of playing around with ideas, not so much of critically evaluating them (this comes later), but rather of getting all the ideas one can and tossing them around. 'Lateral thinking', a storm of mental energy!

(−) Going everywhere and arriving nowhere. Ideas are confused and not related to practicalities, one is simply trying to do far too much. An inability to concentrate; distractions and one's own distractibility. Impotence in action caused by a total lack of practicality and attempts to develop ideas as opposed to fantasizing and coming up with half-baked notions. Also, the possibility of a cruel and capable thinker, one who uses his energies and intellectual prowess to belittle others. This Knight has a warrior-like aspect; his horse wears barding, for a start, and look at how it rears up, with the glint of impending battle in its face!

The Knave of Swords

Unarmoured, and with his sword in his left hand (rational and irrational combine here), the rather plain-looking Knave combines sensation and thinking. The earthy/worldly quality of his sensation function is what protects him from having the moon-face his male companions in this suit wear on their robes!

(+) The power of practical thinking, the ability to take ideas and concepts and imaginings and sculpt them into useful forms. A favourable card for builders, architects, planners, anyone working with material objects and designs. However, even in positive aspect this card suggests some limitation of intelligence by the practical world, so that there may be a blunting of imagination because of over-practical and over-cautious attitudes.

(−) One possible meaning is that of impractical thinking, but the more likely meaning is that of retarded thinking. Imagination, flair, insights are all diminished or lost because of an habitual preoccupation with the here-and-now practical realities of life (and especially work). Staid, stolid, and unimaginative would be the formula for this card. Progress is impeded by lack of imagination.

The Suit of Cups

Notably, all the figures shown in this suit hold the Cup in the right hand, that of the conscious mind. There is none of the symmetry of King-Queen/Knight-Knave that we saw in the suit of Swords, and this is also true for the two other suits, with one major exception – the Knight of Clubs (Wands) who holds his wand in his left hand. What the Tarot is surely showing us here is the pervasive problems that attend the over-emphasis of the thinking function. It achieves this by showing the illusion-producing Moon affecting the King and Knight of Swords, as if the power of reason is an illusion (the King is most affected), and also by stressing the need for a balance with the (left) unconscious in the suit which represents the thinking function. The other cards are right-handed people; the Tarot has exalted the other functions to the status of consciousness, as if to balance the over-valued, typically superior function (thinking). The one exception, which is the *power of pure intuition*, is a perfect Jungian symbolism, for intuition is arguably a perfect opposite to thinking-irrational as opposed to rational, concerned with examining all possibilities and potentialities, amplifying rather than analysing. One might perhaps have expected the single remaining left-hander to be the Queen of Cups – after all, she is pure feeling, and isn't feeling the function which is opposed to thinking in the Jungian scheme? Possibly, but the Queen of Cups has a complex and intriguing symbolism all of her own as we shall shortly discover. This strange little grammar of handedness in the Tarot came to our attention when looking at the Major Arcana, and it surfaces again now.

The King of Cups

A sympathetic, almost sad-looking, old man sits berobed on his throne, holding a huge golden cup. He brings together the thinking and feeling functions, but in a rather different manner from the Queen of Swords, for his position of authority is greater and this puts a stronger emphasis on more social (as opposed to personal) matters.

(+) Ethical and moral concerns, judgements and expressed views which are rooted in feeling-based thinking about problems. A wise and kindly adviser of some kind, someone who is in a position of authority or who commands respect from others.

(−) Difficulty in making moral evaluations; being unsure about one's own values as these are used to judge others. The card may also indicate someone who is secretive and scheming, who harbours some grudge or discontent, and works in slanderous and/or covert ways to harm another. Such a person has no moral sense other than their own self-interest, and will act in an expedient way to get what they want.

The Queen of Cups

This card is a much more complex one than one might expect; one would anticipate that, as the prime representative of the feeling function, the Queen would stand for abundant and flowing emotion. Not so; probably, the card which comes closest to that would be the Ace of Cups. Rather, the Queen has two quite unexpected attributes which we see at once in the card. Certainly, she is smiling and kindly and is comfortably seated on her throne, berobed and secure. But the cup she holds is *sealed*, unlike those held by her three male companions in the court cards of this suit. What is more, in her left hand she holds what is certainly a short sword or very long dagger, even if it is not a sword as such (compare her with the court cards of the Sword suit). These two elements certainly take one aback on first viewing!

The fact that her cup is sealed surely suggests that she does not dispense her emotional gifts easily, and that there is a secretive or hidden quality about the emotional strengths she symbolizes. A possible view might be that excessive display of emotions blunts the finer sensibilities the Queen embodies. These interpretations obviously affect the divinational meanings of the card.

The dagger? This clearly is not a sword and has no connotations of the thinking function. Perhaps this shows something similar to the astrological symbol for the sign most strongly associated with feeling – Cancer, the crab. An important and often-overlooked part of the crab is the claw; when Cancer is threatened these claws can be powerful weapons. Likewise the Queen has a dagger, a weapon more dangerous than it might seem, just as the crab's claws are. Feeling is not a function to be exploited without its having the means of self-defence and vengeance when necessary!

(+) Affection and protection, emotional nurturing, fantasying and romantic feelings. There is something secretive, protective, or even other-worldly about this emotional process. At its best, this may inspire artistry, creativity, altruism, the finest feelings and emotions.

(−) Untrustworthy emotional fantasies, emotional manipulations of people in a way which does not involve conscious scheming but which is highly effective anyway. Unpredictable moods, capriciousness, perversity. Possibly, emotional revenge and emotional blackmail, cruelty.

CAVALIER-DE-COUPE

The Knight of Cups

Seated on his high-stepping horse, the Knight holds out a cup which has a wider brim than any of the others shown in the court cards of this suit. He is bareheaded, an unusual quality in the court cards which suggests his openness to experience, and a possible vulnerability. He seems to be smiling rather sadly, almost regretfully – perhaps this is due to his awareness of possible impending loss (see the interpretations below). Bringing together the functions of feeling and intuition, this is a reflective figure, almost a melancholy one.

(+) A tricky time when all kinds of emotional possibilities seem open; one is intuitively aware of feeling-relationships with others. Interactions and personal relationships take on new qualities and their emotional qualities strengthen and/ or change. There may be a conflict between one's desire to reach out to others emotionally and a natural reticence and passivity which makes one hang back. An unstable time when one has trouble making firm decisions and commitments in the emotional sphere. Restlessness and a continual craving for emotional stimulation may also be pronounced.

(−) Emotional restlessness and dissatisfaction are fuelled by fantasies about life and other people. Fidelity and constancy are almost impossible; dishonesty, presenting a wide-eyed appearance and lying behind the backs of others may also be involved. A card of emotional duplicity and faithlessness, fickleness, possible emotional loss due to one's own lack of honesty.

The Knave of Cups

Rather like the Knight, the young Knave seems a somewhat melancholy fellow, walking along his path. Yet his cup of feeling is open, and he wears a garland of flowers about his head as if to emphasize his affinity with the earthy world of sensation. Uniting feeling and sensation as this card does, one might have expected to see a figure more obviously joyous and celebrating pleasure; perhaps, again, he is saddened by the darker side of himself.

(+) Sensual and sexual experience and pleasure, the expression of emotion in direct and straightforward ways. The card may suggest a lack of refinement or subtlety in some way, and a quieter side of the Knave is his reflective nature. This is not analytic, but simply a re-creating of the pleasures he has enjoyed; there may be a nostalgic and melancholy aspect to this.

(−) Emotional loss, sensuality and sexuality in abeyance, pleasures which have cloyed and no longer give the satisfaction they used to. Jadedness, world-weariness, a feeling that one has experienced things fully and that one is only going through the motions. Anhedonia, the loss of the ability to feel pleasure, depression (more often, nostalgic melancholy). A time when the emotional world 'weighs heavily' on one, the earthy quality of sensation no longer giving the pleasures and delights it once did.

The Suit of Coins

The King of Coins

A prosperous and contented figure sits casually on a throne, holding the symbol of his wealth and prestige, the coin. He looks every inch the successful businessman – he has authority, but he doesn't really look *regal*. The King brings together thinking and sensation, the application of thought to the material world, and he has clearly done pretty well for himself.

(+) Material success and prestige, which is gained by very practical efforts. This is a card of the craftsman and the persistent worker, and not the inspired entrepreneur. Loyalty, trustworthiness, caution, patience, and being satisfied with reasonable rewards are qualities indicated here. There is no real innovation, but then no deviousness and cunning either. A stolid, reliable figure.

(−) Dull materialism, over-valuing the things of this world, reliance on material support as a crutch for inadequacies of feeling or imagination. An inability to change, a lack of flexibility, poor adaptability to changing circumstances and new demands. Insularity, habit-formed stereotyped thinking which cannot understand what is outside its own narrow system of values.

The Queen of Coins

REYNE·DE·DENIERS

Unlike the Knave of Cups, who unites feeling and sensation as the Queen does, this is a figure of authority. The Knave wandered along his own path, but the Queen is an established figure with influence and power. Her sceptre, held in addition to the coin, emphasizes this fact.

(+) Comfort, pleasure, sensuality, the good things of life. Contentedness and enjoyment of good food, wines, all mod cons. There may be some ostentatiousness about this card, but this is balanced by the generosity which is also indicated. The Queen is not particularly intelligent or wily, but she is no fool, and her judgements about whether people *feel* good or are untrustworthy are accurate ones. Responsibility in material affairs is also part of this card, taking good care of what one has.

(−) Either of two pathological extremes: the miser or the profligate. The miserliness is a hoarding of material gains, denying material support and also denying emotional support (the two often going together), a narrow-minded materialistic outlook. The profligacy is self-advertising; 'Look at me, how wealthy I am,' sometimes (but not usually) characterized by gross bad taste. Usually, however, opulence and extravagance are the order of the day.

The Knight of Coins

A young man fair of face rides out on a sturdy-looking horse. Intriguingly, save for the Queen of Cups, this is the one court card where the figure seems to be carrying the symbol from another suit. As the Queen held something rather like a sword (even though it wasn't one), the Knight seems to be carrying a club in his right hand. We can't be absolutely certain about this, for the court cards in the club (wands) suit all show figures carrying rather varied clubs. Still, it certainly looks like a club/wand and the Queen of Wands holds one not dissimilar to it. Clearly, our intuitive Knight has decided to take the symbol for his function along with him; perhaps he is determined not to be repressed by the earthy nature of the coins suit. Indeed, alone among the court cards here he is not even holding onto his coin!

(+) Energetic involvement in many projects in the material world, enthusiasms, a touch of the Jack of all trades. This card suggests that, at the present time at least, there are many opportunities for material success which are opening up if one can perceive them, and that with dedicated work one can exploit these to good effect.

(−) Too many involvements in the material world; spreading one's energies too widely so that no single project really gets the support which is necessary for it to succeed. An inability to concentrate on one thing for any length of time, rushing from one thing to the next, ending up running round in circles. Abundant energy which is simply not getting used usefully. Sometimes the card suggests that this energy is (or will be) crushed by the demands of the practical, material world – but these demands will have built up precisely because one has been wasting one's time, in the immediate past at least.

The Knave of Coins

A purposive and determined-looking young man carefully scrutinizes the coin he holds before him. Interestingly, this court card shows *two* coins, the second on the ground, as if doubly emphasizing the Knave's complete adherence to the earthy, material values of the sensation function. There is no doubting where the Knave's interests lie!

(+) Material gains, especially financial. Thrift and conscientiousness in financial matters; having an eye for the main chance. Honesty and trustworthiness are virtues close to the Knave's heart (and pocket). Good business sense, avoidance of speculation and risk-taking, sticking to well-trodden paths of financial management which one knows well. Also a good card for financial planning and administration.

(−) Completely hidebound materialism. Total preoccupation with financial gain, amassing far more than one needs, and being wholly impervious to the needs of others. Feathering one's own nest; the natural card of habitual Tory voters. Allied to this is a complete lack of any imagination or even intelligence; there is a definite dim-wittedness about this card which distinguishes it from the King. The possibility of using financial resources as a tool to bully others and manipulate them exists, but this will not be done with any subtlety or real insight, and it can certainly be outwitted.

The Suit of Wands (Clubs)

The King of Wands

ROY·DE·BATON

There is no mistaking the nobility of this King; holding a huge and ornate wand, he wears golden armour and fine, rich robes. These are not symbols of material wealth and affluence, but rather the outer insignia of his undoubted mental prowess and natural authority. The King combines the power of reason with the awareness of intuition, and the energetic quality of Wands make him a kingly character, one who has been given power in recognition of his own powerful qualities.

(+) Swift mental action, based on a full awareness both of the way things stand and of the ways in which they could develop. An intuitive grasp of the essentials of almost any situation, and the ability to act swiftly and decisively to achieve what one wishes. A natural conviction and confidence in one's views and abilities which communicates itself to others and impresses them. The one possible weakness is that one may hang back from necessary action precisely because one can see so many aspects of it and may want to ponder all possible outcomes! However, this is almost always a powerfully positive card in any reading.

(−) Overbearing and even tyrannical attitudes and actions, someone acting on the basis of their own beliefs and ruthlessly pursuing what they want at the expense of others. Opposition which is very hard to counter. Sometimes, vacillation, an inability to make one's mind up even though one is aware of all the important facts – the exact opposite of the other negative meaning.

The Queen of Wands

REYNE·DE·BATON

A woman who is clearly mature in years sits with a kindly smile; she too has a large wand, although it is not so ornamented as that of the King. She wears no armour as he does, but is dressed in long, flowing robes. She brings together the feeling and intuitive functions, and her maturity makes her a more auspicious figure in some ways than the Knight of Cups (who combined the same qualities); her maturity gives her a better ability to combine these two functions.

(+) Emotional fertility; compassion, kindliness, friendship, sympathy and nurturance. Someone who is keenly aware of the feelings of others (and of his/her own) in all their complexities. This is a card which emphasizes a real absorption in emotions and relationships; energies naturally flow into such concerns and the effects of this are positive and rewarding. Emotional protectiveness of some kind is often indicated.

(−) Mothering which is smothering; an overbearing, dominating, matriarchal figure, who sticks her nose into the emotions and relationships of others. The accuracy of emotional perceptions does not guarantee helpful actions, for this person is motivated (at least in part) by a desire to emotionally control and dominate others and to diminish their independence. There is a capacity for cruelly accurate emotional slights which home in on the weaknesses of others.

The Knight of Wands

Astride his horse, the Knight of Wands is a particularly interesting figure. His horse is like no other, for it is white, and it is also almost completely covered by a long cloth; the horses of the other knights were all brown and had but little in the way of decoration (and barding in the case of the Knight of Swords, on his destrier). He also holds his wand left-handedly. This completes the four-fold uniqueness of the 'pure' function types: King of Swords (his twin moon-face epaulettes – or whatever they are – and what *is* that strange sigil underneath his throne? If we only knew!), the Queen of Cups (with her uniquely closed cup and her dagger), the Knave of Coins (the only court card with *two* coins shown, the second being unique in being *on the ground*) and now our intuitive Knight of Wands. This is a delightful symmetry!

(+) Energies which seem to be going all over the place, but which are directed towards worthwhile goals. One's instincts and intuition are the best guide as to what to do; do not give too much weight to the advice of others or to logic and reasoning. Often, the wisdom of one's actions will be seen in retrospect even if what one is doing now is seemingly unpredictable and even a little chaotic!

(−) Diffusion of energy, running around in circles and getting absolutely nowhere. Wilful ignoring of the advice and help-fulness of others, a stubborn attitude of 'I'm going to do what I like,' petulance and lack of amenability to reason. Sometimes, a delight in chaos and disorder, destroying useful things because they are associated with some order or lawfulness to which one takes an irrational dislike. A card of disorder and wholesale lack of discipline.

VALET · DE · BATON

The Knave of Wands

A stocky young man stands holding a wand which is very much rooted in the ground – maybe even a growing stave. Uniquely, he holds this with both hands. Since this is a unique representation in the court cards of the Minor Arcana, any interpretation of what is being meant here must be speculative. But he does combine the here-and-now, take-it-as-it-is earthy quality of sensation with the intuitive, look-at-everything-this-could-be quality, and these two are opposites. Perhaps he needs both hands to hold onto such a tricky combination, and a further puzzle is that his arms have been drawn very awkwardly – almost two-dimensionally, it seems at first sight. It's plausible that his double-handed grasp emphasizes the unity of opposites he is trying to create, but then none of the other figures which show opposite functions have this two-handed grasp although the Knight (intuition) of Coins (sensation) *did* carry a wand, the only figure of the sixteen who *is* carrying an emblem of his function. He is the parallel figure in the Coins suit to the Knave here, so there is *some* symmetry in the intuition-sensation pairing and how these are marked out as being unusual in the Tarot symbols. An intriguing puzzle to end our survey of the court cards!

(+) Energies directed towards, and an intuitive grasp of, the material world, but this tends to be comforts, home, indulgences rather than necessarily financial affairs. Taking pleasure in many involvements in the material world, by no means major affairs in most cases. Getting the most out of what one possesses, enjoyment in fulfilling the potentials of one's involvements.

(−) Impracticality, trying to use one's energies and express-iveness in ways which don't fit with practicalities and day-to-day details of living. Fretting over little things, blowing things out of proportion, being unrealistic about the rewards one might reasonably expect for one's efforts in life.

Personality Theory and the Minor Arcana

First, we can sum up the role of the court cards of the Minor Arcana. I identified the four suits with the four Jungian func-tions (this applies to the entire Minor Arcana, of course), and also argued that King, Queen, Knight and Knave were also symbols for the functions. The only problem with this formula in general is that wands and intuition are not perfectly aligned; wands have a quality of energy and activity which does not fit well with intuition, but on the other hand wands also have the quality of exploring many things, looking at all possibilities, which is very much the nature of the intuition function. So, if the match isn't exact, it's pretty close.

This claim is supported very powerfully by the symbolisms of the sixteen court cards. Most importantly, the four pure function types are unique within the set. This is very striking with the Queen of Cups, with her uniquely *sealed* cup and dagger. It is blindingly *obvious* with the Knave of Coins, with the *two* coins in the picture – as an added bonus, one is on the ground, stressing the earthy quality of the sensation function. The pale horse of the Knight of Wands marks him out as unique, as well as the fact that he alone carries his wand left-handed. Finally, the King of Swords has those delightful bemooned robes and if only we knew what that strange symbol below his throne meant! No other figure bears such a glyph.

The intuition-sensation figures also are marked out as

unique; the Knave of Wands has his unique two-handed grasp on his wand, and the Knight of Coins is the one and only figure carrying a symbol of his own function (a wand) with him in addition to the coin shown on the card – *and*, just to force the point home, he alone isn't holding his coin! We do *not*, though, find any similar pattern of symbolic symmetries uniting the thinking-feeling figures. Possibly, this is because the Tarot has already drawn attention to this polarity for us in the way it has used the motif of left-handedness in the suit of swords (thinking), as we saw earlier.

Now, there are one or two correspondences here which aren't perfectly satisfying. The wands=intuition match isn't perfect. There isn't a perfect symmetry of intuition-sensation *and* thinking-feeling figures (but I think that the reason given for this may explain this fact). Nonetheless, other correspondences are very striking indeed. It seems to me quite astonishing that the match between the Tarot symbols and Jungian function theory is so very close. After all we are dealing with a pack of cards probably designed some *eight hundred years* before Jung evolved his theory, and there is no doubt that Jung was not influenced by the Tarot (there is, in the nineteen collected volumes of Jung's writings, only *one* reference to the Tarot, and that a very brief one). The strength of the correspondences, taking this into account, is quite phenomenal.

The forty numbered cards also show, within each suit, a series of stages of problem-solving, from the first phase (Ace), to collecting information (2), working with others and evolving strategies (3), then a first practical application of plans (4). The 5 card almost always shows some extra difficulty which is thrown at us by others or by circumstance, so that we have to change our strategies and evolve new coping mechanisms. The 6 shows the better adjusted abilities we gain from this, and the 7 shows that we are homing in close to the core of the problem. The 8 is the successful choice of what strategy to use with which problem – minimizing distractions from competing problems – and the 9 is the attainment, the solution. The 10 shows us our basic need to find another problem to deal with once we have solved one; we are curious and endlessly dynamic creatures. The Major Arcana showed us our endless dynamism as growing, developing personalities and the 10, returning to the Ace, shows us this same quality in our problem-solving.

I've reiterated this sequence in a fairly dry language, the sort of language used by cognitive psychologists, those who study reasoning, memory, problem-solving, and similar phenomena. One could, in fact, give an account of the forty numbered cards in terms of cognitive psychology, in terms of mental strategies we use for problem-solving, at least in the case of the suits of swords (thinking) and coins (material-practical world, sensation). One could most definitely establish an affinity with Kelly's view of man; progressively from the Ace to the 10, we are establishing a better mastery of problems (achieving superior predictive powers, Kelly would say) and also extending our competence to new areas (doing the same thing by applying our constructs more widely and being able to predict a larger and larger array of events). However, the point is that the Tarot is using a richer language than Kelly, attribution theorists, or cognitive psychologists. It is clear that the 'problem-solving' of the Minor Arcana applies to much wider issues than thinking and predicting and controlling. This is obvious from the different natures of the functions allied with the four suits. Thus we could not reduce the Tarot to Kellian language but the Kellian view of matters is reflected in the sequence of Ace to 10 within each Minor Arcana suit.

This is not a correspondence of *content* as we found with Jungian theory, specifically Jung's writings about mental functions. However, it is a clear correspondence of *style* and there is some overlap of content.

We would not expect such dramatic relationships between the Minor Arcana and personality theories as we found for the Major Arcana, for the Major Arcana is a storybook about our lives, and the growth of our personalities, whereas the

Minor Arcana does not have this quality. Still the links are clear enough, and some of the details truly impressive. What a remarkable toolbox the Tarot is! Now we shall discover how to use it effectively.

5
Using the Tarot

5
Using the Tarot

How does it work?

The first question to ask is, *Does* it work?' The answer to this is that there is no scientific work of acceptable quality which has investigated the power of the Tarot as a divinational tool. Having said *that*, I can't see any reason why primacy should be given to the value of scientific enquiry as a means of assessing the value of the Tarot. This is merely the pathology of over-valuing thinking to the exclusion of anything, and everything, else. Science is a very effective tool for planning and executing, say, the construction of weapons of mass destruction. It is a wholly inappropriate tool for exploring the validity of the Tarot since this is an instrument which covers the realms of all four Jungian functions. One cannot measure the value of a superordinate instrument by using a subordinate metric measurement to do this. In any event, there are no scientific studies worthy of scrutiny. We are left with experiential evidence. All that can be said is that many millions of people have found the Tarot a valuable tool. The very fact that the cards still exist and are still used after many hundreds of years testifies to that fact. This chapter is concerned with trying to help the reader to use the Tarot in a way which is helpful for him or her.

If we are not prepared to deny the experience of so many people, then we must surely wonder how the Tarot does work, how it is that it is a useful tool for divination and exploration. There are clearly several possibilities. One is that the symbols of the Tarot are intuitively recognized and understood in a way which reveals to the Tarot reader truths about the person for whom the reading is being made. The

Tarot *reveals* things which the person knows to be true but which may have been evaded, repressed, or simply not recognized. It is also possible that ESP influences the Tarot (or the twin ability of mind-over-matter, PK or psychokinesis). Some paranormal factor influences the spread of the cards or the interpretations which are made in a reading, so that the Tarot serves as a vehicle for the use of psi (psychic) abilities. A third possibility is that the Tarot is a powerful archetypal vehicle for what Jung termed *synchronicity*; that this acausal connecting principle affects the Tarot so that meaningful coincidences in the life of the reader are recurrent within the Tarot reading. These possibilities are not exclusive of each other; more than one factor may be at work. Of course, one may simply adopt the sceptical stance and claim that people simply see what they wish to see in the Tarot and shape their interpretations accordingly. This, I think, ignores the very real discipline of the Tarot, which is implicit in its underlying structure, and it also ignores the fact that the Tarot (and good Tarot readers) may most certainly not necessarily tell us what we wish to hear. The Tarot can throw up unpalatable facts and information about ourselves and others; it can threaten us with 'the return of the repressed', to use a Freudian term, and it may worry us and cause anxiety. In doing so, it is (I consider) being truthful; after all, if we all had perfectly contented lives we probably wouldn't need the help of the Tarot, and how amazingly tedious everything would be in any event.

It is also important that the Tarot is useful in understanding past, present, and future states of affairs, the origins of present problems and the way in which they are most likely to develop in the future. It's possible that there are different roots for its uses in these different ways, although we cannot be sure about this.

A simple summary is: we do not know how, and why, the Tarot works or what the origins of its powers as a valuable tool are. This is an unsatisfying conclusion *only* if you are hung up on the need to have everything explained for you. If you are happy to accept that the workings of at least some things in the universe are irreducibly mysterious or at least cannot be explained at the present time, then you should have no problems. But you may be apprehensive about using the Tarot; let's see if some common apprehensions have any foundation.

Anxieties about the Tarot

A fairly common apprehension concerns the possible 'evil' nature of the Tarot and whether its use doesn't conflict with religious attitudes and beliefs. 'The Devil's Picture Book' is a nasty and wholly inappropriate little phrase which brings these two concerns together in a summary slogan. I hope that, by now, we have seen that the Tarot is in *no way* some kind of Satanic or diabolic instrument, that it is a book of knowledge and an instrument of understanding. Frankly, only those people who think that Eve should never have nibbled at the paradisal apple will have any residual concerns. Surely the whole point is that *informed moral choice is only possible when we are free to choose*, and if the Tarot shows us the darker side of ourselves in cards such as the Devil from the Major Arcana it simply shows us our own freedom to progress to the light of the Sun and the glory of the World. It is ludicrous to berate the Tarot as some dangerous instrument of black magic. The few fanatics left who take this attitude are, literally, afraid of their own Shadow. I hope we have also seen that other cards which are frightening at first sight – notably Death and the Tower – have meanings which are obvious within the context of the Major Arcana and are nowhere near so frightening as they appear so far as their meaning goes. Personally, I always look forward to meeting Death in a reading; he generally shows me something I really should be getting rid of, and he points towards some new and exciting possibilities for me.

So far as more rational religious belief is concerned, I have to confess myself hampered by a lack of any faith of my own and an almost complete ignorance of any contemporary faith other than the Judaeo-Christian tradition, and Buddhism. However, I don't see any reason why a wise religious person should reject the Tarot. After all, the progression of the Major Arcana is surely a rather beautiful story about realizing the angelic inner nature of man; the Tarot shows that man is made in God's image but one could hardly charge it with the claim that it shows man *as* God. The World-dancer has become someone who is at one with and part of something much, much greater than him/herself. Even Calvinists (if they still exist) could regard the process of evolution in the Major Arcana as the actualization of God's grace visited upon the soul rather than the evolution of the individual by his/her own efforts and growth. At a guess, I imagine that fans of Original Sin could treat the perfecting of the soul shown in the Major Arcana in a similar way. There seems to me no rational (or even irrational in Jungian terms!) reason for a religious person to reject the Tarot's usefulness.

A more common anxiety is over the possible denial of free will by the predictive power of the Tarot and, a related concern, about 'bad' readings – what if something dreadful seems to be indicated by the cards when someone is doing a reading for a friend or someone one really cares about, for example?

So far as the free will problem goes, the concern is whether our futures are really fixed and unchangeable if the Tarot is useful in predicting the future. If they are, doesn't this deny our free will? The answer to this is fairly straightforward, I think. The Tarot does *not* foretell the future in some precise, perfectly defined way. What it can do is to indicate the *most probable* state of affairs in the future if things continue as they are at present. In a few cases a reading may indicate a very strong probability which looks more or less unavoidable. If this is so, the Tarot will still not be predicting precise *events* which *must* happen but rather a general state of affairs which will occur. This does not deny free will, for the specific details may be something we can affect and we have the freedom to determine our attitude to the future events which take place in our lives. If the Tarot were a perfect instrument of exact prediction, then the problem of our own free will might be an important one, but the Tarot is neither perfect nor exact. It deals with trends, probabilities, the most likely states of affairs. One would not expect more; no personality theorist, for example, would assert that he did more than describe probabilities and likelihoods in human behaviour. Human beings are simply too complex for anything more precise to be possible! This is a problem – specificity versus generalization – which we'll come back to when we consider how to interpret the cards in a Tarot reading. However, it should be realized that not being perfect or always exact doesn't mean that the Tarot is useless. Far from it!

This fact – that the Tarot isn't a perfect or exact instrument – is also relevant to the problem of 'bad readings', ones which seem to point to a disastrous state of affairs. This is a standard prop of B-movie writers who have old gypsy women delivering dire warnings of impending doom as they flip over the Death card for some unfortunate. Also, some of the old Tarot writers classified cards into weak/strong, good/bad; they were stuck with a pair of highly impermeable constructs, to use an appropriate Kellian term. We have seen from our study of traditionally 'negative' or 'bad' cards such as the Devil, the Tower, and Death that these too have their positive sides; the meaning of a Tarot card in a reading may almost always be negative or positive depending on its context. Again, this is a point to be developed when we come to the issue of interpreting the cards in a reading. Still, it is possible to have a Tarot reading which looks pretty negative and promises a fairly bleak and difficult state of affairs, although I *don't* think that one can predict, with any certainty, inescapable and disastrous events like major accidents or deaths. Many potential users of the cards will be anxious about this; somehow, many of us feel as if, in describing some unfortunate state of affairs, we have somehow become responsible for what may happen. This is certainly a worry which many people who have had experiences of precognition (ESP of some future event) feel; it is as if by forseeing some disaster, they might even have had a part in it. It's no good saying that of course there is no logical link involved. This is simply a feeling people get which is troubling to them and not to be easily swayed by reason.

I think one simply has to accept that the Tarot is only reflecting reality; life is not a bed of roses and sometimes even when it seems to be so the Tarot may decide that it's time the thorns got into the picture as well as the pretty flowers. Perhaps the key to matters is that the Tarot has a potential warning function which is valuable. Rather than saying, 'The future is going to be disastrous,' it says, 'If things go on as they are then the future is not going to develop well.' It *warns* us about errors in the present which affect our futures. The Tarot can also tell us how we might work to avoid this negative future or, at the very least, to mitigate it. It can show us both the nature of our current errors and the changes we need to make to improve things. The Tarot does *not* point to some fixed and immutable future state. The Tarot reflects a *dynamic, evolving* future if we use it for prediction. Of course it does! After all, *we* are dynamic and evolving personalities with many options and resources. The Tarot is simply reflecting this fact.

So, to sum up, the Tarot may indeed show some unpleasing state of affairs, but it also shows us how to avoid or lessen unpleasant developments in our lives. The 'bad' reading can be a vital warning to us of the need for change. Such a reading can be very important, and very valuable to us!

There are other anxieties people may have about the Tarot, but these seem to me to be the main ones, and I hope the reader is reassured about them! If there are other lingering worries, then the section on interpretation will hopefully answer them.

There are now the practical questions about using the

cards: which deck to use? are there special rituals which are needed for keeping and using the cards? when should readings be made? and so on.

Practicalities of the Tarot

The first question is, simply, which Tarot pack to use? In this book, I've based interpretations on the Marseilles deck produced by B. P. Grimaud. This is fairly easily available from shops which sell Tarot cards. Games shops will usually stock a range of Tarot packs, and of course 'occult' stores will generally keep them also. If you haven't got either kind of shop near you, then many mail-order services will supply them and you can generally get an illustrated catalogue from them which will enable you to make your choice; the bibliography at the end of the book lists some such sources. But it is best, I think, to actually get to a shop which does keep Tarot cards since you can then look at a variety of packs and choose from full-size specimens rather than the smaller, partial, illustrations most catalogues actually show.

For a first choice, whatever you do choose (if you don't want the Marseilles pack), I strongly suggest you select a fairly 'traditional' design. Packs such as the New Age or Aquarian decks are confusing for the newcomer with their radical reworking of many traditional designs and you won't find it easy to use them. They also reflect to a large extent the idiosyncratic beliefs of their designers, which is another reason for not considering them until one knows the fundamental, traditional Tarot well enough to feel secure in understanding the changes such a new design makes. The Waite-Rider deck is a popular (and beautiful) pack, and the Oswald Wirth deck is another traditional design (but a rather ugly one, I think). The Waite-Rider, Golden Dawn, and Thoth packs are *esoteric* decks; that is, their symbols are constructed so as to stress occult wisdom and the relationships between the Tarot and other systems such as astrology and the Qhabbala. I don't think these are too suitable for the beginner.

Still, it's probably a fair rule that if you feel drawn to one particular deck and like it, it will probably work for you. It's also true that different decks may be useful for asking different kinds of questions, although using Tarot decks in such a flexible way is arguably easier when one is moderately experienced with the Tarot. To start with, pick one deck. Go for the Marseilles, or for one you really like, and don't ignore practicalities! For example, the Thoth deck has cards so large that they are the very devil (no pun intended) to shuffle!

Many Tarot readers have rituals regarding the keeping and use of their cards which they feel quite strongly about. Examples of these would include keeping the cards in a particular box in a particular place, not allowing others to handle them, wrapping them in a silk square, and so on. Every user of the cards has their own individual preference. For example, in my own case I use two decks – the Marseilles and the Thoth decks. The Marseilles I simply keep in its original and stout box. I use it for day-to-day work and addressing practicalities, as it is so eminently suitable for such work. I have no particular rituals about this. The Thoth deck I keep in a sandalwood box and after using it I generally say a mental 'thank you' to the pack for having been useful. I don't think that there is any particular recipe to be handed on here; the user can devise his own rituals or just dispense with them. I think it *is* a good idea to do something with the pack which marks it out as special and different, such as going to the trouble of buying a nice wooden box for it which also protects the cards. It may be a superstition but it is a practically helpful one. Generally, it is just a question of doing whatever you feel comfortable with and which makes you feel happier about using the cards. However, if you don't want other people handling the cards then you should probably make an exception to this when a reading is made, for good psychological reasons, as we'll shortly see.

One form of ritual which definitely *should* be cultivated is allowing yourself time to study the cards and their meanings, and look at the symbols and try to learn more about them.

You need to develop an affinity with the Tarot, and to understand it from within. In part, that knowledge and affinity will come from using the deck, but also from reading more about it (hopefully the bibliography will be useful to you). Although reading about the Tarot and looking for, and studying Tarot symbols in other places, is helpful, don't treat this as some kind of academic exercise! Use playful imagining, daydreaming, fantasizing about the cards, free-association, trying to relate your own dreams to the imagery of the Tarot. All these techniques are helpful in understanding the Tarot better, and you should be having fun doing this.

Preparing to use the Tarot

A first question is, when to use the cards and under what conditions? Again, many readers have rituals for this, such as working by candlelight or burning a little incense when the cards are being used. Personally, I don't think this is necessary, but it may be appropriate if a reading is being made which might be particularly important. If some difficult problem is being addressed or one feels that the reading might be very valuable, then a little ritual to mark out that reading as something special is a good idea. Again, do whatever you feel comfortable with. You will certainly evolve your own style and preferences as you become more familiar with the cards you are using. What is very important, I think, is the psychological atmosphere in which a reading is made. Mood is an important element of this. There are times when, I think, it's a waste of time doing a reading. If you are feeling very bored, in an irritable or very frustrated mood, this is not the best time to be using the Tarot. If there is a formula for this, it is *if you don't feel like using the cards, don't*. If you do you may very well end up with an inconsistent or even silly reading. This certainly happens! So you might as well know how to minimize the chance of its happening. Try doing a reading for yourself once or twice when you really don't feel like doing one and see whether the cards don't come up with something which is incoherent or plain daft. *Explore* the cards through your own experience; this is the best guide as to how to use them to best effect. You never know; *you* might be the unusual reader who gets very good results in a negative mood. The Tarot may turn out to work for you by showing you how to get out of it, or underlying problems which have led to it. Just because *most* readers don't get good results with the Tarot in such a mood state does not mean that everyone will be the same.

If you are doing a reading for someone else (or, possibly, even for a group), then this mood factor will be less predict-able and controllable; if you've arranged to do a reading in some place at some particular time then you don't have the option of waiting until the mood is right. Under these circum-stances, when one can't wait for the right mood to come along, it's important to try to *create* the conditions which make a good atmosphere most likely. There are several ways of doing this.

First, rituals are useful here in many cases. The odds are that the person who has asked for a reading will be looking forward to it, or they wouldn't have bothered to ask. They may be a little apprehensive and unsure but, after all, they are with you to have the reading done! Consider what kind of setting will help create *expectancy* on the part of that person; not gullible believing-anything, but simply a state when they are comfortable with what is going on. Also, creating a relaxed state is important – doing a Tarot reading isn't likely to work so well if you're buzzing simply because you need time and a quiet, reflective state to interpret the reading. So, try to set the scene in a way which both you and the other person will feel comfortable with. For example, you might sit facing them across a table, or sitting together on the floor. The person might feel that a stick of burning incense is a part of scene-setting which they like, or they might regard it as the affectation of an old hippie. It's good to think about what will feel right to them. A simple practical point is that you need a smooth, firm surface to lay out the cards! A table is an obvious choice but if you prefer to sit on the floor to use the cards something else will be needed.

Particularly if you're doing a first reading, it's important to discuss what the other person thinks about the Tarot. You can use that discussion to correct any misconceptions they have about it, and to defuse any worries they may feel. This is particularly important, I think; if you think in one way about the Tarot and they have an entirely different set of beliefs and preconceptions then the reading simply is not going to be helpful. They may think, for example, that the Tarot is something which will show them the immutable workings of fate in the future with absolute certainty. If this is so, you'll need to correct that set of misconceptions, explaining why this is not so. You're not going to get anywhere if you and the other person have completely different ideas about what it is that you're actually doing!

It is also important to try to get *some* idea of the problem or concern the person has, if there is one. There are two reasons for this. The first is that the broad nature of the problem may determine the nature of the layout of cards you're going to use (see below on this). The second is that knowing a little about the concern will enable you to be more helpful than if you're just shooting in the dark. *Don't* go into all the details of anything; it can actually make it more difficult to do a reading if your head if full of knowledge and 'rational' awareness of the details of a problem. If you are like this you may end up forcing the pattern of the reading into your preconceptions of what the reading *should* be showing. After all, the Tarot may well show some unexpected opportunity or state of affairs which is not obviously linked to the concern at hand, something which the person has overlooked or not seen, or which is an unexpected event with external origins the person has not (or cannot have) anticipated. You're not going to pick this up if you're trying to squeeze everything to fit the precise problem the person mentions. Also, the person may not *want* to discuss the problem in full. It's better to learn that the problem 'involves relationships' rather than getting all the intimate details. It may seem strange to say that privacy should be respected when one is hoping to cast light on matters, but since the Tarot isn't a tool which deals with absolutely precise, nitty-gritty detail this paradox is more apparent than real.

Some people may, however, just want a very general reading or be testing you or just be generally curious, so that no problem area is indicated for the reading. If this is so, fair enough – and, after all, in some cases the Tarot may show a problem which someone is not actually aware of in any event!

Laying out the cards

There is an infinite number of ways of laying out cards for a reading! I think it is valuable and useful to devise one's own layouts, but we can start by considering some common layouts which are easily understood and used by a beginner.

The first step is taking the pack and shuffling it. Many writers seem to think this is a simple matter. If you happen to be as lacking in manual dexterity as I am, it isn't. If you have problems here, two hints: first, avoid using packs with very large cards (like the Thoth deck). Also, after a reading 'randomize' the cards by spreading out the entire pack on a large table and move them around so that they are re-ordered. This ensures that you won't just get the same cards sticking together from one reading to the next. Practice shuffling if you have trouble with it. You may also wish to have the person for whom the reading is being done (if it isn't for yourself) shuffle the cards. Shuffling is always done with the cards face down. Then, cut the pack (at any point the shuffler feels is right) without looking at the faces of the cards, place the bottom part of the pack on top, and lay out the cards.

The nature of the layout will be affected by the questions you want to ask of the Tarot, and you should discuss this with the other person before you do the reading. The Tarot does have an irreducible quality of mystery, but most people will appreciate some understanding of why cards are being laid out in some particular way. It is nice when the structure of the layout matches the logic of addressing some particular problem.

The cards should be taken sequentially from the top of the pack; you can either lay them all out face-down and then turn them up one at a time in the correct order, or you can lay each one down face-up as you take it from the top of the pack. Either method is fine; I prefer to lay down each card face-up as I take it from the pack, since this gives a little extra time to consider what is evolving in the spread of cards as it develops.

Two traditional methods of layout are now given, which are suitable for use by beginners and can be used by any Tarot reader with benefit. At this stage, I'm not dealing with interpreting the cards and their meanings, only with detailing the layouts.

The 'horoscope' layout

Figure 1 shows this; twelve cards are laid out in a circular pattern as shown. This layout can be used in two ways. A first use is as a calendar of future events; the twelve cards correspond to important trends in each of the next twelve months, the first card showing the most important trends in the present month, the second showing the most important trends in the next month, and so on.

The second way in which this layout can be used is to give a mirror of present states of affairs (which obviously have implications for the future) in twelve different (but related) spheres of life. These are the twelve spheres associated with the twelve 'houses' of the astrological horoscope. This use of the layout is particularly useful for someone who knows about astrology, since they will feel at home with it. The twelve spheres of life which are meant here are:

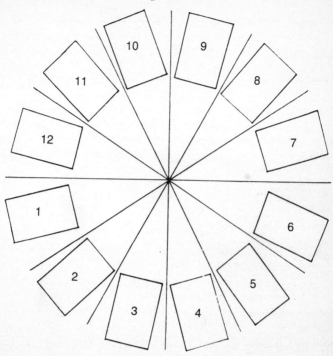

Figure 1   The Horoscope Layout

Card 1: The persona: how one projects oneself to others.
Card 2: Finance, money.
Card 3: Communicating, sources of mental stimulation.
Card 4: Sources of emotional security, house and home.
Card 5: Romance, sex, children (if appropriate).
Card 6: Daily routines (especially at work), personal health.
Card 7: Major partnerships and one-to-one relationships.
Card 8: Deeper emotions, repressed problems.
Card 9: Travel, reading, education, opportunities for growth as a person.
Card 10: Career, reputation.

Card 11: Friendships, groups one is affiliated with.
Card 12: Daydreams and fantasies, possible 'Achilles heel' problems, especially ones associated with self-undoing.

Now, obviously, there are associations between these twelve areas, although none is redundant to the others. For example, Card 6 (day-to-day work routine) will be relevant to Card 10 (career), and Cards 4, 5, 7, 8 and 11 obviously all deal with slightly different aspects of relationships. However, each card has something unique about it too; they don't simply indicate exactly the same thing in comparison with others.

The Celtic Cross

This traditional ten-card spread (actually there are several versions of this but the one here is perhaps the most easily used) is shown in Figure 2. The meanings for the cards here are:

Card 1: The person for whom the reading is being done; the most salient aspect of the person in understanding the reading.
Card 2: The current situation; what is most important about this. Often described as the card which *covers* the person.
Card 3: That which *crowns* the person; their conscious mind, the attitudes and concerns which are paramount there.
Card 4: That which is *beneath* the person; their unconscious, what is hidden from their own awareness.
Card 5: That which is *behind* the person; an important state of affairs in the immediate past, which may have exerted an important effect on the current state of affairs.
Card 6: That which is *before* the person; the most probable direction for general future development, at least in the short term.
Card 7: Strengths and weaknesses. The most important qual-

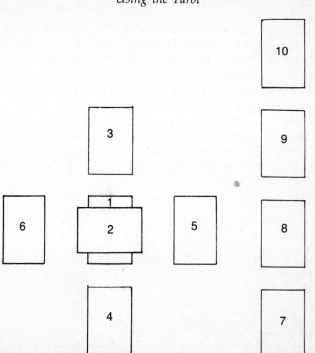

Figure 2   The Celtic Cross

ities within the person which will influence future development and what is happening now.

Card 8: Significant others: the nature and attitudes and possible actions of other people (or one person) who have significant influence on the development of the current concern.

Card 9: Goals and anxieties: what the person wishes, or fears, may happen in the future.

Card 10: Outcome: the most probable resolution of current concerns; this is a longer-term effect than is indicated in Card 5.

This is a versatile layout which can be used to deal with almost any problem regarding the future, and the best course of action which one should consider.

Designing one's own Tarot layout

This is really a very simple matter, once you have clarified the nature of the question you want to ask. This kind of approach is very well suited to asking some specific questions about some specific problem. Let me give some examples of what I mean.

The past-present-future layout

Here you simply lay out three cards, one after another, from left to right; these represent the most salient element of a problem in the past (causes and influences on the present), right now (current state of affairs) and in the future (most likely course for future development). This layout simply tells you about the development of the problem if things go on much as they are doing at the present time. Of course the person may then want to know what to do about the problem if the outcome does not look too good! But this simple three-card layout is a useful one for taking a concrete problem (such as 'How is my career going to shape up?' or 'How is my investment of time (money) in such-and-such a venture likely to be rewarded?'). The past/present cards are important because, while the person may most want to know about future developments, what has happened in the past certainly influences the present state of play and both will affect the future! For example, a bad outcome may appear to be reflected in an original error of judgement of some kind – for example, basing one's judgement on intuition which was wrong and ignoring the advice of others – and this knowledge may be important for avoiding repeating the mistake.

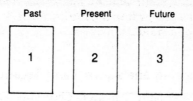

Figure 3 The Past-Present-Future Layout

The Self/other layout

This six-card layout is shown in Figure 4. It's a useful one when a reading pertaining to some problem in a relationship is needed. This doesn't have to be a deeply emotional and intimate one – it can be for a working relationship one has, one's relations with one's boss or anyone.

Card 1 shows the basic nature of the relationship at this time, whether harmony or conflict is involved, possibly the nature of the involvement (e.g., it may be a financial and business one, or an element of this kind of transaction may be important to the relationship at this time). Cards 2 and 3 relate to oneself (the person for whom the reading is being given); Card 2 shows a strength, and Card 3 a weakness *within the context of this particular self/other relationship.* These cards help clarify for the person the nature of positive and negative elements within one's own psychology and behaviour. Cards 4 and 5 show the corresponding strengths and weaknesses for the other within this relationship; these will be qualities, attitudes or behaviours which are seen as sources of strength and bonding in the relationship (4) and difficult aspects of the other (5) by the person for whom the reading is being done. Card 6 shows the nature of the best positive development which can be hoped for within the relationship in the present and foreseeable future. It can indicate the easiest way in which one can achieve a more harmonious and rewarding quality of relationship with the other person.

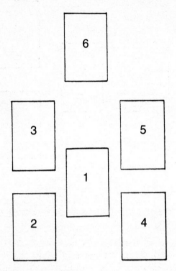

Figure 4   The Self/Other Layout

The problem-solving layout

This simple (abbreviated) six-card layout (shown in Figure 5) is a nice building-block which one can develop into an expanded layout. This is a good layout for taking any practical problem and expanding understanding of it and deciding what to do about it. The meanings of the six cards in the layout are:

Card 1: The cause. What underlay the development of this problem?
Card 2: Current status of the problem: the most pressing aspect of it or the most important one.
Card 3: What to do? The best course of action to be followed in trying to achieve a satisfactory outcome.
Cards 4, 5: Possible blocks. Card 4 indicates some weakness within one's own feelings or behaviour which may present

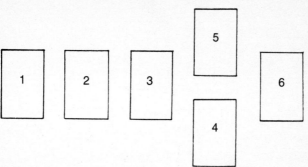

Figure 5   The Problem-solving Layout

difficulties for solving the problem. Card 5 shows the nature of some external difficulty (another person, circumstance, etc).

Card 6: Probable outcome. This gives an idea of the most likely outcome for the problem, if the person makes efforts to deal with it as suggested earlier in the layout.

Building up the layout

The past-present-future, self-other, and problem-solving layouts are good for straightforward questions and answers. But often this is not what you wish to use the Tarot for, and yet the more general and traditional horoscope and Celtic Cross spreads don't quite seem right either. In this case, develop your own layout. After a little familiarity with using the five shown above, this won't be too difficult.

It's important to consider the problem one is going to deal with and try to develop it into a set of questions by brainstorming about the problem and then getting down to a list. For example, someone concerned about their job might reduce their concerns down to a list of queries such as the following:

What's right in my job?

What's wrong in my job?
What are my prospects in my job?
What kind of alternative would suit me best?
Is this a good time to be looking for an alternative?
What should I do to find the kind of job I'd be good at and happy with?
What difficulties would looking for a new job entail?
Would I be likely to be successful in getting a new job?
What would be the most likely outcome of moving to a new job?

Clearly, it is possible to take almost any problem and reduce it to a set of questions like these, and then consider the layout one might use. One might end up with a layout like that shown in Figure 6. Here, some of the questions have been refined in the layout. For example, the question about job prospects might need answering both right now and for the next few months or so as well. One needs to know if these prospects might change. This would obviously be important! Also, the question about looking for another job is so important that it might be helpful to split this into two related questions: about the person asking the question (resources, how well he/she might come across in interviews, and so on) and also external opportunities (are any openings available, how might others react to the job applicant, and so on). The question of 'difficulties' in looking for a new job also needs more careful examination. Obviously, such activity always involves expenditure of time and money to some extent, but one wants to know more than that. These difficulties should again be split into two; internal and external, oneself and the reactions of significant others who have influence over the job-selection process. The other questions are all self-explanatory.

Just experiment with this kind of layout building yourself. Take a fairly clearly demarcated problem of some kind and try to set out a list of questions which reflect what you really want to know about this problem. From that list, you can

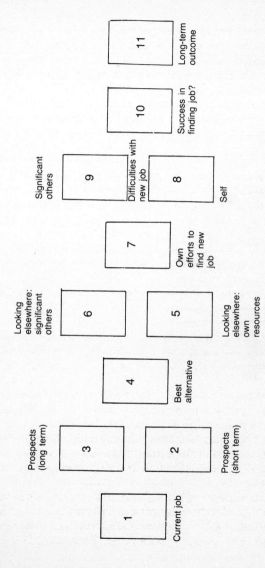

Figure 6 Your Own Layout

specify the most important questions and whether they have more than one aspect you need to know about – like self/ other, or past/present/future, perhaps. Then, take the questions in an appropriate order and build a developing layout to match the way the questions develop (in time from past to future, and from self to others, and in other ways).

As I suggested, experimenting with this exercise for yourself, in doing your own readings, will make it easier for you to build your own Tarot layouts. Take simple problems to begin with, ones which can be reduced to just a few questions – only three or four. More complicated ones you can deal with later and complex questions can be reduced to a number of simpler ones if you're lucky in any event. Do this with your own readings a few times before trying layout building with other people's questions. Try also to keep a note of which layout patterns really work well for you; go through these to see what they had in common and keep a note of ones which didn't, to examine these for contrasts with the successful layouts. Doing this may give you some idea of how you've been able to ask questions of the Tarot successfully; there may be some personal style of inquiry you've developed, almost certainly without realizing it, which works well for you.

We now need to deal with interpretation of the cards in a reading, and the problems which can arise in readings – seemingly meaningless readings, inappropriate ones, and readings which simply look plain wrong! These difficulties are ones which a surprising number of books on the Tarot tend to avoid. From reading some of them, you'd never believe that you ever got a reading which was nonsense, and you certainly do, sometimes. But before you know whether you have got such a problem on your hands, you obviously need to be able to interpret the spread of cards in a layout in the first place.

Interpreting the Tarot layout

For all the seventy-eight Tarot cards, both positive (+) and negative (−) meanings have been given. When you first start working with the Tarot, there is always going to be an element of interpreting by numbers, looking up the suggested interpretations for each card and using these like the elements in a recipe, trying to build a coherent whole out of the disparate parts. Later on, much as happens with a recipe, you become familiar with things and you don't need to look up in the book any more. But this takes a lot of experience and practice. Don't feel intimidated by the sheer number of cards whose meaning you have to remember; with experience you'll understand these rather than simply needing to look up the words for the meanings. It may not seem so at first but it will happen!

In trying to synthesize a coherent reading from the different cards in the layout, with the different themes and images they show, there are three dichotomies of some importance.

Major and Minor Arcana

When a Major Arcana card appears in a reading, it *always* indicates something of particular importance for the person for whom the reading is being given. Sometimes, this may not be obvious; the card may appear as an indicator for a minor part of some problem, if you defined the position in the layout which it occupies in this way. If this happens, then the card points to an unexpected importance, if you like; something (or someone) which is more important, has greater influence, than one would have expected or is immediately apparent. Major Arcana cards should always be given more weight in a reading than Minor Arcana cards, and a layout which features many Major Arcana cards (about one half, or one third if the reading contains a dozen cards or more) is concerned with something of major importance.

If this importance isn't apparent, it may be that the future events which occur as a result of what is shown in the present layout may be very important – this will be particularly likely if future-trend or goal-outcome cards are Major Arcana cards.

Positive and negative indicators

In the text, positive and negative indicators for cards were given. There are two ways of dealing with this polarity, but in either case we have to deal with another polarity – whether cards have appeared *upright* or *reversed* (that is, upside-down) when dealt. Traditionally, many writers have ascribed the negative meaning to the reversed card and the positive one to the upright card.

This is a perfectly feasible approach to take if you are using a layout which, like the horoscope or Celtic Cross layouts, is a general one which addresses non-directive and non-evaluative questions. However, I've also suggested the problem-solving approach, of defining within a layout which cards will indicate difficulties and which will indicate positive qualities and opportunities (like, 'What's wrong with my job?' – negative, or 'What's the best I could hope for in a new job?' – more positive). If you use this kind of layout, then you have defined what aspect the card will show by its position and context within the layout. Under these circumstances, you can dispense with reversed/upright differences, simply righting any upside-down cards. Whether the card has a positive or negative meaning will depend not on whether it is upright or reversed but rather on its position within the layout.

There is another option for this which you should perhaps defer until you've gained some experience with the Tarot; that is, you can still deal with upright and reversed cards within a problem-solving spread. In this case, upright cards in a positive position will have a strong (+) meaning; reversed cards in a negative position will have a strong (−) meaning; and ones which are mixed (reversed card in a positive position or upright card in a negative position) will have a 'neutral' meaning, indicating that both the (+) and (−) qualities are indicated as possibilities. Doing this tends to increase the uncertainty of the layout, for there will be fewer clear positive and negative trends. It is always more difficult to interpret a layout with more uncertainty in it, which is why I suggest deferring this for a while!

Specifics and generalities

The Tarot deals with trends and probabilities. There's a tricky dividing line here, between being too specific and being so vague that what one says is valueless. It is usually better to stick to trends, to indicate that such-and-such is *probably* the case, except with cards which are powerful indicators and have very clear meanings. Some cards, by their nature, can *only* be interpreted in a general way. The four Aces would be good examples, for they simply indicate that *some* new opportunity is opening up and that something new is beginning or about to begin, in the affairs of the suit involved. The rest of the cards may give more details of course.

If there is a general rule, I think it is this: it is possible to be more specific with more clearly demarcated problems. In a very general reading, like the horoscope reading as a twelve-month forecast, one can't be incredibly specific about dates and precise events. But wouldn't information like 'next month is not a good one financially. You've got fingers in too many pies and you aren't likely to make the right decisions about financial options. Don't take risks!' be useful? (This would be the interpretation of the 7 of Coins reversed/ negative, for example.) You can't tell the person specifics − such as which particular investments to avoid − in a layout which by its very nature deals with general trends as the horoscope layout does.

With a more specific, problem-focused, layout then you can hope for more specific answers, although obviously you aren't addressing such a wide range of possible issues. For example, using an element of Self/other in a layout you might be able to tell the person that an important part of the financial problem (as indicated by the 7 of Coins if it appeared here) might be bad advice from others, or being preoccupied with some other concern and not giving enough time to financial concerns, depending on the cards involved.

As an analogy, the Tarot works *like* a microscope. A general reading is low magnification; you can see a lot but you don't get fine-detail resolution. Zero in at high magnification and you get much better detail of a much smaller area, but you can only look at a certain part of what you would have looked at with low magnification. Obviously the analogy is not that appropriate in other respects, but in understanding specificity versus generality in Tarot readings it's not a bad one.

A sample interpretation

For space reasons I can only give one example here. There are three other ways of learning more about making interpretations. First, study the cards! Second, read other books on the Tarot and look at examples given there. Third, experiment, especially with your own readings. You're *bound* to be insecure about this when you first start – this is only natural. You may not find the interpretations given for this example (or those in other books) quite right in your view. If so, that's fine! Clarify for yourself what you don't understand and what you think doesn't seem to fit in other people's examples. Go back to the descriptions of the cards involved to see if differences are resolved. If not, you're already beginning to learn your own style of interpretation. Interpretation is part science and part art, and must *always* involve a subjective component. It is no more a question of one style being right and one wrong than it is a question of which chef has the right recipe when two of them cook the same dish in somewhat different ways, so long as they both produce something delicious at the end!

We'll consider here a layout for a person who was contemplating taking up a new job and no longer working as a freelancer. This would be quite a dramatic change, moving back into the 9-to-5 rather than being self-employed. This is obviously no trivial problem, and that fact is reflected in the six-card spread, for no fewer than four of the six cards found in the layout are Major Arcana cards. Even if he had not told me that the problem was of major importance this would have shown it to be so. Let's consider the layout used and the interpretation; it's important to realize that this man had been offered a definite job with a company, he wasn't just thinking about such a career move in the abstract.

Card 1: The situation now (while still being free to choose). The card here is Justice. Refer back to the first line of the positive (upright) meaning for this card: 'Formal judgements, contracts, agreements, arbitration, negotiations.' This suggests a time when contracts and agreements are on the horizon and integrity and fair dealing (Justice also) are important. We also saw that Justice embodies a call to develop further, and thus the situation at present offers such opportunities. This matched well since the man was waiting for an employment contract from the company and had also just signed another contract with them for freelance work he was doing in the interim. The auspicious nature of the upright card shows that fair play and a chance for development will be offered also.

Card 2: What if I took the job (short term)? The card here is a reversed High Priestess, a difficult card with a negative meaning. Most generally, this card implies some emotional instability and a failure of rational action: impulsivity which is disruptive. This card gives a warning that moodiness or over-exuberance is likely to cause problems in the early stages of taking up this job. It stresses the need to be careful, cautious, and to curtail one's feeling-based expressions. Why this should be so will be clearer when we look at Card 5 in particular.

Card 3: What will I lose if I take this job? The card here is the Lover, which is not reversed but which has a negative quality because we have defined this position as one of loss (however, that it is upright may suggest that the loss is not so keenly felt as it might have been). At the most general level the Lover is a card of choice. Inability to choose is the nature of the loss. While the negative reading of the card suggests factors within one's own personality which can lead to this, in the context of this problem the nature of this loss of choice is obvious; as a company man, the man's freelance freedom will be much curtailed. This is a very good example of why knowing something about the problem is important for a Tarot reader. Given the situation, only one particular part of this card's total meaning is appropriate for this reading.

Card 4: What will I gain if I take this job? The card here is the 5 of Coins. This card indicates (even in positive/upright aspect) that the person is unsure about material security and that an upsetting and unsettling change is in the air. However, as we saw, 'The card suggests that there is the promise of better things to come, but this may not be seen for a while, since one is too fretful and anxious to look for positive trends.' So: short-term material insecurity and upset with the promise of better things to come. Again, what was unsettling for the man was the worry of having to move house and home (coins aren't just money!) and anxiety about loss of income from freelancing. The better prospects were at the company – the initial salary was not good but the fringe benefits and, especially, promotion/salary prospects were notably better. The card also suggests that the company of others with similar concerns would be helpful. The man took this to refer to his prospective workmates who had mostly only been with the company for a short time and who would have similar concerns to his own; he had met and liked them and thought that working with them would be one of the best parts of the job.

Card 5: Other people I'd work with. Specifically, the man wanted to know what would be the most important short-term element of his relationships with others and the values they would look for and espouse. The card here is the King of Swords, upright. This now begins to make sense of Card 2. The King of Swords is the prime representative of reason, mental speed, mental prowess and flexibility. These would be the qualities which the significant others would most value. This was an important revelation for the man, for his job brief included both creative and more linear-thinking work. This card suggested that the latter element would be more important to those who were significant others in the new job, and that this should be where he should make most effort. The card also showed why the reversed High Priestess was a problem: such hyper-rational others would react negatively to any impulsive/emotional displays; 'Even in positive aspect there may be an ignoring of values which are not "rationally" based so that the desires and needs of others may be misinterpreted or pushed aside.' This card is less alarming than it might be, for it concerns the short-term and the King of Swords looks beneficent even if he does have a narrow mind! Also, this card is clearly linked with Justice – the rational mind of the King of Swords is associated with the contractual aspect of Justice, the getting-it-on-paper, black-and-white detailing element. That both cards are upright also shows that matters are basically well disposed towards the man, and that unfair censure is certainly not part of the picture.

A further element in the symbolism of the King of Swords is important; this is a monarchical figure, a man in authority. Now, the 5 of Coins showed us that at least so far as material matters were concerned, workmates could be helpful to discuss problems with. The pure-thinking role of the King of Swords, and his nobility, suggest that this desire for highly rational values and behaviour will be more typical of authority figures in the new job; management. This division is also of obvious importance for the man.

Card 6: Long-term outcome. Exasperatingly, the Fool has to pop up here – he does this to me far too often. It's as if he's saying to me, 'Until you can deal with *me* you can't really break through to a complete understanding.' In this reading, the Fool is immensely paradoxical at first sight (well, it is his nature, after all). The Fool is a card of endless possibilities and yet a concern the man has is that taking the job and curtailing his freelance work will do the exact reverse – reduce the possibilities open to him (and the Lover seemed to stress this also). The Fool may show that in the long term (this is how we defined this card) the opposite happens – through this job more possibilities will open up. I suggested this to the man, who said that he really had not seen this (the Fool always has this quality) but that on reflection it was more than possible. Perhaps the short-term concerns of the 5 of Coins blocked his foreseeing the opportunities the Fool suggests, although as we will now see there's more to it than this. He would certainly be coming into contact with many others who worked for other companies, including foreign ones, with whom his company had various licensing arrangements and the like. Because of the nature of his work he would certainly have much to discuss with them, including creative work, not just formal dealings. Obviously all kinds of creativie possibilities might open up, on reflection. What is also crucial about the Fool is that while one's own imagination is valuable, entirely unexpected developments from outside may suddenly present great opportunities. Clearly the long term was very promising!

However, I have to confess to a lack of skill and a problem of my own here. Looking back (and we went back to the Fool later and understood him better), I bowed to my own inner insecurity regarding the Fool and judged that this final card didn't make it clear whether taking the job would be a good idea in the long term; I didn't know one way or the other. (Actually, of course, the upright Fool shows that it is not just a good idea but that in the long term it may offer unparalleled opportunities.) So I took an extra card to get a clearer verdict on the change. This was the 10 of Cups, upright. A 10 always shows that one cycle of involvement has ended and that there is a need for a new beginning. 'One can wait for the possibility of change and growth to come along in the form of someone or some new interest which will stimulate that growth and development . . .' and of course that new interest had already come along. The involvement of Cups also shows that the change is one which will be good for emotional harmony, and this strengthens the meaning of the Fool. If there was a problem, it was the conflict of cards 2 and 5, the possible over-valuing of 'rational' qualities in the man by others at work, but the Fool promised long-term creative possibilities and the 10 shows this too.

The man took the job and is enjoying it greatly after a slightly tricky first few weeks.

This reading was a productive and useful one, and I think it emphasizes the value of having some clearly defined problem and designing a layout around that, isolating the key questions one wants answers for. But not every Tarot reading works as easily as this one did!

Some common problems with Tarot readings

Certainly, things can go wrong with readings. They may seem hopelessly wrong, confused, impossible to interpret. If this happens, then regard this as a possible challenge. After all, it is largely true that we learn through our mistakes, so try to find out what understanding might be extracted from these seeming disasters!

Readings which can't be interpreted

You do get these. Sometimes the sequence of cards in a reading just seems not to fit at all. Cards which are linked to events and others and things which should be associated (e.g., in time) are so disconnected in terms of their meanings that it seems impossible to synthesize them into a coherent story. You might find a couple of cards from the Minor Arcana coins suit (which generally have a nice, concrete meaning) next to one of the more abstract Major Arcana cards in a reading where it seems impossible to see any link between the meanings, for example.

In some cases, this may just be due to the atmosphere of the reading having been completely wrong. If this is so, you'll know it. Under these conditions, it is as if the Tarot is telling you to go away and come back at some more suitable time when you can do business together! Try a reading immediately following the first uninterpretable one and you'll get another which is much the same or even more pointedly rejecting. When I used to make this mistake, the Marseilles deck had a notable habit of throwing the Fool at me in a second reading in a way which clearly directed this card at myself. Take the Tarot's advice.

But in some others, you may have felt that the conditions were right and still the Tarot produced gibberish. In these cases, there are two possibilities, I think. First, it may be that the problem which was being worked on isn't the whole story or is even a cover for other concerns. So the Tarot may throw up stories about two quite different problems (the one you were told about and the other one) which seem disconnected. Well, they may be! It is good to be frank with the other person and ask whether there isn't some other concern they have; say that the Tarot seems to be telling a story about different problems and that the spread of cards reflects both, so that you cannot synthesize matters. If this is indeed true, then you can either try to read the current reading at two levels, for the two problems, or you can reshuffle and try again, taking each problem separately.

But *still* this may not be the answer. You may have a good atmosphere, a clear problem area, and still the reading is seemingly impossible to interpret. If the other person isn't denying a secondary concern, then you should frankly admit that the reading is one you cannot interpret right now. You should be honest and say that either this is due to your lack of understanding at this time, or that the reading may simply be wrong (on 'wrong' readings, see below). This is obviously not something one wants to admit, but I think it's best to be frank about it.

Keep a note of the reading; write down what the spread of cards actually was. At some later time, when you feel in a reflective mood, lay the cards out in the same way again and just look at them. Rather than trying to interpret the reading again, just let your mind wander around the spread and let associations and ideas flow. Play around with the concepts and meanings of the cards. Write down any new ideas about any of them (and their links with each other) which occur to you. You're not doing a reading now; you're using this puzzling problem as a tool for understanding the Tarot better. Don't use linear thinking, don't try to synthesize things, just *play*. You might not end up by understanding the reading second (or third, or even fourth) time around, but you may develop one or two new ideas about certain cards or patterns which will be helpful to you in the future. You may get lucky and crack it and be able to go back to the person the reading was done for with at least a couple of scraps of information your imaginative mental play has produced for you!

Inappropriate readings

This is when a reading has been asked for with respect to one problem area, but the spread of cards clearly does not seem to be addressing it. However, it is also clear that the spread is giving some intelligible messages with respect to some other problem area! For example, one might be addressing some emotional relationship issue and get a spread packed with cards from the suit of coins.

There are two major possibilities here. First, the spread may be saying, 'Actually, it's *here* that the problem lies.' In the example I've given, the emotional problems may be rooted in the practical/material world of coins. Since one's home is associated with this suit, domestic matters may be important. Financial concerns may be very relevant to the problem – one only has to consider how marriages suffer with the constraints of unemployment to realize how obvious this is. In such cases, the Tarot may be showing that the underlying causes of a problem may be different from what one might imagine, or that it is necessary to see the problem from a different angle. This can be an important insight. Discuss this possibility with the other person.

It may also be that the Tarot is simply showing a quite different problem! This may be one which is being over-looked or ignored, or has been ascribed a secondary import-ance whereas it is actually quite important and needs some attention. This, too, has obvious value.

Getting it wrong

You may get a reading which looks coherent enough and yet it doesn't apply to the person. Assuming that their prot-estations of irrelevance are honest enough (and I think it's pointless to query this), then there are several possibilities.

Again, the atmosphere of the reading may have been nega-tive or inappropriate, but you're likely to know this. You can say to the person that this was the case, and that it would be better to try again at some time when conditions are more favourable. Now, this may very well be regarded as a cop-out by that other person and you may not feel too happy about matters, but it's obviously ridiculous to expect the Tarot to work every time you use it, especially to begin with. If the person seems to take a very negative view about this, a swift lesson from scientific psychology will hopefully put them straight.

Let's indulge in a digression concerning experimental personality research. One popular theory concerning the nature of extraversion-introversion is that this personality trait has its roots in different patterns of brain function. Specifically, it is argued that extraverts have low levels of arousal in the brain cortex while introverts have high levels. Since subjective feelings of pleasure and comfort tend to be associated with intermediate levels, extraverts attempt to increase their arousal level – so they're risk-takers, sensation-seekers, and they like parties and stimulants and exciting company and unconventional sex and all kinds of other activities which increase arousal level. Introverts are the reverse, liking peace and comfort and the quiet life. So much for theory. As it happens, there is quite a lot of support for the theory from various experiments and surveys, *but* there is also a large body of experiments which *completely fail* to support the theory. When I worked in the Department of Experimental Psychology at the University of Cambridge, a PhD student of mine surveyed all the available evidence and found that only about thirty per cent of the experiments clearly supported the theory (this is far more than chance would predict with the statistical criterion psychologists use, by the way). His own certainly didn't do so. The point about this is that psychology in any form *never* deals with one hundred per cent probabilities and absolute certainties. The *balance* of evidence supports the theory but there are many, many exceptions. This is true both at the level of different experiments and of different individuals, and the latter case is obviously the most directly associated with the psychology of the Tarot and how successful it is. One will *always* find the gregarious extravert who, unusually for his type, is *not* a risk-taker and eschews gambling, dangerous physical sports, and the like. *There are always exceptions to any psychological rule* and they're usually fairly common. In fact, Tarot readings which simply don't get it right are probably a lot rarer than exceptions to scientific psychological theories! You should explain this to the person you're doing a reading for. In fact, it might be better to go into this in the discussion you have before doing a reading rather than having to use this line of argument after a failure has been suffered.

Even so, the 'error' may be more apparent than real.One distinct possibility is that the person rejects the reading because he/she isn't actually aware of what is shown in the cards. This is particularly likely if the spread contains several cards which suggest secret, hidden or covert actions – cards such as the High Priestess, the Hermit, the 5 and 6 of Wands, the King and Knight of Cups, and several others may indicate such a state of affairs. It is worth exploring this possibility with the other person. After all, isn't it an obvious major value of the Tarot if it *can* show us something we don't know about?

One can sometimes get a tricky state of affairs when a person strongly rejects a Tarot reading with a quality of emotional force which suggests that they don't *want* to accept what the cards are saying. This is simply evidence of some quality of repression, a suggestion that the Tarot is touching on something the person doesn't like about themselves and doesn't wish to be made aware of. It's best to be tactful and end the reading, suggesting that the person might like to go away and think about it for a while. Often they will come back and accept the reading in part. But don't see evidence of this kind of psychology all over the place. It doesn't happen *that* often and you will be fooling yourself if you put denials of validity down to repression every time they happen. Sometimes readings really are wrong!

And, finally, your skill may not have been up to it. You may have given an erroneous reading because you felt that such-and-such a pattern was appropriate for that person, your own preconceptions leading you astray. It's worth giving this possibility some consideration at some stage after the reading.

Clearly, the 'mistake' of an erroneous reading can be a learning experience in many different ways. Don't be discouraged by this, and remember that mistakes are always most frequently made when we are first learning to master some new skill.

Doing one's own readings

Different Tarot writers disagree about this. Some take the view that this is not a good idea, for one is more dispassionate about doing readings for others, so that one is less likely to project one's own wishes and desires into the interpretation and the layout. Such writers would suggest that it is always better to have readings done for yourself by others (although asking the reader to use your pack, if this is OK with both of you, is a good idea). I think this is a doubtful stricture. For one thing, I cannot see that one should be necessarily less honest with oneself than with others, and I can't see why possible problems with one's preconceptions, wishes and desires should be more likely to influence one's own reading than a reading done for others who one cares about. Doing your own readings also gives you the chance to experiment and play, and to learn from your own mistakes without the embarrassment a beginner will surely feel when making mistakes with a reading for someone else. One's learning is going to be facilitated in part by doing one's own work, so I think doing readings for oneself is a good idea. Hopefully, from what's gone before, the value of this type of exercise should be clear enough.

A final word

The Tarot is a wonderful and versatile tool. It is a theory of personality development and growth which has all the important insights of personality psychology, and it is a problem-solving kit into the bargain. It has the power to reveal what is hidden, to clarify what is known, and to show matters in perspective. It reveals, divines, illustrates, symbolizes and clarifies. What an amazing instrument of knowledge this ancient picture-book is. I only hope that this book has been able to inspire in the reader something of the respect in which I hold the Tarot, and to lead him or her to the pleasures of learning, creating, playing and understanding which the Tarot offers.

Concise Bibliography

Butler, Bill, *Dictionary of the Tarot* (London; Rider 1987). Exactly what it says it is: a dictionary of the interpretations which a number of major writers on the Tarot give for the cards, plus an introduction and guide to divinational methods. Butler also gives his own interpretations, which are not generally in keeping with majority views!

Campbell, Joseph, and Roberts, Richard, *Tarot Revelations*. My copy has no indicated publisher, but is a 1969 copyright. You can get a copy of this from specialist bookshops. This book is ninety per cent Roberts's essay on the esoteric symbolism of the Waite-Rider Tarot. A real tour de force. Brilliant and all-embracing, a phenomenal piece of work. Not a first book to try by any means but a must for anyone wanting to learn the Tarot's more arcane wisdom.

Crowley, Aleister, *The Book of Thoth (Egyptian Tarot)* (New York; Weiser 1969 reprint). Standard Crowley fare, if there is such a thing: part brilliant, part funny, part plain daft and part unintelligible. But the cards are very beautiful and it's impossible to read this without learning something of value. There is also Crowley's *Tarot Divination*, a paperback reprint of an article from *The Equinox* which Weiser have reprinted, which is useful.

Douglas, Alfred, *The Tarot; The Origins, Meaning and Uses of the Cards* (London; Gollancz, 1973; New York; Taplinger 1972). Also a paperback from Penguin Books. A very fine guide to the Tarot in all respects; particularly good as an introduction to esoteric approaches.

Huson, Paul, *The Devil's Picture Book* (London; Abacus 1972). Apart from the appalling title, a useful general book on the Tarot, managing to balance practicality and esoteric approaches pretty well.

Jacobi, Jolande, *The Psychology of C. G. Jung* (London; RKP 1942). Easily the best introduction to Jung, a book which makes a very difficult author accessible.

Maslow, Abraham, *Towards a Psychology of Being* (New York; Van Nostrand Reinhold 1968 second edition). A good general exposition of his personality theory, written with a deft touch, a very honest openness towards its limitations and some very amusing and witty observations. Psychology can actually be fun!

Matthews, John (editor), *At the Table of the Grail* (London; RKP 1984). Essays on the symbolism of the Holy Grail, which has a very definite affinity with the suits of the Tarot and other mythic motifs. For the person who is getting interested in the symbolisms of the Tarot in some depth and is beginning to stray into related areas. Varied topics but every chapter is worth reading. Engrossing stuff.

Nichols, Sallie, *Jung and Tarot* (New York; Weiser 1981). An excellent comparison of the Major Arcana with the Jungian theory of archetypes and individuation. The last word on the subject really. Wonderfully written too, a real pleasure to read.

Pollack, Rachel, *Seventy-Eight Degrees of Wisdom* (Wellingborough; Aquarian 1984). Two volumes in paperback, one on the Major and one on the Minor Arcana. A good general book which is especially strong on parallels for Tarot symbols and also in discussing psychological themes within the Tarot.

Waite, A. E., *The Key to the Tarot* (London; Rider 1910; still in print as a paperback). Useful reading if you plan to use the Waite deck. Since a lot of it is Waite sniping at contemporary writers it's pretty dispensable otherwise.

Wolheim, Richard, *Freud* (London; Fontana 1975). Probably the best introduction to Freud, although it's hard going. Lots of philosophy and similar indigestibles but worth the effort.

I could add many books to this list, but this is enough for the beginner to be getting on with! Also, many of these books contain very useful and longer bibliographies which can be used by the reader.